MASQUERADE

Joanna Taylor

piatkus

PIATKUS

First published in the US in 2015
First published in Great Britain in 2015 by Piatkus

1 3 5 7 9 10 8 6 4 2

A CIP catalogue record for this book
is available from the British Library.

ISBN 978-0-349-40728-9

Typeset in Garamond by M Rules
Printed and bound in Great Britain by
Clays Ltd, St Ives plc

Papers used by Piatkus are from well-managed forests
and other responsible sources.

MIX
Paper from
responsible sources
FSC® C104740

Piatkus
An imprint of
Little, Brown Book Group
Carmelite House
50 Victoria Embankment
London EC4Y 0DZ

An Hachette UK Company
www.hachette.co.uk

www.piatkus.co.uk

Joanna Taylor is a best-selling cross-category author, who has sold over 150,000 books. She teams fiction writing with a successful and award-winning journalism career, working for *The Times* and the *Mirror* in London. Her first adult romance, *Spotlight*, became an Amazon bestseller, and Joanna ranks in the top ten adult-romance writers on Amazon.

To Simon,
my everything

Chapter 1

wake to a hammering on the door, and a sinking feeling.
I'm still wearing my corset, stockings and shift.
Though I did at least heave off my great dress, before dropping into
exhausted oblivion this morning.

I can tell by the pitch of the afternoon sunlight that I've over-
slept.

Did Kitty leave already?

My eyes flick to the floor. The money we earned last night is
gone.

I sit up on the dusty double bed. We've decorated it to look like
a four-poster, and arranged sheets and silks. But it's still a cheap
mattress. The straw filling pokes into my legs as I slide back the
covers.

'Open the door!' calls a voice.

I wince, moving a tentative hand to my head, which is pounding from last night's wine. Then I swing my legs over the side of the
bed where Kitty usually sleeps.

We only have one room, so we share. Though in a fit of

cleverness, I had a false door and doorframe nailed to the far wall. It gives the impression there is a room beyond. So male guests might imagine that Kitty and I have a chamber each.

My bare feet knock against empty wine bottles, sending them clattering, and the banging outside reaches a fever pitch.

'Open up!'

I stand, smoothing my white linen shift, so it falls to my ankles. My stays are laced rigidly and I can feel where my ribs are bruised, from them digging in as I slept.

I move towards the door, which is now reverberating dangerously, due to the pounding fist on the other side.

No decent woman would open the door dressed as I am. But that is no concern for a girl like me. My only thought is, no one should see for free what he should pay for.

I turn the key, and the knocking falls silent as I lift the latch and open the door.

'Yes?' I set my face haughtily. The man on the other side is not fooled. My visitor is a heavy-set, beefy-faced kind of man. He wears the plain clothing of a debt collector.

'Five guineas,' he says, without preamble.

I shake my head, remembering the pile of money missing from by the bed. Thanks to Kitty, I have nothing but my wits to trade.

'You are wanting Kitty,' I say. 'It is she who owes a debt, not I.'

The man frowns and brings out a dog-eared roll of paper. He unfurls it, licks his lip and scans it with a sausage finger.

'Kitty French and Elizabeth Ward,' he says. 'Both runaways from Mrs Wilkes, Mayfair, London,' he adds, stating the address as if legal fact of our guilt. 'You think you can hide in Piccadilly?'

'I paid my debt,' I say evenly. 'Before I left. I owed nothing to her house.'

'And did you leave Mrs Wilkes stark naked?' sneers the man. 'You girls bite the hand that feeds. You ran away, wearing the clothes that Mrs Wilkes fitted you with. Those belong to her, and she will be paid out for them.'

He leans close enough that I can smell pipe tobacco.

'I mean to leave here with money, or a girl for the debtors' prison,' he says.

I feel fear slide into my stomach.

'I did not steal clothes,' I say, trying to imitate the boldness that Kitty would muster. I take a step back into the room. The man moves towards me, as though fearing I might run. Though I am trapped by him in this small room.

'I will show you,' I say, backing towards the large trunk where we keep our dresses.

I'm gambling that Kitty is wearing her stolen silken gown today. Otherwise I'm about to give her only fine dress to a debt collector.

I open the trunk. To my relief, there is nothing but my plain cotton dress inside.

I pull it up.

'I stitched this dress,' I explain. 'In secret, every morning, for a month, while I worked in Mrs Wilkes's house. I bought the cotton myself from Cheapside, and I can sew well enough, for I was raised to make my own clothing.'

The man looks at the cheap printed cotton and then back at my face.

'What of the rest,' he says, after a moment. 'The shift and the stays.' He's pointing at my half-dress.

'The shift was always mine, since I came to London at seventeen,' I say. 'The stays have been paid for. You may ask Mrs Wilkes.'

I swallow, because this situation can still turn on me. And if Kitty is already out drinking, she won't think to look for me in the prison. Perhaps not for days.

'And what of Kitty's clothing?' he asks.

'That is between you and her,' I say evenly.

3

He steps forward and grabs my arm.

'You will tell me where I can find her.'

'I do not know where she is,' I lie. 'She has a new gallant, a lord. She is under his protection. He often takes her away for days.'

'You share a room,' he insists. 'You must know where she is.'

'I do not know,' I say. 'I swear it.'

It sometimes amazes me, how adept I have become at lying. It was never a skill I sought to learn. I suppose necessity is the best teacher.

His fingers dig in.

'You are her friend,' he says. 'You will take me to her.'

I take a breath and go for a bluff.

'Sir,' I say, 'if you bruise my arm, you do damage which must be paid for. I am in keeping with a merchant, who regards me as his own property. He will come for you and he has heavy men to make his case.'

The debt collector's face shifts to uncertainty. But his hold remains firm. His eyes roam the room, assessing if I am wealthy enough to be telling the truth.

I hold my breath as he takes in the modest chamber that Kitty and I rent. It's decked out best we can, to look like a high-up boudoir.

Besides the conjurer's trick of making our plain bed look four-poster, our furnishings are meagre. What's more, the smell of the cheap straw mattress sneaks through, so we hide bushels of lavender beneath the bedding. It's a feint to fool aristocrats, but it won't wash with this man. The smell hangs accusingly on the air.

I see the debt collector take in our mirror, then fix on our trunk. Kitty begged this item of furniture from an old suitor. It bears his household crest, so it looks grander than it might. For a moment I think this will swing things in my favour.

Then the debt collector's eyes flick to the ageing casement window and down to the floor.

We no longer have a rug to disguise the dusty floorboards. Our old one was bought cheap at London Bridge and had fleas. Since there are two of us, and men do not like to share a bed, Kitty and I could not do with the flea bites from rolling on the rug.

The man's eyes move up to the false door, assessing the illusion of a second room beyond.

The charade is convincing enough in candlelight. But it's late afternoon, and dying sunlight streams through our little diamond pane window.

I wait, with my breath held.

Slowly, the fingers ease away from my arm. I move my hand to the place reflexively, rubbing it.

'You may tell Kitty,' he says, 'she must pay her debt. I will find her out, whether she has a suitor or not.'

'I will tell her.'

The man tilts his head slightly. He's still standing a great deal too close for comfort.

'If she does not pay,' he adds, his eyes sweeping my body, 'I will come for you, and you will work off her debt with me.'

I swallow, keeping my face neutral. He's regarding me in that way men do when they decide you might be useful to them.

'And believe me,' he adds, with a leer, 'I will make you work hard for it.'

My expression must hold, because the light in his face dies a little, as though I didn't react in the way he was hoping for.

He turns and spits.

'Whores,' he mutters as he leaves. 'You think yourselves fine when you're young and beautiful. But you all end up gutter-beggars in the end.'

Chapter 2

As the door closes, I realise my heart is pounding. I'm furious with Kitty. She promised me she would not steal clothes. But on the night we ran away, she arrived dressed in the finest silks, announcing she wore this or went naked.

Rose, the only other girl brave enough to run with us, had earned out her own dress long ago. She regarded Kitty's theft with silent terror, clearly regretting her decision to join our escape. But it worked out very well for Rose, in the end. Better, at least, than for Kitty and me.

Willing my body to calm, I turn back to our little room. I have slept too long, and need to get dressed and working.

Carefully, I ease out my own fine dress from its hiding place beneath the straw mattress.

It's linen. But I chose a deep blue colour and the best weave I could afford. From a distance, or in the dark, it could be mistaken for silk. I had it made from my first street earnings at a bargain dressmaker, who understood why it should be cut so very low at the front, and made no judgements.

I stand before our long mirror – the first tool of our trade Kitty and I bought, when we moved into this room. Before even a bed.

I set my dress down, and the skirts are so wide they stand half up on their own, spreading out like great wings. As though a ghostly girl is sunk into our bare floorboards, trying to fly her way to freedom.

I step into the confines of the dress, pulling it up and around my body, and settling into the practised restriction of it.

Mrs Wilkes gave us daily lessons in how to walk gracefully, bearing the weight of our great dresses. But though I learned the walk well enough, I have never felt easy with the heavy fabric crushing me.

I tie the back myself with the great dexterity street girls learn, from doing without maidservants. Regarding myself in the glass, I tighten the bust, pulling my breasts so just the tiniest edge of nipple is visible. This is a trick I learned from Kitty, since neither of us has the pillowy bosom of fattened ladies.

I have never quite lost my country skinniness. And since Kitty and I live hand-to-mouth, my arms and legs have become thinner, these past few months.

My special banknote, which I carry with me always, is tucked down, just out of view. Pressed against my heart. Touching it with my fingers, I make myself the same promise I have made ever since I earned it. That one day I will have my own independence.

I examine the half-moons of my breasts, then reach for my powder, sweeping blush to make my cleavage unavoidably eye-catching.

With my professional advertisement taken care of, I direct my attention to my face. Which is probably the best part of me. It was my pretty face that convinced Mrs Wilkes to take me in, when I was brought ruined and weeping to her door.

Do not think me conceited to think myself fair. Mrs Wilkes only takes girls who are very beautiful, and I was not the most pleasing of her harem.

Rose, who ran away with Kitty and me, is far more lovely than I am. And Belle was so enchanting it would make you sick. Yet she was so nice with it that you could not help but like her. Everyone loved Belle. She was the real thing, beauty and purity.

Belle was the one who warned me to keep my special banknote safe when I first came to the house. She pointed at the other gaudy, loud girls, of whom I was sick with fear at having to imitate, and told me beware.

They may dress like ladies, Belle had whispered, *but many come from the gutter, and they steal as naturally as breathing. Keep anything dear to you tied in your stays.*

Of all the girls I came to know, I had loved Belle the most. Mrs Wilkes sold her in secret just before we ran away and we never found out who bought her.

Besides Rose and Belle, my face was the next best in that house. Better than Kitty who looks brazenly seductive. I have been told my countenance can be almost genteel in the right context. Though I have not lost all of my country mannerisms.

In any case, I have perfectly even features, with wide-apart hazel eyes, a straight little nose and a generous mouth. My grandmother always called me her little elf, with a pixie nose and my eyes always dwelling on mischief.

My nose is a bit big for a pixie now, but it's right for my face, and my eyes still sparkle in the right circumstances. With my wide mouth I fancy I still look a little impish. Not voluptuous like Rose, or perfect like Belle. But attractive enough to turn heads.

I also have good skin, and though it has a tendency to tan, I have not had smallpox. So I have an advantage over many fine ladies who were poxed in childhood. Especially in candlelight.

'Take note from Elizabeth,' Mrs Wilkes would say, as we applied make-up at our dressers. 'She is not the most beautiful here. But men do not mind if a girl is a little brown, or does not fill a bodice. They care for a girl who looks healthy and lively, and game for the sport.'

Mrs Wilkes liked me, because, despite everything, when I settled in, I was always laughing. She said that was what rich old men liked.

I have a few other advantages. Besides my face, I am tall, which is good, and young, which is better. But my figure has not much else to recommend it. I do not put on weight easily like some girls. I cannot yet afford to feed myself up.

So I make the very most of my face, because my whole life I've always made best use of what I've got. And in this strange midnight world, which I never imagined for myself, my face is my greatest asset.

I pick up my lip paint and notice it has almost run out, again. I sigh, spreading the red pigment as meanly as I can across my lips. A hazard of having a big mouth is using a lot of lip paint.

I tug my dress tight closed and reach for my shoes, which are handmade and expensive. They're dark blue, to match my dress, with a little heel.

I pick up my gloves from where I laid them out before the mirror.

Gloves are a habit we all learned at Mrs Wilkes's house. She taught us to scorn the poor wretches who were not educated enough to realise a pair of gloves could double a girl's worth.

Mine are almost worn through on two fingers and not as clean as they could be. But I don't dare wash them, for they might fall apart entirely. Kitty and I have run out of credit with the haberdashers.

I reach for my hat, which is wide-brimmed in the shepherdess style – a fashionable prop to keep the sun from my face.

I wear the hat low, so my eyes peek out flirtatiously beneath, and arrange my hair so it seems to tumble from the brim. My head grows masses of chestnut curls, which are abundant enough that I can pass them off as an expensive wig with the right hair ornaments.

I push in my favourite pewter comb, which is decorated with little butterflies and feathers – both blue to match my dress and shoes. Then I take up my hanging purse. Since Kitty has absconded with our main earnings I have only a few small coins. Enough to buy a little cheese and bread if I get too hungry.

Assessing my reflection, I give my breasts a final heave. Then I powder my face white as I dare and rouge my cheeks.

My hazel eyes sparkle back in the glass, as if daring me to do something wicked.

Tonight could be the night, I tell myself, as I do every evening. *Tonight could be the night when I meet the right man, and everything changes.*

Chapter 3

Kitty will be in the gin shop. I can't quite bear to see her there yet. So I walk instead to the bird market a few streets away.

Piccadilly, where we rent our room, has a good-sized pavement, which means us street girls can keep our shoes clean without paying for a sedan chair.

Our area is not as grand as Mayfair, where Mrs Wilkes keeps her famous house. But the street attracts a fair influx of younger aristocrats, looking to entertain themselves any way their money takes them.

Since it is now early evening, traders are clustering on the street to hawk their wares. Girls with baskets of fruit or shrimps on their heads mill around. Men draw carts laden with trinkets for drunk city folk.

The bird market is closing up as I arrive, and sellers are throwing cloths over the larger enclosures. Smaller cages for sale hang on clotheslines, or line the dirt floor. There are teardrop-shaped wicker cages, chaotically wrought wire creations and the occasional elaborately crafted aviary. Still more randomly fashioned holders house the birds themselves.

I walk through the narrow tracks and find out my favourite seller. He's an old man in a patchwork of barely held together clothing. But his blue eyes are happy, as though he doesn't notice his low surroundings.

'Good day to you, Queenie.' He doffs an imaginary cap, grinning.

Queenie was a nickname given to me because some drinkers at the gin shop think I act above myself. It's usually meant as an insult. But I don't mind it from the birdman. I think he imagines it differently.

'Come to buy a bird?' he asks.

I nod. His old hands are already fumbling with the catch on his large cage of birds. I watch as the raddled fingers swoop in at lightning speed and capture a starling.

He manoeuvres the frightened bird out of the entrance, seals the cage and presents me with it, in one dextrous movement.

'Like the look of this little fellow?' he asks, holding up the chirruping starling.

I examine the creature, which the birdman holds with remarkable gentleness.

I nod again and smile.

'He's going to join the others?' asks the birdman, with a wink.

'Yes,' I reply, handing over my penny. The birdman pockets the coin and inserts the bird into a roll of paper, twisting both ends shut.

'Here you are.'

I take the parcel, marvelling, as I always do, at the lightness of the warm paperbound little body. Then I cross the street to St James's Park and find myself a patch on the grass where no one is walking.

Closing my eyes, I settle myself to calmness. I draw a picture of a new life into my head. One that is free from heartache and horrors, debt collectors and false suitors. I see myself well-fed, in fine clothes, with my own independence and maybe even a man to treat me kindly.

Slowly I twist open the paper.

'Out you come, little bird,' I whisper, unstopping the end and tipping it down.

The bird's tiny claws scrabble against the paper and then he's out on the grass, twisting uncertainly in the light.

The bird reminds me of us girls, when we first fled Mrs Wilkes. Blinking in the sunlight, afraid of the sudden big wide world before us.

The creature takes a few bobbing steps, growing bolder now, hardly daring to believe his luck. And then, in a split second, his wings are open and he streaks through the air, vanishing into a large leafy oak tree.

I close my eyes and feel my heart go with it. Then I hear birdsong. I open my eyes again and now I cannot tell which bird was mine, from all the other starlings chattering in the oak. I smile.

The memory of my last failed liaison still aches. But I know I will survive. I'm going to get up again. I'm going to try harder.

And one day, I promise myself. *One day. I will be as free as that bird.*

I crumple the paper prison in my hand and stand, feeling happier.

It's time to find Kitty. And get to work.

Chapter 4

I am always glad of my resilience. My soul feels lighter as I walk towards the gin shop.

Perhaps the men from last night will seek us out again. Or Kitty and I will find our way into a ball. We did that once, and you could barely move for drunk and wealthy men believing you to be a real lady. Were it not for Kitty's temper, throwing drink in a man's face, it would have been rich pickings.

I turn off Piccadilly into a smaller backstreet. A jumble of overhead signs announces this is a cork-cutting street, and the squeak of the working knives closes around me.

I catch sight of a familiar face, huddled in a doorway, and for a moment my brain struggles to match the image.

Then it does and I feel a sickening surge of recognition.

Emily-Jane.

I knew her from the gin shop, last year. When she was fresh-faced and charming.

Now she holds out a hand, begging. Now her face is sallow and sunken, and she has only a few teeth left in her mouth.

I struggle for the memory of why she left Piccadilly.

She was put in the debtors' prison less than a year ago. It has aged her ten.

The woman does not recognise me, but assesses from my powdered face and low-cut dress that I am not one of those ladies who can afford to give charity. So her attention is elsewhere as I approach.

I move nearer, meaning to offer her some sympathy. But at the last minute I change my mind and walk on. It would be cruel to stop and raise her hopes, with no money to give her. She is in need of more than kind words.

Kitty's favourite gin shop has an innocent-looking door and a large sign, displaying a bottle. I push my way inside, to the familiar acrid smell of liquor and the din of drunks.

The gin shop has a sturdy bar in front of a neat row of barrels. The owner, a vinegar-faced woman known as Gin Joan, is filling a glass bottle from the nearest barrel. She turns as I enter and begins refilling the glasses of a cluster of drinkers who are crowded in.

Into the night, the gin shop can get full to busting. But it is early evening and only a handful are here. So the atmosphere is yet to turn unruly.

I scan the collection of drinkers for Kitty. A young woman with bad teeth is raising a glass to be filled in one hand and holding a ragged toddler with the other. She wears the relative finery of a streetwalker and, judging by the stoic look on her face, is steeling herself for a long night.

A middle-aged woman in a plain wool dress has her arm looped around a man I take to be her husband. They are both shouting cheerfully across the general din. Other little pockets of men and women play at cards or dice. A few rough-looking characters are lounged around with far-away looks, sipping gin like it's a reflex movement.

I see Kitty by the bar. The contrast of the other plainer women makes her appear even more striking. Her feline features are deepened by the gloom of the gin shop, blackening her eyebrows to dramatic arcs over her sultry green eyes.

Kitty has black hair, deep pink lips, high cheekbones and a gap between her front teeth, which adds a roguish air to her seductive appearance. As though she's ever-poised to say something shocking.

She catches my eye and her wide-apart eyes come alight like a cat's. Her delight in seeing me is closely followed by a false, guilty smile. Kitty is famous for having a smile that makes men want to go to bed with her. But her allure stops short at the bedroom. Men want her for a mistress, but she's too much trouble to be a wife. And she somehow belongs more to this crowd than anywhere else, despite her fine silk dress.

'Lizzy!' She raises her glass and straightens with effort. Kitty is slight, with small breasts pushed up towards her collar bone and a narrow waist that emphasises the wide bulky span of her stolen skirts. Her movement in grand clothes is never completely easy.

As usual, she has a little bevy of reprobates around her. She is arm in arm with Susie Sweetlove, who she must have made amends with, because they clawed each other's faces last week.

Pete and Leo, two card sharps from London Bridge gambling house, are hanging around her, hoping they will get some of Kitty for free if she drinks enough.

I move towards the bar and see Kitty is not so drunk as I feared. Perhaps she hasn't yet spent all of yesterday's money.

'Do not allow her credit,' I whisper fiercely as I pass Gin Joan, who has taken a break from pouring to tip a slug of gin down her own throat. Joan swallows, wipes her mouth, then points wordlessly to a chalked line of numbers.

I make out Kitty's scrawled initials next to the spiralling column of figures and my heart sinks.

Kitty sees me looking at her debt.

'Lizzy!' she announces with exaggerated cheer, throwing out an arm to pull me close. In the process she drops her hold on Susie Sweetlove, who glowers at me as an interloper.

'Come join us,' says Kitty, though she knows I do not drink gin.

As always, Leo attaches himself to me the moment I step near Kitty.

'Come for a gin today, Queenie?' he asks. 'Or are you above us again?'

His hand snakes around, pressing into the small of my back.

I try to make my face belie my feelings. In my current mood, Leo's poorly judged seductions are the last thing I need. But he is vengeful when crossed. Angering him is unwise.

'Maybe later,' I lie.

Leo considers, and I think for a moment he is displeased. Then his face breaks into a predatory smile. 'A woman who doesn't like gin,' he says. 'You will make a fine wife, Lizzy.'

Leo could be handsome, were it not for his weasel-like expression and a lurid knife wound running from ear to chin. He always reminds me of some feral creature, forever sniffing for a way to press an unfair advantage.

I make a face at Kitty, and to her credit, she registers my meaning immediately.

'Liz and I will talk outside,' she announces, taking my hand and tugging me out of the darkly fragrant confines of the shop.

We break out onto the street and I turn angrily on Kitty.

'A debt collector visited today,' I say.

'Oh?' She looks unconcerned.

'For *you*,' I say, 'for the dress you took. From Mrs Wilkes.'

Her gaze drops to the dress she wears. A huge silken thing, many times more valuable than mine. Though Kitty has managed to lose her gloves and no longer bothers with a hat.

In fact, Kitty seemed to throw off as many of Mrs Wilkes's teachings as she could, with reckless, riotous abandon, revelling in her descent to street level. I remember the lessons as best I can. But it is hard, for we have less chance to practise them than we did in Mrs Wilkes's house.

'You need not be always so fearful,' says Kitty. 'She must forget the debt soon. It has been months. This is freedom, Lizzy. We've made it. We escaped.'

She gives me a wide grin.

'It doesn't feel like freedom to me,' I mutter, looking at the sloping eyes of a few drinkers who have arranged themselves on the street outside the gin shop.

'Would you go back?' asks Kitty. 'Would you rather work for Mrs Wilkes, like a slave? On your back ten times a night, for any decrepit old man who pays her the right money?'

'No. I would not,' I reply. 'I should rather we lived in hope that some young lord or duke will fall in love with us. And I did not like it that we had to give Mrs Wilkes part of our money.'

'*Most* of our money,' corrects Kitty. 'The old hag took almost all.'

She runs a hand through her long black hair. Mrs Wilkes also brought in very rich men. We do not earn as much on the streets as we did in her house. But I have lost the will to argue.

At least we make our own destiny, I remind myself.

Then I remember the beggar girl.

'I saw Emily-Jane on the street,' I admit, my fears suddenly returning in lurid detail. 'Remember her? From the gin shop last year.'

Kitty rubs her forehead foggily.

'Oh. Yes,' she agrees.

'She is begging on the street,' I say. 'She looks over forty and can only be twenty-five.'

Kitty looks unconcerned.

'Emily-Jane had no one to bail her,' she says. 'Else she would never have spent a year in the Fleet Prison.'

My face must look distraught, because Kitty's face twists. 'Has she lost all her looks?' she asks.

I nod, the terrible image of the haggard face floating before me.

Kitty puts her arm around me and squeezes me tight.

'Half the women in London prostitute themselves at one time or another,' she says. 'Not all are made for Piccadilly.'

'Neither are we,' I insist. 'We will rise above all this and find ourselves fine men. Men who will keep us and give us an annual wage.'

Kitty only shrugs. Then her eyes widen suddenly.

'Holy Mary!' she says. 'Did you ever see such a thing outside Westminster?'

I follow her gaze and see a glossy racing stallion bearing a handsomely dressed rider, who seems to be struggling for control in the noisy mayhem of Shaftesbury Avenue.

'That is a thoroughbred,' I murmur, taking in the shape of the fine-looking horse. 'That is a foolish animal to ride in a city.'

'The rider must be a lord,' decides Kitty. 'Look at his boots and coat. And he cannot be above thirty.'

I had been preoccupied by the horse, but now my gaze takes in the rider. There is something striking about him, even from this distance. He has a solid poise that hints at a muscular frame beneath the lordly clothes, and a quiet determination, even as he grapples with the temperamental horse.

Kitty nudges me, her eyes shining. 'Rich pickings.'

I nod slowly, following her line of thought.

London attracts young titles. They come to town to spend their money and avoid their lady wives. A girl who catches a newly arrived lord might do very well.

Kitty licks her lips, considering.

'You should go,' she decides. 'You have more grace with fine folk.'

I can tell she's thinking of the five guineas she owes. Her eyes slide along the pavement, taking in the array of painted faces that have also seen the rider. 'I will make sure none come to trouble you,' she adds.

I am frozen with self-doubt, aware of my poor quality dress and worn out gloves.

'Lizzy, you are the most beautiful girl in Piccadilly,' Kitty reassures me, reading my uncertain expression. 'Men see faces before finery.'

She leans in, fanning my chestnut curls across my shoulders. Then she adjusts my shepherdess hat so the brim comes a little lower.

'Go,' she adds, pushing me into the street. 'Before another girl gets to him.'

Chapter 5

I move from the pavement onto the dirt of the road, picking my way between the muddy patches to spare my shoes.

The horse has stopped moving forward now. It stands, tossing its head and flexing its legs as if working up to rear. The rider seems to have temporarily given up on urging it onward, running his hands soothingly through the animal's mane.

I'm close enough to get a good look at the man now. His shoulder-length brown hair falls into a slight wave. And as my eyes reach his face, I see his features are fine, with high cheekbones and a straight nose. You could almost think it a feminine face, were it not for the broad jaw.

I am struck by his eyes. So deep brown they are almost black. A girl could get lost in those eyes. They seem to tell a story all of their own.

The rider's attention flicks to where I'm standing, and I realise I am staring. Instinctively I look away. The focus of that dark gaze is so intense that it seems to pierce right through me.

My eyes drop to his well-worn riding boots. The butter-soft leather has faded to grey, looping in large folds at mid-thigh. The pirate style suggests he's new here. City lords wear stockings and shoes.

Courage, Lizzy, I admonish myself, *you are not a girl to be cowed by an aristocrat.*

Frowning at my lowered gaze I force myself to look upwards. I take in his long black frock coat, hanging open at the front, with large rolled cuffs, and French lace at his wrists and at his neck. My eyes flick defiantly to the rider's face and I see his expression has changed. Before it seemed as though he was assessing me very deeply. Now there is something almost challenging there, as though he is waiting for me to disappoint him.

I take a determined step forward and his horse snorts as I near the flank. I reach out a hand to pat, feeling more confident. I've got a way with horses. This animal is wet with nervous sweat and I rub him soothingly.

When I look back up to the rider his head is tilted and the dark eyebrows are slightly raised. Perhaps he is outraged that I have been bold enough to touch his horse but I cannot tell. 'Are you looking for business?' I ask, the universal question of prostitutes all over London.

He sweeps me with that appraising stare again. I cannot decide if it is unnerving or flattering to be the object of such undivided attention. This time I refuse to look away.

'I am looking for an ostler,' he replies eventually, giving no indication my lack of servility offends him. The horse twitches beneath him as he speaks. 'I need blinkers to get this animal to Mayfair.'

His voice is not loud. But it has a smooth authority that makes his words resonate easily through the Piccadilly hubbub.

'What is your horse's name?' I ask, trying not to be unnerved by the command in his voice. His accent is upper-class with a slight country burr making him sound warmer than most aristocrats. There is a calm power there.

The rider frowns, studying me, as though I could be working some confidence trick. 'Samson,' he says, after a moment.

'Easy, Samson,' I whisper, patting the flank. 'Easy.'

The horse lets out a disgruntled snort. As though he'll take pacifying for the moment but it won't wash in the long term.

I look up to the rider. 'Your horse thinks to bolt,' I explain. 'You will not easily get him to an ostler, and blinkers will not help. It is the noise that frightens him, not the sights.'

I consider for a moment.

'If you like, I will guide him to Mayfair, with you atop. It is only a few streets from here. He will be easier with another person alongside.'

The man nods, acknowledging the truth of this. 'I would be grateful,' he says. The tone suggests he is not used to being beholden to people.

I make an assessment of his hanging pocket. 'You must pay me three shillings,' I add.

The man's eyes widen and I see him make a swift calculation of his options. I'm on surer ground now. We both know he will not easily get to Mayfair alone. He must take my offer or risk injuring his horse.

'Very well,' he says, after a pause. For an instant I think I see a glint of admiration in his face, and then it is gone.

'You should be ashamed of your lack of charity,' he adds, his face hardening to an expression more familiar to men of his rank. 'I am a visitor to the city.'

I take hold of the bridle.

'It is not you who needs charity,' I say easily, wrapping the reins around my hand. 'And shame costs money.'

We set off in silence, at a slow walk, and Samson calms considerably with someone to lead him. I plot a path to avoid the squawking cockfights on Cockspur Street and away from the hustling sedan chair carriers on St James.

'What is your name?' I ask the rider, since he's making no effort to speak.

'Edward,' he says. But he does not ask mine. He seems transfixed by the squalor of Piccadilly, and I wonder how often he visits the city.

We walk on a little more.

'Samson is a fine horse,' I say, reverting to the easy small-talk that has become part of my working girl persona.

'How do you know about horses?' Edward asks after a pause. I get the feeling he would rather not ask. But his curiosity has got the better of him.

'I grew up in the country,' I explain. 'My grandfather bred horses and I learned a little. Yours is an Arabian thoroughbred,' I add, by way of illustrating my knowledge. 'It is the finest I have seen.'

'Do you ride?' he asks.

'Yes.'

'Side saddle?'

I shake my head. 'Only astride,' I admit, not liking to confess I cannot ride the lady's way. 'I have never ridden in London,' I add, reasoning he might as well know the whole. 'Or an animal as beautiful as this. You must be proud to own him,' I conclude wistfully.

I glance up and the expression on Edward's face is thoughtful.

It strikes me anew how handsome he is. Many lords have a certain look after generations of inbreeding – exaggerated noses or pronounced overbites. Or they are florid with wine and swollen with gout. Edward's features could be described as refined.

'It is not my horse,' he admits. 'I am usually a better rider.'

'You must have good credit,' I say, 'to have the loan of him.'

'He belongs to a friend.' His tone pronounces the topic is closed, and I let the subject drop. I do not mind. I have no sensitivities and expect no courtesy where rich men are concerned.

Samson tosses his head agitatedly and I let him some slack, and then wind the reins back in.

'Thoroughbreds are temperamental,' I explain. 'If you sit a little further forward, you will help him feel easier.'

I do not know what it is that makes me so outspoken. Only that he does not seem so arrogant as most lords.

Edward frowns in reply, and I think perhaps I have misjudged and spoken too free.

We reach a junction.

'Which street in Mayfair?' I ask.

'Clarges Street.'

I consult my mental map. Though I lodged here with Mrs Wilkes, we slept by day and worked by night. The only way I know for certain is through a busy street.

I move around to catch Samson's head between my hands, and blow gently in his nostrils to calm him.

He snorts back, lowering his head, and I press my forehead to his.

'It will be a little noisier here,' I explain to Samson apologetically, fixing on his uncertain eyes. 'But I will take good care and no harm will come to you, I promise it.'

I release his head when I'm confident he's taken my meaning, and move to take his bridle again. It is only then I realise Edward is looking down at me with a slight smile on his lips. I look away, embarrassed, concluding fine folk do not talk with their horses.

I'm about to walk on, when Edward slides down from the saddle in one agile movement. He lands directly next to me and his sudden proximity makes me catch my breath. Edward appeared statuesque on the horse, but now his height is daunting. I am not used to men being this much taller than me. His muscular frame has a coiled energy that is almost palpable. There is an easy grace to him that puts me in mind of a predator. Without meaning to I take a slight step back.

Edward takes the reins from my unprotesting hand. His face is completely neutral; though he must know the effect he has on women.

I look up at him questioningly. Perhaps my conversing with his horse was the final straw. He has decided that I am too strange a companion to brook any further association with.

'Will you walk on yourself from here?' I ask.

He wraps the reins around his forearm but shakes his head.

'I thought you should ride,' he replies.

'What?' My first thought is he is mocking me.

'I should like you to ride,' he repeats patiently. 'The horse seems to like you. I think he would be easier.'

I point to the shining coat of the thoroughbred, thinking I have mistaken his meaning.

'You want me to ride your friend's horse?'

He nods patiently, as if explaining to a child. And there is that disarming smile again, very faint, but unmistakable. As though some deep part of him is amused beyond measure.

'This horse?' I clarify, trying not to be disconcerted.

'Unless you think I have some other horse hidden about my person.'

It takes me a moment to realise he is in jest. I break into a wide grin, and unexpectedly, he smiles broadly back. Then his features recompose themselves quickly, as though the expression took him by surprise too.

For an instant he looked much younger than the thirty or so I judged him to be.

'Do you need a hand up?' he asks, reaching forward to offer his arm.

The bare skin of his hand brushes mine and I start slightly. The unexpected contact makes the hairs on the nape of my neck stand on end.

I realise I am transfixed by his dark eyes again, and now they seem to hold a question. As if something in me has confounded him.

To hide my confusion I step quickly away and put my hands on the horse. In a moment, my foot is in the stirrup and I've swung myself full over Samson's sturdy body.

'You have a more confident mount than many lords,' Edward murmurs approvingly. All his lordly poise has returned now, and I wonder if I imagined the moment that seemed to have passed between us.

Atop the fine horse I sit taking it all in, smiling delightedly. Samson's black coat has been groomed to a high shine. His mane is fastidiously plaited close to his neck, revealing the prominent muscles that join to his broad back. I can feel the power of him, solid and expectant.

I am beaming at my chance to ride him.

'Such a beautiful creature,' I murmur, leaning forward to run my hands across Samson's wide neck.

I know I must look a fine sight. A gaudily dressed girl on top of this magnificent beast. But I don't care. Not in the slightest. This is the finest horse I have ever seen in London. And here I am about to ride him.

I let my eyes wander, taking in my elevated view. The city looks a great deal more regal from this height, with the mud and the squalor safely hidden away.

Edward gives a little smile, but doesn't say anything.

'To Clarges Street then?' I ask, uncertain of myself again. He gives a little bow, and I touch my legs against Samson, urging him softly forwards and marvelling at my good fortune.

This is starting out to be a good night after all.

Chapter 6

We are almost to Clarges Street when Edward speaks again.

'You are a good horsewoman,' he says. 'How did you end up in Piccadilly?'

I hold my gaze ahead, concentrating on keeping the horse calm.

'I was kidnapped from a masquerade,' I say, reciting the familiar rehearsed story. 'By a masked man I thought to be my brother. He forced himself upon me. And once ruined, I was too ashamed to return to my family. And so I rely on the kindness of honest men.'

Edward raises an eyebrow. 'I mean your real story,' he says, 'not the one you tell drunk young lords.'

He is more astute than he looks.

I hesitate and then I give him a sideways grin.

'I grew up a country girl near Bristol,' I admit. 'My father sold our farm. So I ran away, rather than become a rope worker like my mother. I hoped to gain maid's work in London. But it was harder to find and poorer paid than I had been led to believe.'

This seems to satisfy him and he turns silent again. There is something compelling in his introspection. As though beneath his surface calm a whole world is turning.

'You do not speak very much,' I observe, in my usual habit of letting words fly out of my mouth unchecked.

He smiles at this. 'I like to consider things, before I say them.'

'That is not like me,' I admit. 'I toss around my words like wedding rice. That is what my mother used to say. And Mrs Wilkes. She said I was like a chattering monkey.'

'You were in Mrs Wilkes's house?' He is looking up at me.

'Yes.' I look down at him, registering his interest.

'I have heard of it.'

'Every lord in London has heard of it,' I reply.

Suddenly his gaze is completely on me and I find myself locked in it.

Those eyes.

A girl could fall deep in his black eyes. A lucky thing he does not seem to often apply them. I feel myself discomforted, under his stare.

'Wilkes House. I can see that,' he decides, after a moment. And I wonder what he has seen in me that leads him to that conclusion.

We've reached the top of Clarges Street now and I draw Samson to a halt.

I slide down, feeling strangely disappointed to be ending the meeting. Not to mention I'll have to tell Kitty that I only made three shillings from the arrangement.

We stand looking at each other.

Suddenly a male voice echoes down the street and I see a stableman walking towards us. We look away from one another.

'Lord Hays,' calls the stableman, approaching Edward.

My eyes widen, seeing him in a new gold-hued light.

Lord Hays. He is from one of the wealthiest families in England.

'You are Lord Hays?' I manage, looking at Edward.

He nods. The stableman is taking Samson's reins and addressing himself to Edward.

'You would have him stabled here, Your Lordship?' the stableman is asking.

'Yes. He is to be returned to Berkshire tomorrow,' says Edward. 'Please arrange a rider to deliver him back.' He is speaking in the clear tones of a man used to giving orders. Nothing in his tone suggests that my presence needs to be explained, and his absolute authority makes my arrival here seem perfectly normal.

The stableman nods his head. 'Yes, Your Lordship.' He keeps his eyes firmly on Edward, risking not the slightest glance in my direction. Though I know he must have assessed me as a street whore as he approached.

The stableman escorts Samson away, and I decide there is no reason to question Edward about being one of the richest men in England.

I see the stableman give a little backward glance at me and am struck anew by how odd an arrangement this must look. The Piccadilly street girl and the lord.

I stand awkwardly, wanting to leave. This is a fine part of town, and my low-cut dress and vulgar face paint do not fit. I see Edward's eyes linger on my uncovered bosom and the cheap cut of fabric surrounding it.

Not knowing quite what else to do, I hold out my palm for payment. A ghost of a smile plays on Edward's face and he reaches for his hanging pocket.

'I nearly forgot,' he says, removing coins.

'I would not have,' I reply.

He pauses, with the coins held over my palm.

I tilt my head, trying not to show my impatience. I hate to wait for money.

'I do not know your name,' he says, as though this is the first time it had occurred to him to ask.

'Lizzy Ward,' I say, flexing my fingers meaningfully.

'Elizabeth,' he says thoughtfully, dropping the coins into my hand.

'No one calls me that.' I close my hand into a tight fist around the coins and drop it to my side.

He regards me carefully. I feel myself fidget under his scrutiny.

'How much would I need to pay,' he begins, 'to enjoy more of your company?'

In my great surprise, I feel my face break open in a wide grin.

I'm dimly aware that his enormous five-storey house is standing behind us. But the grand façade is turning hazy as I take in his question. As though it's underwater.

Lord Hays is asking to pay for my company.

'Five guineas,' I say, blurting the first ridiculous figure that comes into my head. I straight away regret it. No sensible man would pay that price. Not even a lord of the Hays family.

His eyebrows shoot up and his eyes drop to my worn gloves.

'Five guineas?' he repeats.

I nod, deciding, in a rush of recklessness, to hold my nerve. Something tells me he would not respect my backtracking.

'That seems a high price,' he says, regarding me coolly.

'Five guineas is the price.' I raise an eyebrow at him and drop the tiniest, most irreverent curtsy. 'You would pay double in Mrs Wilkes's house. Your Lordship.'

A smile creeps onto his face. He turns very slightly on his heel and for a moment I think he means to walk away. But he hesitates.

'Five guineas?' he repeats slowly. 'Five guineas.'

I stay silent, hardly daring to breathe.

He jangles his hanging pocket thoughtfully. Then his dark eyes are on mine.

I hold my nerve, meeting his gaze. And then his arm extends and locks into mine.

'I would be delighted,' he says with exaggerated courtesy, 'if you would join me this evening.'

'Of course, Your Lordship,' I say, sinking a little against his arm, as though I receive such requests on a daily basis. 'Please lead the way.'

Chapter 7

We walk up the steps of his grand townhouse and the door is pulled back by two liveried servants.

I step into the marbled lobby and it is as much as I can do to stop my mouth falling open.

'This is where you live?' I am staring up at the towering elaborate ceilings, finished in frescoes and gold leaf.

The floor is more marble than I have ever seen in my life. And it extends into an enormous staircase, with winding mahogany banister.

A chandelier large enough to light a grand ball hangs from the ceiling, dripping with candles to make it almost bright as day inside. Huge gilded frames bearing oil paintings are lit separately, with gold candelabras dotted on crafted ebony tables.

'It is my London home,' he says, smiling at my reaction. 'My family estate is in Berkshire.'

'It's . . . It is so big.' I wander over to one of the huge candelabras and run my hand across the candle bases, watching as the flames flicker. I turn to him. 'These must have cost a king's ransom. And you have ten of them.'

He tilts his head to one side, watching me. It occurs to me, I'm showing myself very low, admiring all his rich things. It's against Mrs Wilkes's teachings. But Edward doesn't seem to mind. In fact he looks almost pleased.

I notice the servants are staring at me. Edward turns to follow my gaze, and they instantly glance away.

'Excuse me,' he says, and the nearest servant turns towards us again, with a nervous, furtive look.

'Yes, Your Lordship.'

'My guest and I will be using the parlour. Have Sophie bring us up some wine and sweets. Make sure we are not troubled with any other disturbances.'

The servant nods and now he doesn't seem sure where to look. His eyes flick to my rouged cleavage, my powdered face and then to the floor.

'Yes, Your Lordship,' he says, his eyes glued to the marble.

Edward nods and puts out his arm for me.

'Upstairs,' he says, and it is both an explanation and an instruction.

I rest my weight on him as we climb the stairs, feeling all at sea in this enormous grand house and wondering what on earth is expected of me.

We walk along a seemingly endless corridor, and then Edward produces a large key and unlocks one of the doors.

He gestures I should walk in first and I am greeted with a room that seems even more spectacular than the lobby.

It reminds me in some ways of the larger rooms at Mrs Wilkes's house. The furnishings are sumptuous, deeply coloured. Silk, mahogany and gold leaf feature prominently. But it is so much grander than anything I have ever seen before.

The room is simply enormous. I can hardly take in why anyone could need this much space. I let my gaze travel around.

It has a great bank of enormous windows that reach twelve feet to the towering ceilings and elaborate cornicing. The curtains are rich silk and run to a few extra feet of fabric at the bottom. The price of a single pair could support a labourer for the rest of his life.

There's a deep chaise longue, an ornate little table with chairs for tea service and the largest four-poster bed I have ever seen.

'This is your bedroom?' I ask uncertainly.

'It is my parlour,' he corrects.

'Your parlour has a bed?'

'It is commonplace to have comforts of this kind in larger town-houses,' he explains.

There's a large bookcase and I step towards it with a thrilled gasp.

'You have so many books!'

I let my thumb wander across the titles. He has some books on agriculture and farming, but also some fiction.

Reverently, I lift out a leather-bound copy of *The Faerie Queene*.

'You have read this one?' I ask.

He nods very slightly.

'All five volumes?'

He smiles. 'All five volumes.'

I look away, realising it was a foolish question to ask an educated man. He would have been privately tutored in all the great English books, and taught French and Latin besides.

I let the book fall open in my hands and he frowns slightly.

'The spines are delicate,' he says.

'Oh.' I close up the book again chastened. 'This is my favourite book,' I say, by way of explanation. 'I always like to see how it is printed on the page.'

'You can read?' he sounds surprised.

I nod, my eyes on the bookcase, scanning the titles.

'Most of us seduced maidens can read,' I say with a smile. I turn away from the titles to face him.

He looks uncertain. As if not sure whether to believe me.

'I was educated at a country school for a little while,' I explain, to the unasked question. 'It was provided as charity, for poor children who showed ability.'

'How long were you schooled?' he asks.

I move my gaze back to the books.

'Not long. My mother discovered I could recite Edmund Spenser, but could not card wool as fast as the neighbour's daughter.'

I say this with a little laugh, keeping my gaze fixed on the bookcase, so he cannot see my face.

'What can you recite?' he asks.

'Many of his poems,' I say, my eyes on the books. 'My favourite was a sonnet from *Amoretti*. The poem of enduring love.'

I pause, remembering the words.

'"My verse your virtues rare shall eternize,"' I begin, '"And in the heavens write your glorious name."'

'"When Death shall all the world subdue,"' rejoins Edward, '"Our love shall live, and later life renew."'

We look at each other and for a moment something seems to pass between us.

'You know that one by heart?' I blurt.

He nods.

'I did not realise lords learned poetry,' I mutter, to hide my surprise. His recital of my favourite verse was moving.

'Nor I street girls,' replies Edward, his eyebrow raised. 'So your favourite poem is about immortal love?'

I smile a little. 'It was. As a girl I believed in fairy tales.'

'And what do you believe in now?'

'Now,' I say, returning the book to the shelf, 'I believe in a reliable income.'

He laughs. 'Then we are the same in that,' he says.

There's a pause as we regard each other and suddenly I sense the atmosphere has changed.

Our talk had become so easy, I had forgotten why I was here.

I eye the bed cautiously. Edward catches my uncertainty. He steps towards me, guiding me away from the bookcase. I am used to men groping me wherever they please. But he is the only man who has taken my hand as though I were a lady. As his fingers meet mine a strange fear runs through my body. I realise how intimidated I am by his gentlemanly poise. I am used to something quite different, and his courtesy wrong-foots me.

Edward's hand is cool, dry. There is nothing strange about the way he leads me across the room towards the chaise longue. So why is my heart beating a little faster?

There's a knock at the door and I freeze.

He squeezes my palm reassuringly and my heart flutters in my chest.

'The wine,' he says softly. 'Come in, Sophie,' he adds, raising his voice.

The door opens and a girl in an expensive maid's dress enters, carrying a bottle of wine and a little dish of marzipan sweets. She looks so small and young to be dressed in such finery I fear for her. For she looks very anxious as she approaches.

Sophie seems to be walking a determined path towards Edward, taking very good care not to let her eyes stray to me at all. But at the last moment her resolve deserts her and her gaze openly roams my brazen dress and make-up, as if she is wholly unable to decide what to make of it all.

I stare back at her and she looks away.

She has a pretty little face, with mousy brown hair and blue eyes. Not good enough for Mrs Wilkes, but sweet in her own way.

'Thank you, Sophie,' says Edward, taking the bottle.

'Will that be all, Your Lordship?' Her eyes are on me again, drinking me in.

Edward smiles slightly and gives the tiniest incline of his head.

Sophie turns abruptly and swishes out, with her silk skirts swinging.

The door closes a little too loudly.

'May I offer you wine?' Edward asks, gesturing I sit.

I nod, feeling my way in this unusual situation. 'I should like it very much,' I manage.

He manoeuvres himself to a large desk, which holds two wine glasses.

I watch as he removes a corkscrew from his hanging pocket and eases the bottle open. The movements are so smooth and measured that they calm me, and as he pours wine into a glass, I feel back to my usual self.

He proffers the dish of sweets. I take one eagerly.

'These are my favourites,' I confess, taking a happy bite of a marzipan fruit. 'I used to buy them every week, when I was trying to fatten my arms.'

He smiles at my confession and I feel suddenly so out of place, in Lord Hays's parlour with my mouth full of sugar paste.

I swallow my sweet with difficulty.

'Why do you have so many books on agriculture?' I ask, bringing the wine to my lips.

'I have ... projects that I like to understand as fully as possible,' he explains. 'Family business.'

'I did not think lords troubled themselves with business,' I say, lowering the glass a little. 'I thought your occupation was spending money.'

I am unsure of what to do with my hands. So I toy with the glass of wine.

'Not all lords,' he says. There is a sudden bitterness in his tone that brings me up short.

I change the subject to something I'm more practised at.

'Should I take off my dress?' I ask, setting down my wine. 'Or would you rather I only put up my skirts?'

He frowns a little, but doesn't answer the question.

'How long were you at Mrs Wilkes's for?' he asks.

I pick up the wine glass again.

'A little under a year.' I begin nervously kicking my feet against his chaise longue. I do not want to talk about Mrs Wilkes.

He looks down at my feet. I follow his gaze, and still my feet.

'Did you like it there?' he asks.

'Very much,' I lie.

He gives a little laugh, as though he's rather charmed by my blatant mistruth.

'What brings you to London?' I ask, my curiosity getting the better of me. 'If not to spend money?'

'Aside from the five guineas for your company?' he smiles. 'Why do you think I am here?' There is something playful in his tone.

I assess him carefully. I have had a great deal of practice judging men.

'I think you have something to do with riding and horses,' I say. 'You are not pale and thin-shouldered as most lords. You look to spend time outdoors.'

Edward considers this.

'You are right in part,' he says after a moment. 'But that is not my business in London. I am here to buy a ship. I mean to begin importing from the colonies.'

'Oh.' I don't know what else to say. I know nothing of such things.

He moves to sit next to me and carefully removes the wine glass from my unresisting fingers, setting it down.

39

His dark eyes are on my face and I feel myself gazing up at him, unable to break away. In the candlelight of his parlour, the high contours of his face are dropped in dramatic shadows. Once again I am struck by the intensity of his eyes. There is a sadness and a sweetness about them, all bound up in one.

I wonder, dreamily, why a man who looks as he does is paying for a street girl.

His hand moves to touch my cheek.

My eyes are on his and for an instant I'm tumbling into the dark depths of his gaze. Then habit reasserts itself and my body slips into the established ritual of bedding men for money.

My hands move to slide along his thigh. His eyes slide shut as I caress higher.

I continue this teasing, counting the strokes. Then I stand.

His eyes open.

'Might I use the screen?' I ask, a seductive smile playing on my lips. 'To undress myself?' I am on familiar ground now and my earlier unease steadies.

He nods, and his eyes follow me as I walk towards the screen and then disappear behind it. Now he can no longer see me, my smile drops and my hands work rapidly to unlace my dress.

I kick off my shoes and roll up my skirt, extending a naked leg for the benefit of my audience beyond the screen. I peek out my head, while running my bare foot seductively along the edge of the screen.

Edward is watching me, his expression dark.

I lick my lips, keeping my face sultry, but working rapidly with my hidden hand to unlace my bodice and pull off my shift.

I take care to ensure my special banknote is hidden carefully among my clothes.

Then I emerge from behind the screen.

I flutter my eyelashes at him, letting him take in my nakedness unabashed.

'You are very lovely,' says Edward. But he makes no move to run at me, as some men do.

'I am yours, to do as you wish with,' I say, stepping a little nearer.

Edward nods, accepting this.

'Did you learn your tricks with Mrs Wilkes?' he asks.

I move to stand over him, and seat myself on his lap.

His hands move to hold me there.

'Some things I learned at Mrs Wilkes's house,' I say, planting a slow kiss on his mouth. 'Others I learned for myself.'

I slide off his lap and twist down, so I am now kneeling between his legs. I hear him take a breath.

'Perhaps you can decide for yourself,' I say, 'which of my tricks you like best.'

41

Chapter 8

$\mathcal{I}$ wake in a deep soft bed. And my first thought is that I am back in Mrs Wilkes's house and have fallen asleep in one of the guest rooms. Then I remember. I'm in Lord Hays's parlour. In his big bed. The thought gives me a strange thrill.

I sit up, taking in the sumptuous surroundings, the deep horsehair mattress, linen sheets and duck feather eiderdown.

I could get used to this, I think to myself, with a little smile. But since his lordship made no suggestion I stay beyond one night, it's back to Piccadilly.

My stays are back on and loosely fastened. Having satisfied myself of the shape of my banknote, I turn my attention to other things.

I slide out of bed, wondering what to do next.

Edward went to another room in this great house to sleep. It seems sharing a bed is not an aristocratic pursuit. This is strange to me, having shared since being a baby, first with my mother, then either friends or lovers.

I pad across the large Persian rug and open the door softly. The corridor beyond is empty and silent, save the distant noises of staff a few floors down. It seems to go on for ever, with various blank doors, and it occurs to me I might even get lost in this vast place.

Then I hear Edward's voice. It seems to be coming from one of the rooms. Not far away.

Growing bolder, I step into the corridor and follow the sound. It takes me a little onwards and then to a door that is slightly ajar.

Edward's voice trickles in starts from the opening. He sounds to be making orders, in the same confident and courteous tones I heard him use with the servants last night.

My curiosity gets the better of me and I peek through the crack in the door.

Edward is already smartly dressed, though it can hardly be nine in the morning.

I peer more closely into the room and make out another person.

Edward is talking to a man who is clothed in spectacular opulence. The man's high white wig is tied with green silk ribbons – in stark contrast to Edward's natural brown hair, which is tied with a black ribbon.

The rest of the visitor is a similar riot of decadent colour: blue breeches, a red waistcoat, jewelled rings, and ruffles and lace at every opening.

I guess immediately that this is the person who loaned Edward the thoroughbred. It is just the kind of swaggering animal such a man would own.

At Mrs Wilkes's house, we called men who dressed like this 'peacocks'. For all their preening, we usually found them the least generous and the most trouble.

'You are sure it is wise to meet Vanderbilt?' this peacock-man is saying to Edward. I do not like his voice. He sounds grasping. Untrustworthy.

I tilt my head to see him better. His face is even featured enough to be called handsome. Though his eyes are small. And he is nothing to Edward's fine features and dark glimmering eyes.

I would guess him to be the same age as Edward. Thirty, perhaps.

Edward's head is bowed, as though in thought.

'Better I meet Mr Vanderbilt on my own terms,' he says, 'than risk seeing him at the Exchange. He is a hot-headed man. I wish to buy his ship. Not to duel with him.'

'But dinner,' winces the man. 'Such a coarse seafaring man would discomfort any ladies.'

Edward smiles at this. 'Mr Vanderbilt may have been born low, but he became an admiral by his own talent. He must have learned social manners to rise through the ranks.'

There is a pause as Edward looks at the man. 'That is something you should well understand, Fitzroy.'

The man lets out an uncomfortable little laugh.

'With respect, Edward, my own upbringing was rather higher . . .'

'Yes, of course,' says Edward, but his voice suggests the similarity amuses him.

'Can you easily arrange a dinner, with so little time?' says Fitzroy, as though trying to investigate every avenue of impossibility.

'It is already done,' says Edward. 'I have asked Lady Montfort. She will bring her daughter.'

Fitzroy lets out a barking kind of laugh. 'Then you will spend your night fending away marriage proposals from her ladyship.'

Edward raises his hands slightly.

'Do not concern yourself with that.'

Fitzroy's mouth falls like that of a surly child. By conscious effort, he twists it back to a courtier's smile.

'I should also like you to extend an invitation to Lord Rivers,' continues Edward.

'Perhaps you had not heard,' says Fitzroy. 'Lord Rivers is rumoured to have a lady companion who is not his wife.'

'I know it,' says Edward shortly. 'That is why I wish him to attend. Such a scandal will help keep her ladyship occupied.'

Fitzroy nods at this. 'Very clever,' he says with grudging approval. 'You play this game well, Edward.'

'Thank you.'

There is a slight pause. 'Have you decided who might be your lady companion at this dinner?' asks Fitzroy.

'Not yet,' says Edward.

'You might consider asking my sister,' says Fitzroy, in a wary tone. 'Since you and she are to be married one day, it would be a fine way to introduce her—'

'Caroline will be introduced to my society soon enough,' says Edward bluntly, cutting him off.

Fitzroy drops his head contritely. 'Yes, of course.'

I hear a foot on the stair, far back down the corridor, and start. It would be dreadful to be caught eavesdropping, in only my shift and bodice besides.

I turn hastily and dart back along the corridor to the parlour room. I catch a glimpse of a housekeeper's mob cap ascending onto the landing just as I close the door behind me.

Did she see me? I wait a few moments with my breath held and then sigh out in relief.

There's a hard knock on the door and I twist in alarm.

'Who is within?' demands a high female voice.

I am struck dumb. Should I answer? I have no idea how to comport myself in a lord's townhouse. For want of a better plan, I race to recover my dress and at least attire myself decently.

'Announce yourself!' demands the voice, growing more menacing. The tone suggests the housekeeper suspects a burglar has got inside.

I step clumsily into my dress, dragging it up. Then I pull my laces tight enough to secure it, in a single fast movement.

I've mostly fastened it when the handle turns and the door opens.

A finely dressed housekeeper enters, holding a live chicken cradled in the crook of her arm. She is an older lady – I would judge her to be forty. She is trussed tightly into a grey silk dress, with French lace at the edges and around her cap.

For a long moment, we all stare at one another.

Her, the chicken and me.

My eyes soak in her fine attire. Every aspect of the housekeeper's appearance is pin-neat, from her well-proportioned little figure to the silver buckles of her spotless shoes. Her hair has been bundled so ruthlessly under her headwear that not a single strand escapes. And though she wears the apron of a servant, it is snowy white, as though she stitched it new this morning.

The chicken, still closed tightly in the crook of her arm, clucks loudly.

I realise what a fright I must look. I still have on my make-up from last night. And the white face and overly rouged cheeks mark me out so clearly as a whore, I might as well have the word branded on my forehead.

This is matched by my half-closed dress, which barely conceals my breasts and is likely made of the cheapest fabric this household has ever entertained. For even the lowest servants, in this wealthy household, wear modest coloured silks.

We stand stock still, neither sure of what to do next.

It is the chicken that moves first. Sensing a chance for escape, it makes a squawking flap for freedom. The distracted housekeeper loses her grip and the bird drops free, landing with a bounce and scurrying for cover in a flurry of feathers.

Instinctively I dive for the escaping animal, making a chirruping cluck in the back of my throat. The bird pauses in confusion at the noise and I launch forward, securing it by the feet.

I stand, tucking the chicken into my arm, murmuring a little childhood farm song to stop it scrabbling and spoiling my dress.

'Coo, coo, coo, Mrs Cluck Cluck Cluck,' I croon. 'Do not cluck, cluck, cluck, for the pot, pot, pot.'

The chicken wriggles a little and then settles more calmly against my body, with one last disgruntled cluck.

I look up to see the housekeeper staring at me in utter amazement and behind her, I realise to my absolute mortification, is Edward.

'You did not tell me you could sing so sweetly,' he says. His face seems to be fighting a smile.

I never blush. But I feel my face growing hot. As a girl I did all manner of embarrassing things and as a woman more still of which I have cause to be much ashamed. But somehow, nothing quite amounts to the humiliation of having Lord Hays witness my chicken song.

'I grew up on a farm,' I say weakly, as his dark eyes watch me holding the bird.

'I remember.' His voice sounds flat-calm, but his eyes say something different. As though I've amused him beyond all measure.

The housekeeper, who seemed to be paralysed until this point, suddenly speaks.

'I was taking a chicken to the kitchen, when I heard footsteps,' she says. 'I knew you were in the far room and so I thought I should look. In case a robber had got inside.'

Her eyes are on me now, confused – an emotion I sense is rare in this neatly dressed lady.

Edward takes charge, stepping towards me.

'You may take back your chicken, Mrs Tomkinson,' he says, pulling the bird from my unresisting hands. His eyes light on my face, pausing for a moment.

Then he turns to Mrs Tomkinson, delivering her back the chicken, as though nothing could be more normal. She takes it expertly around the wings, her hands working to habit, her face showing that she is still trying to work out what is happening.

'This is Elizabeth,' says Edward, gesturing towards me with his palm.

To my amazement, the housekeeper makes me a slightly confused curtsy. The chicken clucks in alarm.

'I announced her to Sophie last night,' says Edward smoothly. 'But perhaps it slipped her mind to inform you.'

Mrs Tomkinson's face darkens.

'I will have strong words with the girl,' she promises.

Edward shakes his head.

'Sophie might have thought some privacy was necessary,' he said. 'She should not be punished.'

Mrs Tomkinson is looking from Edward to me and back again.

I am deeply conscious of my heavy make-up and cheap, low-cut dress.

'But in any case,' continues Edward, as though this kind of situation were perfectly regular, 'Elizabeth will be joining me for breakfast. I should like the dining room to be prepared.'

I am joining him for breakfast?

I look at him questioningly. Edward makes a slight motion at me with his hands, suggesting he will explain things in due course.

In possession of both her chicken and a viable instruction, Mrs Tomkinson seems to collect herself. She straightens, shrugging on authoritative competency like a familiar cloak.

'As you wish, Your Lordship,' she says, dropping us both a perfect curtsy and managing to make the chicken look as though it's a deliberate part of the manoeuvre.

'I will have the maids add another setting to the breakfast

service,' she says. 'Will Miss Elizabeth be taking chocolate with her breakfast?'

I wonder, suddenly, if perhaps I have not yet woken up and all this is some strange dream.

Edward looks at me.

'You should try the chocolate,' he says, deducing from my blank face that I am not sure of the correct answer.

'Yes please,' I say, adopting my best speaking voice for Mrs Tomkinson's benefit. 'Chocolate with breakfast would be delightful.'

Chapter 9

I expect Edward to explain why he wishes me to attend breakfast. Instead, he advises me to make my toilette and leaves me alone in the parlour. Since I am not certain what this means, I seat myself nervously on the chaise longue, picking at a loose thread on my dress.

I am all in a quandary as to Edward's motives. Perhaps he will ask to see me again. Though I am under no illusions that he could be interested in a long-term arrangement. A girl like me could hardly become his courtesan. Things like that do not happen to whores in hand-stitched dresses. I should first need to establish myself far higher than I am now.

I chew my lip in thought. It could be that he simply takes pity on my poverty. That he gives me a meal out of charity. Or maybe it is some ploy to trick me out of my money. For he has not paid the five guineas yet.

A knock on the door distracts me from my tumbling thoughts. I rise, expecting to see Edward. But instead a maid enters. The same girl who delivered the wine last night. Sophie, I remember.

She opens the door cautiously, and once again I have the sense of a tiny girl, swamped in her fine adult clothes.

'Hello, Sophie,' I say.

Her eyes widen and I realise she is probably unused to strangers remembering her name. From my memories of Mrs Wilkes's, aristocrats have a wonderful ability to ignore those in their service.

'His lordship thought you would wish to make your toilette,' Sophie says. Her quavering voice is grasping for an official tone.

I nod vaguely.

I know that ladies do such things, but have small notion of what it means.

'Of course,' I say, hoping my voice doesn't betray my ignorance.

She breathes a sigh of relief and turns to the hallway.

'Her ladyship should like the basin brought,' she announces.

I open my mouth to correct the title, but shut it again uncertainly.

To my amazement, three more luxuriantly dressed maids enter, carrying a large porcelain basin, jug, large gilded mirror and various intricately wrought silver boxes on a matching silver tray.

They approach a little table, near to where I sit. I watch, fascinated, as the girls work expertly, setting these artefacts out to some preordained ritual, each in the right position.

Finally, after an endless series of deft little movements, steaming water is poured from the jug and rose petals are scattered in the bowl.

'Please sit,' says Sophie, gesturing to a comfortable chair next to the basin of water. I rise and seat myself as requested, wondering what awaits me. I have hazy memories that ladies are washed all over by their maids and am dreading missing some protocol.

Sophie dips a white linen cloth into the bowl, wrings it out and then approaches my face. She passes it gently across my forehead and down either cheek. Then she repeats the motion, washing away my thick white face paint and rouge.

The hot water is soothing and I close my eyes as she massages my face with the cloth. The water in the bowl clouds as she works.

Sophie makes a final satisfied wringing of the cloth and nods for a maid, who holds up the long mirror.

I stare at my face in the glass, feeling vulnerable without my armour of make-up. A whore can take liberties with social graces. But people might expect manners of this fresh-faced girl in the mirror, which I do not possess.

'Thank you,' I say to Sophie. She looks surprised and nods in reply.

Another girl steps forward with two small silver boxes. She opens them and holds them towards me.

My gaze darts to Sophie, uncertainly. The boxes seem to have a kind of grease inside.

'Would you take rose perfume, or bergamot?' asks Sophie, registering my confusion and saving me.

'Rose please,' I say, opting for the more familiar word.

Sophie leans forward to dab perfume at my throat.

'Shall we pin your hair?' she asks.

I nod, thrown again into a ritual I do not wholly understand.

A maid steps forward with one of the silver boxes. She opens the lid to reveal an array of silk ribbons, delicate lengths of lace and coloured feathers.

'Which should her ladyship like?' asks Sophie.

'Oh,' I say, feeling too ridiculous to continue with this particular lie. 'I am not a lady.' I smile at them. 'You can call me Lizzy,' I add.

The maids seem both pleased and disconcerted by this. Sophie makes the first address. 'What should you like in your hair, Miss Lizzy?'

'I am not used to such finery,' I admit. 'Perhaps you could select for me.'

Sophie looks pleased at this. 'Of course, Miss Lizzy.'

She scoops up a handful of my chestnut hair and lets it fall through her fingers admiringly.

'I think some French lace,' she decides. 'Your curls are so pretty they need hardly any ornament.'

I am not sure what to say to this, so I smile gratefully and stay silent. Seeming to need no answer, Sophie and the girls set to work on my hair, pinning and twisting.

They are finished quickly and the glass is held for my approval. My eyes widen, taking in my new appearance.

'It is not so very fine,' apologises Sophie, 'for we have no hair-dresser and no hair pieces to make it proper. But I think it looks well enough.'

'You have done very well,' I assure her, turning my head to take it all in. My face is framed by a cloud of high hair, ornamented with exquisite swoops of lace. Two thick curls have been left to fall free over each shoulder. The overall arrangement makes my brown eyes look striking and my wide mouth more prominent.

It is not elaborate, as very fine ladies style their hair. But it is much nicer than I usually have it. I look like a merchant's daughter, I decide, or a country debutante.

I breathe out. I realise, with a sinking heart, that my cheap dress looks even worse fitting against my neat-pinned curls.

Sophie and the girls begin packing up the toilette, with the same deft assurance as when they laid it out. Then they sweep out of the room and leave me alone, and even more anxious than I was before.

I stand, chewing a fingernail and tracing the shape of my special banknote in my bodice.

You can do this, I tell myself. *You can eat breakfast in a lord's dining room. Remember Mrs Wilkes's teachings.*

Before I can work myself into a true state of terror, there is another knock on the door.

'Come in,' I say absently, praying there isn't another frightening aristocratic ritual to be endured.

The door eases open and Edward walks in. I feel myself swallow, alarmed at the sudden thoughts his presence is invoking.

Last night was … business. So why has my heart started beating faster?

I am abruptly aware of how ridiculous I must look. A whore-styled-as-lady half-breed.

'Did I startle you?' he asks, and I realise my face must show all my trepidation.

'Yes,' I admit, alive with awkwardness.

'A bare face suits you better,' he observes. 'And your hair looks very nice indeed.'

I give an uncertain smile.

His eyes drop to the top of my dress. And I realise I am still fingering my special banknote.

'What do you have there?' he asks.

'Nothing.' I give a false smile to pass off my discomfort and quickly move my hand from the top of my stays.

Edward's face tightens and I realise my gesture looked guilty. As though I am hiding something.

'Did you take something,' he asks, 'from this room?' He sounds disappointed.

My face drops in horror.

'No! I …' I am too offended to get my words out. Edward moves towards me.

'I am no thief,' I say hotly, disconcerted now by his proximity. 'I have never stolen. Not even when I was half-starved and homeless.'

His hand is at my stays and before I realise what is happening, his fingers close on my banknote.

'What do you conceal here?' he asks, pulling it out before I can stop him. 'What is this?'

He pauses, studying it. 'A banknote,' he says, more to himself than to me.

I snatch it back from him.

'It is money I earned when first in London,' I blurt, angrily pushing it back into my clothing. 'It is no business of yours.'

Edward looks as though he is understanding something.

'You did not spend the first money you earned as a whore?' he asks.

'It is no business of yours,' I repeat. 'You have no right to accuse me of thieving.'

To my shame, my eyes have filled with tears. But I am furious too. How dare he judge me a thief?

I reach up, meaning to begin tugging out the foolish hair ribbons. Edward's hand closes on my wrist.

'Please,' he says, and his dark eyes are filled with remorse. 'I apologise. I am very sorry to have doubted your character.'

We stand there, my hand halfway to my head, his fingers gently restraining me.

Slowly, I let him draw my arm away from my hair. In truth I am a little taken aback by the sincerity of his apology.

'Please,' he says. 'Take breakfast with me. Allow me to make amends. It was wrong of me to judge you. It is just that ...'

He pauses, his hand still holding my arm. 'I am usually a good judge of such things,' he concludes finally, with a look on his face to suggest he has seen the worst of human nature.

'Well,' I say, some of the anger slipping away, 'you should not judge so quickly. Just because a woman makes her living a certain way does not mean she has no morals at all.'

He looks rather moved by this. 'No,' he mutters, as though thinking of something different entirely, 'I suppose it does not.'

Edward releases my wrist from his grip.

His eyes roam my face and his lips are inches from mine. And just when I think he might kiss me, he turns and exits the room.

Chapter 10

It is Mrs Tomkinson, not Sophie, who arrives to guide me to the breakfast room. And I can tell that every part of her is straining in her effort to remain courteous to me. Her eyes linger on my cheap dress, her mouth set in a straight grim line. As though I am a personal affront to her fine household.

I follow her, keeping my face defiantly happy as she opens the door and gestures me inside.

A long, long table has been made up with a place setting at either end. The space in between is peppered with the various pots and plates of a lavish silver breakfast service.

Edward is sat at the far end. He smiles at me.

'What a very long table!' I announce in a voice deliberately loud and common, to goad Mrs Tomkinson. 'I should not hear a word my sweet Edward says.'

Instead of sitting at my allotted place, I stride down to the end of the table and perch myself on an empty patch of mahogany surface, so I am almost in Edward's lap.

Mrs Tomkinson's face sets in high alarm and her body tightens so much she is almost twitching.

Edward is struggling with a smirk. He inclines his head very slightly to the chair at the far end. A footman dives forward, heaves it up and carries it to my self-appointed place next to his lordship. Another servant arranges a place setting for me.

Mrs Tomkinson leans forward, glowering, and straightens a cup.

'Thank you. You may leave us,' adds Edward, addressing all the servants.

I slide from the table into my new seat.

The servants retract smoothly and as the door closes, Edward raises his eyebrow at me.

'I could not help myself,' I admit.

'Perhaps you should try,' he says. But there is no reproach in his voice.

Something smells delicious, I realise.

'Have you taken chocolate before?' Edward asks, following my gaze and gesturing to a little steaming silver jug, with an ornate whisk beside it.

'No.' I shake my head, peering into the mouth of the jug.

He smiles at my interest and leans forward, taking up the whisk and frothing the contents of the jug. He then pours a high stream of dark liquid into a thin china cup. He passes it to me and I take it gingerly.

It smells like heaven itself. I take a sip and find my eyes closing, as the sweet chocolate rushes over my tongue.

I open my eyes to find that Edward seems to be studying my face. I set the cup down awkwardly.

'It is fine indeed,' I exclaim. 'Delicious.'

He says nothing, but only looks at me with a gentle smile.

'Do you not take chocolate?' I ask, noticing he has no food or cups before him.

Edward shakes his head.

'I rose very early to start my business for today,' he says. 'I have tried a great deal of chocolate already. It is something I mean to begin importing.'

'Chocolate from the colonies?' I guess, piecing together what I know of him.

He gives a little incline of his head.

'So you will deal in the slave trade?' I ask.

He frowns at this. 'No. My ship will carry guns and gold to Africa. That money will buy slaves to send to America. Then America will ship me goods in return. Coffee, chocolate. Goods of that nature.'

'But you still broker in slaves,' I point out, wondering if he has any moral stance on this. There is much talk now of making slavery illegal.

'Not directly,' he says. 'My main business is securing a ship at a good price. That will ensure us good profits.'

'But why should you care about profits?' I ask, taking another sip of chocolate. 'You are a rich lord.'

It is not the kind of question a lady would ask. But he doesn't seem to mind.

'Regrettably,' he says, 'my father was not the best custodian of the family wealth.'

'Ah,' I say, understanding. 'So the son makes amends for your father's poor management.'

'Yes.' He seems pleased by my breezy assessment of his situation. 'In any case,' he adds, 'my financial situation brings me to London. And it might also involve you.'

I cough on my last mouthful of chocolate.

'Me?'

He hands me a napkin.

'You.' His eyes are on mine. I dab uncertainly at my mouth.

'What is it you wish from me?' I ask, wondering if there is some illegal part of his plan he wishes to involve me in.

'I need a female companion,' he says simply.

'A companion.' I repeat his words back slowly, trying to make sense of them.

He nods. 'I need to do business in London. That involves hosting dinners, attending balls. If I go alone, I will be besieged by matchmaking women looking to find me a wife.'

'You do not look to marry?' I ask, thinking of the exchange I overheard.

'Not for the time being.'

'Surely a rich wife would bring you more money than a good ship?'

'I do not intend to take a wife for some time,' he says.

My face twists, trying to make sense of things. Perhaps his betrothal is an informal arrangement.

'Why not take a courtesan?' I ask, thinking of the beautiful women who accompany wealthy men.

He shakes his head. 'They are all well known. And society ladies would not attend an event with a courtesan.'

'A debutante then,' I say. 'Some pretty girl.'

He shakes his head. 'That is far too complicated. A society girl comes with a mother. A mother means all kinds of problems.'

I swallow. 'You would like me to be your paid companion?'

He gives a small nod. 'For a week,' he says. 'No more. After that time, my business in London will be concluded and I will return to my country estate.'

'You want me to ... masquerade?' I say, searching for the words. 'But as what?'

The thought of pretending to be high-born makes me hot with fear.

'People will be too polite to question who you are in detail,' says

60

Edward. 'I will tell them you are a distant relative and a country heiress. As long as your clothes are right, your manners will not be so important.'

'How much would you pay me?' I ask bluntly, deciding money will be the persuader.

'Thirty-five guineas,' he says smoothly. 'Five a day for seven days.'

I suppress a sharp intake of breath. This is a great deal of money. A great, great deal of money.

'You want me to attend society events,' I say slowly. 'Dinners, balls. Things of that nature.'

He nods.

'Then you must pay me more than thirty-five,' I say. 'You do not buy me for company alone. I must act in front of others to be part of your charade.'

'Then how much would you ask?'

'Seventy,' I say, doubling his price.

He regards me coolly for a moment.

'Forty,' he says. 'No more.'

I swallow. 'Fifty is my lucky number,' I reply, using Piccadilly barter.

Edward laughs. 'Fifty it is.' He holds out his hand and I shake it, still reeling with shock.

Fifty guineas!

I can scarce believe it. The sum is enough to leave Piccadilly. To rent good rooms. To buy a fine dress. If I manage the sum properly, I could secure a wealthy suitor within a year. My dream of independent income could come true.

'Fifty guineas,' I murmur, my hand limp in his. 'Fifty guineas.'

I break into a grin. 'Holy Mary.'

Edward rises. 'I will be back this evening and we will both take dinner with some guests.'

'Dinner?' My anxiety levels reach a new peak.

'It is not a formal dinner,' he soothes.

I swallow, resolving to work hard for my fifty guineas. I've had a little training, after all, in gentry ways.

Then my eyes drop down to my dress.

'Yes,' says Edward, following my gaze. 'You will need to get yourself a dress. I will leave a purse of money for you,' he adds as an afterthought. 'It will contain your five guineas for last night and more for clothing.'

I feel a little thrill of excitement. Our arrangement is getting better and better. With a dress to disguise my humble beginnings, I can keep quiet and stay below notice. For I know I scrub up nicely in the right clothes.

'Your wish is my command,' I say, quoting from *Arabian Nights*, since I know he will understand the reference.

'For fifty guineas, I will expect more than three wishes,' he replies.

Chapter 11

*E*dward leaves and as promised I am left a purse of money. I open it gingerly, hardly believing my good fortune. Inside is more money than I earned in a month at Mrs Wilkes's.

My grin, which has become fixed to my face since we brokered our deal, widens further.

Then I remember Kitty. I need to explain things to her. And send money.

After a few moments' thought, I decide to ask Sophie's help.

I wander out into the endless corridors and soon find her manhandling a heavy sack of potatoes through the back door.

'Here, let me help you,' I say, stepping to take the sack. She looks terrified.

'God's fish, Sophie,' I say. 'Look at the size of you. You will never get that sack inside without it breaking open.'

Not waiting for her answer, I pick up the other end of the sack.

'Thank you,' she concedes, her little face red and sweating. 'They usually carry potatoes down, but they have a new delivery boy who forgot.'

I settle the potatoes easily on my hip, the farmyard way. Sophie waddles uncertainly forward with her end.

'I want to get a message,' I say, 'to a friend in Piccadilly. Do they collect the penny post here?'

'No,' replies Sophie. 'His lordship uses servants to send messages.'

I should have realised that. Of course a lord would have a liveried man to send messages.

'But I can call for a message to be sent,' adds Sophie.

'Could you?' I ask gratefully.

She nods, still straining under the weight of the sack.

'I need to send money,' I say. 'Will it be safe?'

Sophie looks shocked. 'Of course, Miss Lizzy,' she manages, making the final waylaid step into the cellar.

Now we have reached the bottom of the stair, she indicates a pile of similar sacks. I turn towards it.

'Where should the message go?' she asks.

'Kitty French at number seventy-three Piccadilly.'

'I will ask right away,' she adds, as we heave the sack to the ground. 'What would you like said?'

'Only that this is some money from Elizabeth Ward. And I am safe and will be back in a week,' I say.

Sophie nods slowly, memorising this.

'It will be done,' she says.

'Thank you.' I beam at her. I take out Edward's purse and give her three of the five guineas I earned last night. Enough to pay rent and keep Kitty's creditor at bay a little longer. I have already decided to send more, if the arrangement works out. So that Kitty might pay off her dress and finally be free of Mrs Wilkes.

'You will be sure it is put into her hand directly?' I ask, seized with fear that one of Kitty's shady friends will pocket the money.

'You have my word, Miss Lizzy,' promises Sophie. 'I will make sure the money gets to her.'

Once I have taken care of Kitty, my head returns to my own affairs.

A silk dress. New shoes and gloves to match.

It is all so exciting. Already I have decided on the colour and the style.

But the situation also presents me with a problem.

I came from the country almost direct to Mrs Wilkes. I have very little idea of how to find good dressmakers in the city.

I puzzle on the problem. I am in Mayfair, after all, I decide. I will take to the streets and hunt out the right fabric myself. There must be dozens of fine shops for the ladies in this part of town.

I sneak out of the house, avoiding Mrs Tomkinson, who I feel sure would make some remark. But it is much harder than I thought to find a place to have a dress made. Mayfair seems to have none at all.

I spend the best part of the morning searching, but see nothing that resembles a dressmakers.

I am trying to think where to go next, for I only know low dressmakers. I am considering broadening my search to Westminster when I spy a city beadle approaching me. Beadles police the streets and so this one must be able to help.

'Good day, sir,' I say, as he nears. He is a stocky sort of man, with a close beard and mean little eyes that seem to be regarding me in full derision.

'What are you doing in Mayfair, girl?' he asks. He is staring meaningfully at my cheap dress. I swallow, trying to remain dignified. I have a great purse of money about me, after all.

'I look to buy a dress,' I say.

'This is not the place for your kind,' he says. 'You had better go to Cheapside.'

I shake my head, blood beginning to hammer in my ears.

'I have money,' I stutter. 'I am here to buy a silk.'

'Cheapside is the place for you,' repeats the beadle. 'Now you had best stop roaming these streets, Missy. Before I have you whipped for plying your foul trade.'

'I . . .' I open my mouth and close it again, lost for words. In Piccadilly, in my face paint, I am ready for any cruel remark. But the man's vitriol has taken me by surprise.

I blink back the tears of shame that prickle at my eyes and without a word, turn from the beadle and stride away.

I arrive back at Edward's grand townhouse burning with shame. I have failed utterly. I could not even buy a dress for this evening and have been chased off the streets as a gutter whore.

The hurt of it goes deeper than any I have felt in a long time. And it pains me that the thick shell I worked so hard to build seems so easily pierced.

The hallway is empty as I enter and I walk quickly to the stair, with an uncertain plan of heading back to the parlour.

'Elizabeth!'

A sharp voice calls me back and I turn to see Mrs Tomkinson. My heart sinks.

'What?' I say, my painful day making my tone harsh.

'Come with me,' she instructs, making clear that she is under no illusions that I am a lady.

When I pause, Mrs Tomkinson takes my arm and leads me officiously into a small reception room. She closes the door and gestures for me to take a seat.

'What do you want with me?' I demand, sinking bad-temperedly into a chair.

Mrs Tomkinson does not sit.

'I have heard that his lordship wants to make a guest of you,' she says.

I regard her face, refusing to reply. She has dark features, foreign-looking when you consider her closely. I wonder vaguely if she came from somewhere far away. There is no note to her accent.

Mrs Tomkinson sighs at my silence.

'This is a fine house, for a fine family,' she begins. 'What his lordship does is his own concern. But I should not like to see the good name besmirched.'

I keep my eyes fixed on the floor.

'His lordship has left no instructions as to your status in the household,' she continues. 'Do you have anything to tell me that might save the servants gossiping?'

I stay silent, not quite sure what she is asking me.

'I will tell the servants that you are the daughter of a country family,' she continues, after a moment. 'They are all London born and if you are on your best manners, the illusion may hold.'

I look up, to see she is regarding me steadily, as though she thinks me unlikely to master this particular disguise.

'But your dress,' she says. 'It is very cheap. No one will believe you are anyone at all if you insist on wearing such vulgar attire.'

This final insult sparks some new spirit in me.

'Then tell me how a dress can be got in Mayfair!' I cry exasperatedly. 'For there are no dressmakers and no fabric sellers.'

Mrs Tomkinson blinks at me.

'You went looking for a dressmaker in Mayfair?'

'Yes,' I say. 'And my feet ache from searching.'

I do not tell her about the beadle.

'Edward, his lordship, wishes me to have a dress for dinner,' I add, tears of hopelessness springing up. 'But I have none and no time to have one made.'

To my amazement, Mrs Tomkinson's face softens.

'Men know nothing about such things,' she tuts. 'There are only a few dressmakers in London who could accomplish such a feat in a day. And *you* could hardly be expected to know them.'

She shakes her head, her eyes falling to my figure, judging my inadequacy all over again.

'Sophie!' she shouts.

I start in my chair, thinking she means to turn me out of the house.

The door opens almost instantly. I realise Sophie must have been listening outside. I suppose I must make a rare drama for the servants.

'If you mean to turn me out of doors—' I begin.

But Mrs Tomkinson cuts me off, speaking to Sophie. 'I have a better task for you than listening at doors,' she says tartly.

'Yes, ma'am.' Sophie's face is guilty.

'Go to the yellow chamber,' commands Mrs Tomkinson. 'There are some dresses there that were left by Lord Erwing's niece when she last visited. Bring me the purple silk.'

Sophie curtsies and exits.

Mrs Tomkinson eyes me again.

'I think it should fit you,' she decides. 'You are tall, so the skirt may run a little short. But the lady was slender and had good colouring. I think her dress might do nicely.'

As it dawns on me what Mrs Tomkinson is proposing, a new rush of tears rises up.

'I . . .' I try to reply, but there is a dangerous lump in my throat. 'Thank you,' I manage. 'Truly.'

Mrs Tomkinson nods and I feel a rush of warmth towards her.

'No need to thank me, child,' she murmurs. 'Let us first see if you can carry such a garment off.'

Chapter 12

For all her tutting and poking at me, I can tell Mrs Tomkinson feels a sense of pride as she examines me in the borrowed dress.

'It looks very well on you,' she concedes with a satisfied nod. And I realise this is high praise, coming from her.

'Is it not too low at the front?' I ask, tugging nervously at where my bust is on display.

She shakes her head. 'The richer the garment, the more you can display without cheapening yourself. You have a lot of beauty to recommend you. We women must play to our strengths.'

'What will the dinner tonight involve?' I ask.

'A lot of hard work for me,' she says, stooping to arrange my hemline.

I smile. 'Will there be dancing?'

'Yes. French dancing,' she adds. 'It took me all morning to find the musicians.'

My face falls.

Mrs Tomkinson looks up from her manipulation of my hem.

'You do not dance French?' she guesses.

I shake my head limply, feeling flat. Mrs Wilkes taught us English dances for ageing lords.

Mrs Tomkinson stands fully upright and puffs out her cheeks in a sigh. She appraises me for a long moment.

'You dance English?' she asks.

I nod listlessly.

'You can dance well?' she demands.

I shrug. 'I have been told so.' There's no point in being modest. My talent hardly helps me here.

'Come with me.'

Mrs Tomkinson leads me into the large ballroom of the house, where a harpsichord stands.

'The musicians are not here yet,' she says. 'We shall have to sing it ourselves. That should not be hard for you,' she adds, and I realise she's referring to my chicken song.

'You would teach me the dances?' I say, overwhelmed with gratitude. 'You think I could learn the steps?'

'It depends how fast you learn,' she says. 'French is complicated. But if you are a good dancer, then you might be able to learn enough to pass. Sophie will partner you,' she adds. 'The girl spends half her time watching dances when she should be working. She knows the steps.'

I nod, chewing my lip.

'Thank you,' I say in a small voice.

'We shall have none of that,' says Mrs Tomkinson. 'You will learn nothing at all with that littleness.'

She frowns. 'Keep your face straight,' she instructs. 'Stand taller. Show your good figure to its advantage.'

Mrs Tomkinson examines me critically.

'You are very lovely,' she adds without sentiment. 'People will be looking at your face, not your feet. You may be able to fool them yet.'

Chapter 13

I am so alive with nerves that the long preparation for the evening is over before I realise. Sophie and an army of maids flock around me, lacing my dress and ornamenting my person.

Motivated by Sophie's instructions, the girls have spent a solid two hours building my curls high over my head. So I have my first taste of the weight that fine ladies carry on their heads.

I am so grateful for their help I hardly know how to express it. But the maids seem to take a quiet delight in styling me for dinner.

As the time for Edward's return nears, I descend the wide staircase and wait anxiously in the hall, my neck muscles stiffening under the weight of my tall hair.

The servants are all in a flurry now, racing back and forth between the kitchen and the dining room, fetching and carrying.

I spy Mrs Tomkinson heading to the kitchen.

'We shall take three kinds of wine before dinner,' she announces to a passing servant. 'A Bordeaux, a burgundy and the cellared Haut-Brion. Have them decanted and ready.'

'Bridget!' I hiss, as she races past.

Mrs Tomkinson stops, noticing me for the first time.

'Well,' she says, breathing out, 'you look quite the lady.' She steps forward, fussing over me and adjusting my dress a little.

Then she catches my terror-filled face and tuts.

'Breathe slowly, stand tall and smile,' she advises.

Suddenly, I hear Edward's voice.

'Do we have a guest, Mrs Tomkinson?' He sounds confused.

I turn and his face looks blank, before dawning recognition sets in.

'Elizabeth?' His expression is one of stunned delight.

I smile uncertainly. He steps forward, taking me in. Then, as if remembering himself, he backs away a step and bows low.

'I am undeserving of such beauty and grace,' he says, directing the words to my feet.

I grin and he straightens, offering me his arm.

'Our guests will arrive shortly,' he says. 'Would you do me the honour of joining me in the reception room? You look beautiful,' he adds. There is so much warmth in his voice that I find myself feeling bashful.

I rest my hand on his arm, allowing him to lead me forward.

'Your Lordship, I should be delighted,' I reply.

We glide away together. And just for a moment, I feel like a real lady.

Chapter 14

*E*dward leads me into a richly furnished room on the ground floor. I have never been inside it before, though I did catch a glimpse from the street when I set off to try to find a dressmaker, and thought it very fine.

The room commands the very front of the house, with enormous windows in the modern sash style. The walls are panelled with gold-leaf edging right up to the towering, elaborately corniced ceiling.

The servants have been hard at work in here and the whole room has a freshly scrubbed and decorated feel.

The huge marble fireplace is adorned with swags of silk, though no fire has been lit, since it is a balmy summer night. The large crystal chandelier is decked with glittering candles and many more shine from the sides of the room.

A colourful Persian rug has been beaten clean to within an inch of its life and the artfully scattered carved-wooden furnishings are waxed to a high shine.

'Tell me about the reason for this dinner,' I say, hoping for something to distract me from my rising nervousness.

'It is partly business,' admits Edward slowly. 'I wish to buy a ship. The owner would rather not sell.'

'Why not?'

'He wishes to make a voyage of exploration with his ship. But a storm sank the rest of his fleet.'

'So he is in debt and his last ship is now owned by creditors?' I deduce.

'How did you know that?'

'I grew up near a port town,' I say. 'Few seafarers land without owing money.'

'You have it right,' says Edward, sounding impressed. 'I arranged dinner to avoid a scene. For he is hot-headed enough to duel.'

I consider this.

'What kind of man is he?' I ask

'Mr Vanderbilt is a buccaneer. A kind of gentleman pirate.'

I grin at the description.

'You know of such men?' asks Edward.

'We sometimes saw them on the Bristol docks,' I say. 'I always thought them the most fascinating of creatures. Dripping with exotic spoils and rugged with far-flung travel.'

Edward smiles a little at my description.

I'm about to ask for more details when an enormous carriage rolls up to the window.

'Our first guests,' he says, though he doesn't sound especially pleased. 'Lady Montfort and her daughter Charlotte.'

'Are they here to husband-hunt?' I ask, joking to disguise my nerves. 'Should I stand close and keep you safe?'

Edward eyes me in amusement.

'Very much so,' he says. 'You may have to fight for me.'

'For fifty guineas I would claw out an eye gladly,' I promise.

He gives a little laugh and then presses my hand as a sign to stay silent. We hear the front door open.

There are high female voices in the hall and then a knock. The door is opened by a footman and two women enter.

Mother and daughter have almost identical faces, with long hooked noses, small eyes and close little mouths. But where the younger Montfort is slim, slight and youthful, the elder is stocky, heavy and imposing.

I curtsy clumsily, hoping this is the required gesture.

'Lady Montfort,' says Edward, bowing low. 'And Miss Montfort.' He steps forward and kisses her hand. The younger Montfort makes an odd kind of simper, which rises to a high-pitched giggle.

'*Char*lotte!' hisses her mother, and the giggle stops short.

'May I present Miss Elizabeth Ward,' says Edward, gesturing to me. 'Miss Ward is an heiress from the country. She is related to my mother's family.'

Lady Montfort purses her thin lips so they seem to disappear utterly and regards me with undisguised disapproval.

'I had heard, Lord Hays,' she said, 'that you had a female guest. Quite a surprise to *us*, you must be sure.'

She eyes Charlotte meaningfully as she says this, but Charlotte is goggling away at me, as though she can't decide which part of me she wants to look at the most.

'London is full of surprises,' says Edward mildly.

I get the impression some charged subtext is going on beneath the polite words.

I turn it over in my mind, remembering my earlier overheard conversation between Edward and Fitzroy. My conclusion is that Lady Montfort was hoping to match Charlotte with Edward.

A bell rings and we hear voices in the hallway. There is a knock and we all turn expectantly to the door.

'Your Lordship,' the servant announces, throwing open the door, 'Mr Vanderbilt.'

A tall figure appears in the doorway. The candlelight falls on the folds of his deeply tanned face and his blue eyes sparkle out at us.

Edward moves forward to greet his guest, while the rest of us drink in his riotous appearance. Mr Vanderbilt is a rugged chaos of a man. A medley of pirate and admiral, in a battered red coat flecked with gold. A bright handkerchief is around his neck, gold rings adorn his fingers, and his large hat sports a huge pluming blue feather from some exotic bird.

He looks on the very edge of breaking into a loud laugh. And he winks when he sees me staring. I wonder if I should be careful of him, for Edward says he is hot-headed. But I feel myself liking Mr Vanderbilt, for all his intimidating appearance.

'Mr Vanderbilt,' announces Edward, bowing slightly. Mr Vanderbilt returns the courtesy, doffing his large feathered hat in an exaggerated bow, which I cannot help but think is mocking.

'Your Lordship,' he says, in a gravelly tone that reminds me of rum-soaked sea shanties. 'Ladies.'

He bows to us.

'Elizabeth Ward, Lady Montfort and her daughter Charlotte,' says Edward, with easy courtesy.

I drop low. Lady Montfort makes the tiniest of glaring curtsies and I realise I am likely saved her scrutiny now. This colourful man is far more transgressive than I am.

She glares at Edward, as if mutely questioning why he has invited such a man to dine. He ignores the look, saving his attention for the newest guest.

Mr Vanderbilt and Edward are eyeing each other, like respectful foes.

'You did not bring your wife?' asks Edward, after a beat.

Mr Vanderbilt shakes his head. 'She does not find herself well-suited to English society,' he says. 'Her understanding is not always good.'

'Your wife is not from England?' asks Lady Montfort, finding her voice.

Mr Vanderbilt turns his full attention on her.

'My wife is a Red Indian. A slave when I found her,' he explains.

Lady Montfort visibly blanches.

We are all silent, then Edward speaks.

'How very interesting,' he says. 'Did you bring a guest in her stead?'

Something about his tone suggests there are games afoot. I look to Mr Vanderbilt. His eyes narrow a little as though he's been out-manoeuvred.

'That I did,' he says. 'My partner, Percy. He waits in the carriage.'

'Please,' says Edward, with a bland smile. 'He is most welcome.' He raises his hand for a footman. 'Please ask Mr Vanderbilt's guest to join us,' he says.

The footman vanishes, as I try and work out what is happening. It seems Mr Vanderbilt has brought a second. Another man, instead of the wife Edward was expecting. I feel a stirring of fear in the pit of my stomach, wondering how this will affect the evening. Has Mr Vanderbilt brought another man to duel?

Percy is shown in and we all study him as the introductions are made. He is a young man, but carries himself as though he were older. His clothes look hastily chosen, and slightly ill-fitting, but he carries a sword at his hip with an ease that suggests he can use it.

'Percy is a naval officer,' explains Mr Vanderbilt. 'There never was a braver one. Our ship would have been lost to the deeps, if not for his sailing skill. And he saved my life twice from pirate Spaniards.'

This explains Percy's dress. He has likely rushed to find civilian clothes for the city.

'Admiral Vanderbilt saved my life three times,' returns Percy with a smile. 'Do not let this old dog fool you. He can still swing a sword.'

Edward nods politely and invites them to take wine.

There is an air of restrained tension as the drinks are poured. As though words are bubbling beneath the surface.

I notice Charlotte's eyes are riveted to Percy and hide a smile. With his blond hair and soft brown eyes, I can well see how she finds him handsome. Lady Montfort has noticed and looks furious.

Her sharp little eyes are taking me in again, as though searching for a foil for her venom.

'You are from the country, Miss Ward?' she says, eyeing the fashionable cut of my dress. 'I have not heard of you. You are well dressed for one so new to town.'

There is a sudden silence and all eyes are on me.

'Oh, this is borrowed,' I admit, 'from a relative of Edward's. I could not find a dressmaker anywhere in Mayfair, though I walked all morning.'

There is a pause and suddenly everyone but Lady Montfort bursts out laughing. They think I am joking, I realise. That I have disarmed her ladyship's barb with a better one of my own. Edward turns to me with pride.

'Lord Rivers and his guest cannot be long,' he says. 'Perhaps you could ask Lady Montfort to lead us in to dinner?'

'Of course,' I say demurely, trying desperately to remember the protocol when there is an older dowager present.

'Lady Montfort,' I say in my best voice, 'we have many delicious things to eat. And nice wines to drink too. The servants have been working all day. Won't you take us to see what wonders they have made?'

This also seems to delight the guests. 'We shall have a lively night with such a jolly hostess,' grins Percy, as Lady Montfort leads us through to the dining room.

The table has been set with an enormous sugar confection, fashioned in the shape of the townhouse. Spanning the sugar-work are plates of cold foods, elaborately decorated and looking almost too pretty to eat.

Servants pass us glasses of wine.

We have barely taken in the display, when there is a knock at the door and our final guests are announced.

'Your Lordship,' says the footman, 'Lord Rivers and his guest.'

I am feeling a little easier now in the company. I take a sip of wine and turn smiling to greet the remaining people.

A great hulk of a man walks in and I take him in uneasily. Then my mouth falls open. Because his guest is all too familiar to me.

The woman accompanying Lord Rivers is Belle.

The girl who was sold.

Chapter 15

*B*elle and I stand looking at one another in total amazement. Then she makes the tiniest little incline of her head.

Do not reveal me.

I nod slightly in return. Memories fork unbidden through my brain.

We were at Mrs Wilkes's house. Men were arriving. Belle was taken off alone.

The introductions are happening around us. I hear Belle's name spoken and curtsy to her.

Mrs Wilkes told us Belle had gone willingly. But we knew she never would have left without saying goodbye.

'A companion to Lord Rivers,' Lady Montfort is saying. 'That word is used to mean all kind of things nowadays. I wonder sometimes what it means.'

Belle has turned slightly pink and I realise Lady Montfort is implying she is a courtesan. Lord Rivers's face sets to dark fury and I interject quickly to avoid a scene.

'I hear Mr Johnson made a book to give the meaning to words,' I say, blurting out the first thing that comes to mind. 'Perhaps that would help you define it.'

This prompts more laughter and a grateful look from Belle. And I realise that I have unwittingly cut down Lady Montfort again. She seems furious. Edward, however, looks as though he is enjoying himself immensely.

When we sit for dinner, Belle is placed at the other end of the table to me.

I try desperately to work out her circumstances. Lord Rivers is a brooding kind of man. Hulking and dark. Certainly, I would be terrified to have been sold into his house. My mind is turning over the possibilities of it all. How was the sale arranged? What did she feel meeting him for the first time?

Does he own her? Is she his courtesan? His mistress?

My thoughts keep me mostly silent, as we are served the hot dishes, and I feel Edward's eyes on me in concern. I smile at him weakly.

All I can think of is Belle. As we eat, she says hardly anything. And she is too far away for me to speak privately to her.

Lady Montfort is holding court and Charlotte has grown confident enough to join the conversation. Though she acts more like a girl of twelve than of twenty. I endure Charlotte's gauche remarks with slight annoyance, wishing dinner would end so I might see Belle.

A girl like Charlotte would drive me half mad with her trivial chatter. I find myself sympathising with Edward's decision not to take a wife. I presume Charlotte's silliness is the result of educating society girls at home, cloistered away from the world. No wonder Edward would rather the company of someone like me.

Dinner is coming to an end, when my thoughts are distracted by the men's conversation.

'Give me two months,' Mr Vanderbilt is saying to Edward. 'I expect a landing in two months, which will let me pay off my creditors.'

'I cannot wait two months,' says Edward. 'I need a ship.'

Mr Vanderbilt glowers. 'My creditors sell my ship too cheaply.'

Edward shrugs. 'It is theirs to sell.'

'You mean to work my vessel in the slave trade,' accuses Mr Vanderbilt.

Edward shakes his head. 'The ship will not carry slaves. It will carry gold and guns.'

'Which will then be sold for slaves,' says Mr Vanderbilt. He strikes the table and we all jump a little. Then he seems to assess his company and calm himself. I realise Edward was right to redirect him to a dinner, rather than a personal meeting. I could envisage swords being drawn, or a duel being brokered.

'You fine men, in your fine houses,' says Mr Vanderbilt darkly, 'you see nothing of the horrors. Slavery is a foul business, Lord Hays. Your soul would be better out of it.'

I look between the men nervously, wondering if this is the point when the tension will spill into duelling. But Edward's face is completely placid. As though Mr Vanderbilt has simply made a reasonable point.

'What business should I be in?' asks Edward smoothly.

'Exploring,' says Mr Vanderbilt. 'Percy and I mean to bring back wonders.' His eyes are shining. 'Half the world is yet to find.'

Percy is nodding in agreement. 'Were it not for the storm,' he says, 'we would have loaded up in Bristol and set sail on a voyage of discovery.'

'But there *was* a storm,' says Edward. 'Sailing uncharted waters is high risk. Trading gold and guns is low risk. It relies on known shipping routes. That is why I choose it.' His voice sounds quieter than usual.

There is a long, uncomfortable silence.

'I still have my ways of thwarting your purchase,' says Mr Vanderbilt finally. 'I may be an old seadog, but I understand this trade better than you think.'

Edward folds his napkin carefully on his lap.

'I take it you are referring to your conversation with Mr Grieves at the Exchange?' he says. 'I am afraid he will not offer you credit. I have made sure of it.'

This time it is Percy's turn to explode in outrage.

'How do you know of our creditors?' he demands. 'You play a low game indeed!'

Edward watches him, coolly assessing. Percy is shaking with anger. My fingers tighten on my glass of wine.

Percy glares, like a trapped animal, with the polite dinner-setting his cage.

I notice Edward's hand shift almost imperceptibly to his sword. And I have a sudden surety that he has no fear, no alarm at the prospect of fighting. If it came to a duel, he would win. But I sense he would not enjoy the victory.

I wonder if he will say anything to soothe Percy's fury, but the hard glint in his eye suggests he is prouder than that. And in the terrible pause that follows, it is Mr Vanderbilt who lays a gentle hand on Percy's arm.

'Lord Hays plays the game well,' says Mr Vanderbilt. 'We must not begrudge him his skill. We deal with a man, not a boy.'

Edward nods respectfully to Mr Vanderbilt.

'It is business,' says Edward mildly. 'You must not think it changes the great respect I have for your admiralty.'

'Most of my admiralty is at the depths of the Pacific,' grunts Mr Vanderbilt, leaning back in his chair. 'But I am obliged to your regard, nonetheless.'

I glance to Percy, who still looks angry.

'Is there to be dancing?' I ask, eager to break the deadlock and get a chance to speak with Belle. 'I have learned steps especially.'

Edward turns to me in surprise and his face shifts as though relieved.

'Yes, of course,' he says. 'We must have you dance.'

Chapter 16

he doors between the ballroom and the dining room are opened wide, and servants rush to remove all evidence of our meal. Within minutes musicians have taken their places.

For their earlier quarrel, the two men seem to quietly respect one another. I notice Edward insisting Mr Vanderbilt is served the best wine. Though, as I've observed at the dinner, he has drunk little himself. The move to the dance floor seems to have broken the earlier tension and everyone is on their best behaviour again.

'You ladies and young men must dance,' says Edward, moving to the edge of the room. 'I will wait out with Lady Montfort.'

I give him a questioning look, but he nods that I should dance without him. I wonder if he means to talk more business with Mr Vanderbilt. But Mr Vanderbilt moves to the floor with Percy and Lord Rivers.

'Edward never dances,' confides Charlotte in a whisper, as we take our places. 'As a boy, he studied mostly farming. It was quite the scandal. His Latin is dreadful for a man of such good family.'

She breathes this last with an air of horror.

I am trying to work out which position will get me closest to Belle in the complicated French dance, but something about Charlotte's remark riles me to reply.

'Edward is an educated man,' I say defensively, remembering his recital of Spenser. 'He is well read. A man due to inherit a country estate is wise to learn farming,' I add.

I do not quite know why I feel bound to defend Edward. His reputation is no concern of mine, after all.

Charlotte's face twists. 'What girl should want to marry a lord who bothers himself in *farming*?'

'A girl who wishes her estate to be well managed,' I reply tartly.

I am annoyed at myself for being distracted by Charlotte. Belle is now at the other end of the line, with Lord Rivers opposite.

I wonder if she might be deliberately trying to avoid talking to me.

I am opposite Mr Vanderbilt and Charlotte dances with Percy. Her face lights up when she realises he is to be her main partner and she looks almost pretty.

The music starts and we begin a bouncing kind of dance, looping our partners and then back down the line.

Mr Vanderbilt appears to know the dance well and he deftly steers me the right way when I make a wrong step. I smile at him gratefully.

'French is harder than English,' he winks at me. 'It took a long time for an old man such as I to learn it.'

I beam as he leads me easily through the steps. At the dinner table, Mr Vanderbilt had a menace about him, but as he whirls me in the dance, he has a kindly air.

We exchange partners and I look anxiously down the line.

The style of the dance means I have the briefest of moments to turn with first Charlotte and then finally Belle.

'Is your stay with Mr Rivers comfortable?' I whisper, searching her face, not daring to ask her outright.

Belle looks uncertain. 'It is as well as I could hope,' she says, after a moment. 'He is a kind man. In his way.'

We dance away from one another for a few turns and then we are back again.

'What of Lord Hays,' asks Belle, continuing our improvised code. 'He is a good host?'

'My stay is very brief,' I say carefully. 'But he is most courteous.'

'His eyes never leave you,' observes Belle.

I turn in surprise to where Edward is sitting. I had expected he would be deep in conversation with Lady Montfort. But while I am right to predict her to be talking animatedly at his side, I see Belle is right. Edward is gazing out at me. His eyes have a softness that I would attribute to wine if I did not know how little he drinks. When he sees me looking he nods a little and smiles. I do not return his smile. Instead I glance quickly away, confused by the affection in his expression. As I contemplate what his attention could mean, the dance turns me away from Belle and towards Charlotte.

My heart sinks as I watch my old friend step away, desperate for more details, but when the dance is ended we move to another kind and I am never alone with Belle.

All too soon, carriages are summoned and I am left with a sick feeling that the evening is unfinished. I wonder if I will ever see Belle again. We embrace tightly before she leaves.

'Take good care,' I whisper, tears rising up. 'You always were the best girl, Belle.'

'You take care, Lizzy,' she whispers back. 'Lord Hays is a good man. He has a liking for you. I see it.'

The guests depart and I notice Edward giving Mr Vanderbilt a heartfelt handshake before the old man leaves.

I watch from the window as Belle's carriage ferries her and her keeper away.

'Mr Vanderbilt has charmed you?' I ask Edward, when we're left alone, 'with all his enthusiasm for adventure?'

Edward gives a half-smile.

'It would make no difference if he had,' he replies. 'I still must buy his ship.'

I nod at this. I, of all people, understand that business should not involve the heart.

'You knew that girl?' asks Edward. 'Lord Rivers's companion. I noticed you talking during the dance.'

'She worked with me in Mrs Wilkes's house.' My voice comes out flat and empty. 'There were five of us who were friends. Belle, Harriet, Rose, Kitty and me.'

'What happened to the other girls?'

'Belle was sold,' I say. 'Since she is with Lord Rivers, I assume he must be her purchaser.'

Edward looks disturbed by this.

'It happened very quickly,' I add. 'None of us expected Belle to leave. When we realised what Mrs Wilkes could do, some of us decided to run away.'

'And that is how you came to Piccadilly?' he guesses. 'You ran from her house?'

I nod.

'How many girls ran?' he asks, frowning as though this is difficult to imagine.

'In the end only three of us. Harriet would not run,' I say. 'She was doing too well for herself. I hear she is a fine courtesan now.'

'Would I know her?' asks Edward.

'Most likely you know lords who do. She is famed,' I say. 'I ran away with the other two girls. Rose and Kitty. We had hoped to set up a house, the three of us. But Rose was spirited away by a fine suitor, the same night we left. He planned to take her overseas,' I add.

'And you and Kitty?'

'We worked the streets,' I say. 'It was bad work. But at least we were free. We half starved ourselves to rent our first rooms in Piccadilly. Close to where I met you. Things were getting better. Then Kitty began drinking gin.'

I stop myself, realising I should not be telling him so much.

'Mrs Wilkes did not try to fetch you back?' asks Edward.

'Yes, she did. But we evaded her any way we could.'

Edward considers this.

'Should you like to see Belle again?' he asks eventually.

'That would not do either of us any good,' I reply. 'She belongs to Lord Rivers now.'

Edward looks thoughtful.

'You did not succumb to Lady Montfort's plans to have you betrothed?' I say, to change the subject.

He shakes his head with a little laugh.

'Your Lordship?' says a quiet voice. We both look up to see Sophie waiting.

The expression on her face suggests she has interrupted some lovers' tryst.

'We wondered if we might clean the room?' she asks tentatively. 'So we might have it ready for breakfast tomorrow.'

'Yes, of course,' says Edward. He takes my arm. 'We will retire to my parlour.' He frowns for a moment, thinking. 'I will be up at dawn tomorrow,' he adds to the servant as an afterthought. 'Please have breakfast ready then.'

Sophie nods, and Edward guides me through the door and up the wide staircase.

Chapter 17

'Y ou did very well tonight,' Edward says, closing the door of the parlour.

Suddenly, we're completely alone. I feel the atmosphere change. My heart begins to pick up in my chest.

'Did I?'

He stands close, his eyes on mine.

'You did.'

Edward studies my face and I think he is about to kiss me. Something in my expression must make him think better of it, for he turns me around instead, to begin unlacing my dress.

I breathe out. Had he kissed me, I might not have known what to make of it.

My dress inches down and his hands roam over my shift and petticoats, feeling out the shape of my body.

He begins kissing my neck softly. For a moment I am caught off guard and my eyes close.

I open them quickly, gently moving my hands to his and turning back to him.

His regards me as though I have puzzled him.

I fix him with a coquettish grin and continue the process of undressing myself. I let my petticoats fall and then reach up, letting my hair down.

Edward strokes a hand through my hair as it tumbles over my shoulders. He pulls away, his face still almost touching mine. I stare back at him uncertainly, wondering what he is expecting.

He kisses me. There is something in the way he does this. As though he wants me to feel something.

I hope he is not one of those men who wants me to enjoy this business more than I do.

I find those men the hardest. For it is a difficult act to pretend you are in love. Though some girls, like Harriet, make it seem easy.

Edward's hands are moving down my waist and I gently stop them. He looks at me questioningly.

I kiss him deeply, pushing my body against his, moving my hands between his legs. My eyes are conveying an unspoken message.

I am here for your pleasure. Not the other way around.

For a moment, I think he may resist my seduction. And then he seems to accept what he sees in my face and relaxes into me.

I give a little sigh of relief and continue my artful work on his body. And after not very long at all, he is all mine.

Chapter 18

_I_ wake to see Edward's dark eyes looking down at me. 'Did you sleep well?' he asks.

I sit up, blinking, taking stock. Edward left for his own chamber last night, leaving me to sleep alone. By the sunlight streaming into the parlour, it is early morning.

'Mmmm. You are dressed already,' I say, taking in his neat attire.

'I rise early,' he says. 'There is much to be done.'

I rub my forehead, trying to wake up.

'I have arranged for dressmakers to come for you, Elizabeth,' he says. 'After you have taken your breakfast.'

He speaks to me easily and I realise we have stepped into a kind of familiarity with one another. It no longer feels so strange to be waking in his fine house.

'Thank you,' I say. 'That is most kind. You do not eat with me?' I ask, not liking the thought of tackling that great dining room alone.

'I often do not eat before midday if I am engaged on business,' he says. 'Now I must go to the Royal Exchange to have naval papers approved.'

'Do you not take time for leisure?' I ask. 'All the lords I have met spend their days drinking and sleeping.'

'I would rather spend my time productively,' he says.

'May I take a little breakfast in this room?' I ask. 'There is no need to lay out a table. It is more work for Bridget.'

He frowns. 'Who is Bridget?'

'Your housekeeper,' I explain. 'Mrs Tomkinson.'

He raises his eyebrows slightly.

'I can ask them to bring you some hot rolls,' he says. 'If you are sure that is all you would like.'

I nod. 'I should not like to trouble the servants unnecessarily.'

He leans forward, hesitates and kisses my forehead awkwardly. Then he pauses. 'It is kind,' he says, 'how you are with the servants.'

I smile a little, not quite sure of his meaning. Certainly a real lady would not refer to the housekeeper by her first name.

'I hope your business goes well,' I say. 'And you are able to buy the ship.'

'It is a delicate game,' he says. 'Only formality and papers are left. But in these last few days every precaution must be taken to ensure the ship is mine.'

There is a strange expression on his face.

'You have respect for Mr Vanderbilt,' I say.

'I think Mr Vanderbilt was a fine admiral,' replies Edward. 'But my admiration for him is of no consequence in this matter.'

I nod in complete understanding. His approach is remarkably similar to how street girls do business.

'So you will play the game and win?' I ask.

'Mr Vanderbilt is trying to block our purchase,' explains Edward. 'And he seeks men to extend him credit. One of my tasks is to make sure they will not loan.'

Edward is looking at me keenly. As though hoping for a particular response.

'I suppose that is a good thing,' I say uncertainly. Though I liked Mr Vanderbilt. I should enjoy the thought of his setting off to the Americas and beyond.

'Yes,' says Edward. But his face looks sad.

After Edward has left, and I have eaten breakfast, dressmakers come in a virtual flood. Six women buzz around me, waving fabrics and tape measures. By mid-afternoon I have seen so many swatches and trays of shoes, I am dizzy from it. Each part of my body has been squeezed and measured. Every conceivable fashion and fit have been debated.

Eventually, the team of women leave with instructions to make over ten fine dresses, for daytime and evening too.

I can scarcely believe it. Only a day ago, I was a Piccadilly street girl in a cheap homemade dress. Now I am about to have an entire wardrobe, which the dressmakers say will be ready for tomorrow.

Until then, however, I am trapped in Lord Hays's townhouse. After the beadle I do not dare walk out in my cheap day dress. So instead I stay in the parlour reading.

Edward arrives home as it's beginning to get dark. I hear him ask my whereabouts from Sophie and then he takes to the stair, heading for the parlour.

I have already planned how I am going to greet him after his long day. But I feel a more than expected amount of excitement at the thought of seeing Edward. I push it away, telling myself it is simply because I have been alone all afternoon.

I quickly strip away my clothes, leaving a trail of stockings, dress and petticoats across the room. Finally I drape my dress over the screen, arranging it so the cheap fabric is not so prominent. Then I hide, naked behind the screen, and await his arrival.

The door handle turns and I peek through a gap to see him enter.

He is dressed in a long grey waistcoat, closed with a row of tiny silver buttons, a white linen shirt and black breeches under high riding boots.

He looks utterly exhausted. My heart goes out to him.

Then his handsome face wrinkles in confusion as he takes in the empty room. I smile. His dark eyes drop to the floor, taking in my abandoned stockings. He looks up, scanning the room with a grin. Then he stoops and picks up the stockings, one by one.

I feel my heart beating faster, excited by the expression on his face.

He scoops up the shift next and walks towards the screen. I hold my breath as he tugs my dress down and folds it carefully over his arm.

Slowly, I step out from behind the screen.

I hear his breath tighten. The tiredness has vanished from his face.

'I thought you should like to see something different, after a day with tired old men,' I explain, standing so he can see me easily.

His dark eyes are roaming my body. 'I like it very much.' His voice comes low with desire.

I take a step towards him and place a single finger on his chest.

'Then you must let me show you something else,' I say, moving forward so that he has to step back towards the chaise longue.

I begin undoing the many buttons of his waistcoat. All the time I'm walking him back, slowly. His face never leaves mine.

I pull open his waistcoat and push him gently down, so he's sitting on the chaise. Then I pull his shirt over his head and undo the top of his breeches.

As my hands do the familiar work, something wholly unexpected shifts through my body. Like a jolt of desire.

It is so unnerving that I pause fractionally.

I shake my head to dispel the thought and concentrate instead

95

on the next part of my act. I mean to make him a little show. This was something we did often at Mrs Wilkes's house.

Edward's lips are parted slightly and his breath has quickened. I know without him speaking, what he is thinking. He has understood what just happened. That some part of me feels more for him.

I toss my head seductively, signalling he should not think such things. This is how I earn my money, that is all. But he only smiles as though he's seen a secret.

I reach up and run my hands across my breasts, my eyes smouldering. Then I run a finger over my lips and draw it softly down my body, over my belly, skimming ever lower.

He makes a tight gasp in his throat. This is something I am very practised at. A large part of Mrs Wilkes's entertainments were for us girls to make naked shows.

The art was in the slow movements. The deliberate tease.

I let my fingers slip between my legs. Edward is rigid. His breath held.

'Would you like to see more?' I whisper, moving closer to where he sits.

He nods, his eyes flicking from my face to where my hand has stopped.

I lean forward and run my fingers lightly over him.

'Then you shall see it,' I promise, pushing him down by the chest. 'I will show you everything you desire.'

Afterwards, Edward takes me in his arms and lies back, staring at the ceiling.

We lie there for a while, enjoying the warmth of one another's arms. And I have an unsettling feeling that some invisible boundary is slipping.

'We should ready ourselves to go out,' he says finally, unwinding gently from my naked body. 'I am in town for only a week and must be seen at every entertainment.'

'Are you not tired?' I ask, remembering his expression when he returned home.

'Maybe a little,' he admits. 'But I have obligations.'

'I had thought lords did what they chose.'

'Not all lords.' Edward's face seems caught halfway between stoicism and humour.

'If I am to make sure Mr Vanderbilt is refused his credit,' he adds, 'I must be seen by those who might afford it.'

'So tonight you must parade your wealth to remind all of your importance?'

He gives a smile at the simplicity of my explanation.

'After a fashion,' says Edward. 'Some aristocracy work harder than you might imagine, to keep the delicate social web aligned.'

'So where do we go tonight?'

'The theatre,' he says. 'Have you been before?'

I shake my head. 'I have always wanted to go,' I admit. 'Since I read Shakespeare as a girl. At Mrs Wilkes's house, Harriet was the only one of us with a fine enough suitor to take her.'

Edward seems interested by this.

'And did Harriet like the theatre?' he asks.

'Oh no. She said it was very dull. We would press her for details, but she hardly seemed to have noticed the play.'

Edward smiles again. 'She is not unlike many lords and ladies in that. And perhaps Harriet has not read Shakespeare as you have?'

I give a snort of amusement at the thought.

'Harriet reads only love letters. And those badly. What is the play?' I ask.

Edward frowns. 'I do not know.'

'Then how can you decide you wish to see it?' I laugh.

'This is not leisure, Elizabeth, it is business,' he admonishes. 'We go so others might see us there.'

I set my face a little more seriously. This is what he is paying me for after all. To be his companion.

'Will the dress from last night do?' I ask. 'I have not yet had others made.'

Edward looks at me as though he is only half listening. And I deduce his mind is already on fulfilling whatever social obligation is expected at the theatre.

'It will do very well,' he says.

Chapter 19

$\mathcal{S}$ ophie dresses me, under Mrs Tomkinson's instructions that the theatre calls for wide skirts and sky-high hair. So a hairdresser is summoned to construct a great column above my head, made from lengths of horse tail and five pots of bear grease.

While my hair tower is hung with swags of ribbon and lace, Sophie manages to find a collection of wicker cages and bulky petticoats to fan my borrowed skirts.

When the style is completed, I can barely move. My neck muscles are already straining under the weight of my hair and I must turn sideways to leave the room. My skirts are so wide I can scarce touch my fingers to the edge of them on each side.

As I arrive in the main hall, Edward seems greatly pleased by my fashionable appearance, but I feel as though I am in a walking prison.

When I see the carriage Edward has readied for us, however, I am distracted from my discomforts and my mouth drops open wide.

The vehicle is a bright blue highly decorated box suspended high above the London mud on four huge wheels. Six plumed horses have been reined in to drive it, and a coachman in a fine coat and hat is in the driver's seat.

'We will ride in this?' I say, stepping forward and running my hands over the shining livery of the door.

'You are the first girl who has caressed my coat of arms,' observes Edward, opening the door and offering his arm to hand me in.

'It is the least interesting thing of yours I have caressed,' I reply, taking his hand.

I eye the low carriage door, wondering how I might get inside.

'How do women get about with their hair so high?' I complain, as I try to manoeuvre my heavy coiffure and huge skirts inside the carriage. 'I can hardly move at all.'

'The carriage is large inside to accommodate it,' Edward says. 'You will be comfortable once you are within.'

I step through, twisting my body, and manage to pull my skirts up and after me. Inside, I take in the plush interior with wonder.

'It is all velvet in here!' I call down to Edward, who is giving instructions to the coachman. He leaps easily in and takes a seat beside me.

'So it is,' he says, smiling at my amazed stroking of the soft seats.

'Real velvet,' I insist.

Edward puts his hand over mine and bangs on the roof of the carriage. The driver cracks his whip and we start with a spurt of movement.

'Oh!' I cry, as I'm jolted forward. Edward's arms automatically grab for me. And when the carriage movement steadies, he releases me slowly, as though he would rather keep me in his arms.

When the carriage arrives outside Drury Lane, I am struck by the milling crowds. I had heard the theatre could be dangerous and now I understand why. Rich and poor are rarely so close together in London. And the undercurrent of discontent that characterises the city's underclass is ever close to spilling over when a mob forms.

I eye the milieu uncertainly. The cheering packs of plainly dressed commoners and the colourful aristocrats, the women like great butterflies with their wide silken skirts.

There are boys selling nuts, gathered from Hyde Park, and girls selling fruit from baskets balanced on their heads. The dirt streets around the theatre have been whipped into a muddy roughness and lining their sides are ragged beggars – scrawny men and women barely clothed in filthy scraps of fabric.

Edward reaches in his hanging pocket and distributes a few coins from the carriage window. A woman with huge ulcers on her legs hobbles up for charity. And as Edward hands her money, I am suddenly shamed by the richness of my dress.

When I left Edward's house, I feared my appearance would be too simple. For I wear a borrowed dress and have no jewelled hair ornaments of my own. Now, among these poorer folk, I wish I were more simply attired.

I do not want to step into this mixed crowd adorned in such finery. It feels wrong. Dangerous. I want to be back in my old cheap dress. To move easily among the crowd. To banter and laugh and swig cheap ale.

Edward must sense my uncertainty, because his hand closes on mine.

'We have a box,' he explains, 'so we shall not be troubled by the crowds.'

I swallow and nod.

Edward's footman has been sent to buy bottles of wine and he returns to the door of the carriage, moving through the thick of the crowd with a determined frown.

The footman opens the door and Edward jumps down, his high

leather boots landing easily on the muddy street. Then he reaches up and helps me down.

I exit laboriously, resting my weight on his hand. Then I am out, looking up at the elaborate façade of the Theatre Royal. It is huge and white, with Greek-style pillars supporting the entrance, like some exotic temple.

I feel exposed, being outside without my usual painted face and wide-brimmed shepherdess hat to hide under. It was part of my armour. In contrast, my tall hair is unwieldy and prominent.

'Come,' says Edward, taking me firmly by the hand, 'we should get inside.'

He pulls me with practised skill through the eddying crowd. Then we are at the doors, through the lobby and into the belly of the lavish tiered theatre.

I breathe in, letting my gaze travel from the bottom to the top.

'It is like being inside an enormous bride cake,' I say, taking in the coloured grandeur of the interior. Gold-leafed decorations adorn tier after tier of boxes and seat sets, rising to impossible heights.

'I suppose it is,' agrees Edward, looking at the sweep of the theatre.

A servant arrives to guide us to the box.

'Should we not have tickets?' I whisper to Edward, as he takes my arm.

He shakes his head.

'I have my own box here. They will put it on my account.'

'Oh.' I am always awed at how aristocrats command credit by their faces alone.

We are led halfway up the theatre and into an incredibly grand box.

I step in sideways for my huge skirts and take in the plush interior admiringly.

'Your box must be the best in the house,' I say, marvelling at the space we have been afforded. 'It is a quarter of the size of the full pit area.'

Edward smiles. 'It is one of the best,' he says. 'There is one other box of this size.'

I lean over the edge, gazing out at the dizzying array of seats and tiers below us.

'I see it,' I say, pointing to a box on the far side that has been sumptuously adorned with hand-painted cherubs in gold leaf. 'Whose is that?'

'That box belongs to His Majesty,' says Edward.

I turn to him, my eyes wide in shock.

'No! Truly?' I look back across, peering, but the box is empty. 'You have the same standard box as the King himself?'

'One of the few advantages of my father's profligacy,' says Edward, 'was he secured our family the finest of everything.'

I take a little step back from the side.

'But your challenge is to keep it?' I guess. 'So the family name is not shamed?'

Edward nods, then smiles easily. 'It doesn't seem like such a hardship when you have someone to share it with,' he says.

I smile at him before returning to my assessment of the theatre.

Aside from the royal box, there are other boxes all around. They are filled with women in the richest dresses I have seen in London. Like mine, their hair is two feet high and their silken dresses are pulled wide. But they have far more elaborate and expensive ornaments than me and their silks are noticeably richer.

My eyes travel down to the pit, where the commoners push and drink and laugh. And then back up to the fine folk.

None are smiling, I realise. The rich women strike me suddenly as captive creatures. Bound tight in their social world and their heavy clothing.

The oppression of it causes me to feel even more restricted by my own heavy hair and wide skirts. I am itching to fly free. To join the easy mix of common folk.

My eye catches a courtesan, easily identifiable to my experienced eyes. She inhabits a box of wealthy men. One I assume to be her suitor is close by her side, laughing with her, his eyes fluttering between her face and her breasts.

He is clearly entranced and she wears the smile of a woman in love. But I can see, even from here, that her smile does not reach her eyes.

I wonder how many broken promises she had to endure to achieve her current success. How much heartache and how much conniving were necessary.

And I wonder for all she undoubtedly went through, if she now thinks her prize worthwhile.

The curtain behind us twitches and a servant appears. He carries a silver tray, a small table and six wine glasses.

Edward moves to the side a little, as the servant sets us up a table, places red wine and a strange bottle with a metal cage on it, and finally steps back with a bow.

'Should you like me to uncork the wine, Your Lordship?' he asks, his head still low.

'Yes please,' says Edward. 'We shall start with the champagne. And perhaps a few nuts and sweets if you can find them.'

'Champagne?' I ask uncertainly. 'What is that?'

'It is a new drink from France,' explains Edward. 'I think you should like it.'

The servant nods and steps forward to uncork the oddly sealed bottle. It opens with a loud pop and I see several heads turn to look up at us.

'This is the purpose of this new drink?' I ask, nodding to the fizzing liquid. 'To have people hear you open it?'

'Exactly that,' says Edward. 'That is the purpose of everything for an aristocrat. We have this box, so people might look at us too. So they might know how preposterously wealthy we are.'

He sounds tired as he says this, as though the game of playing rich is exhausting.

'Has the wine gone bad?' I ask nervously, staring at the foaming liquid coming from the bottle.

He shakes his head, pouring me a glass.

'Try it.'

I take an uncertain sip.

'It is . . . it fizzes,' I say, frowning. I take another sip. The taste is good, but the crackle of the bubbles on my tongue is loud and strange.

'Do you like it?' asks Edward.

'I do not know,' I say, taking another sip. 'I think, perhaps I should get used to it.'

He smiles and takes a deep draft of his own champagne.

'What are the extra glasses for?' I ask, as the servant retreats.

'When you take a large box, you can expect visitors,' he explains.

'Oh,' I say, surprised to find myself a little disappointed. This should be an excellent opportunity to meet more rich men. But the truth is, a small part of me should like to have Edward to myself.

'They will not stay for the whole performance,' he adds.

'What play shall we see?' I ask. It occurs to me that in the excitement I had forgotten to ask.

'*Antony and Cleopatra*,' he says. 'It was written on the board outside.'

I consider this. 'I like that play,' I say. 'I read it as a girl.'

'Have you seen a play acted before?'

'Not in London,' I say. 'We sometimes had travelling players near Bristol. I liked them very much.'

'Then I think you should like this,' he says.

The pit below has filled now and richly dressed young men are being escorted onto the stage.

'Are those the players?' I ask, peering closer.

'No,' says Edward. 'Those are young men who are particularly concerned to be seen. Mostly they are the same pack that favours the gambling club and the coffee shops.'

I watch as the men filter onto the stage. They are swigging wine from expensive-looking bottles and several are arm in arm, talking loudly, waving their hands.

'They look drunk,' I decide.

'Oh yes,' says Edward. 'They have likely been drinking since last night.'

One of the men grabs an orange girl by the waist and she shrieks with indignation.

'They like to show themselves as seducers,' says Edward.

'And their life never appealed to you?' I ask, thinking that he is not much older than they. 'You never thought to drink and whore for sport?'

He smiles a little. 'I outgrew such things. In two years, they shall have the pox, every one of them. Their homes shall be in disarray and their wives shall be sleeping with their friends. Likely they will not know for sure if their heirs are their own.'

'But you do not visit taverns?' I press, thinking of the entertainments lords favour, 'or gambling clubs?'

Edward shakes his head.

'As you know, I enjoy women very much,' he says, considering me with a dangerous smile.

I have a sudden memory of his hands on my body and I hope it does not show on my face.

'But not from taverns,' Edward concludes. 'And I never gamble.'

'Never?' I ask.

'No. I do not like to take risks where money is concerned.'

'Not even for sport?'

'Especially not for sport.'

There is a cough behind us and we both turn.

'Edward?' says a familiar voice.

A man in elaborate dress stands behind a liveried servant. I recognise him immediately. It is Fitzroy. The man I overheard talking with Edward on my first morning in his townhouse. The man whose sister Edward will marry one day.

Chapter 20

I feel myself shrinking back as Fitzroy swaggers into the box.

Once again he is outlandishly attired, in a bouffant white wig almost as tall as a woman's, with elaborate pink ribbons tying his white stockings, silken hose and a coat of eye-wateringly bright green, with gold frogging from neck to thigh.

'Fitzroy,' Edward greets him warmly, moving forward to shake his hand. 'What of business?'

Fitzroy's eyes dart to me and back again. He has a feral quality to him and he is small within his fine clothes. As though he wears the brightest colours and richest stuffs to give himself presence.

'Business goes very well,' he replies, looking at Edward. 'Many lenders from the Exchange are here. Many lords who should like to further their fortunes in shipping.'

He gives Edward an approving smile, showing small white teeth.

'It looks very well that you are in your fine box, Edward,' commends Fitzroy. 'We should easily quash Vanderbilt's objections with a few conversations tonight.'

Fitzroy's narrow eyes are back on me.

'I have not had the pleasure,' he murmurs, scrutinising my face.

'This is Miss Elizabeth Ward,' says Edward, stepping forward a little. 'She is a relation on my mother's side.'

'Is that so?' says Fitzroy, stepping closer. 'May I?' He takes my hand and his lips brush my fingers. There is something so unpleasant about the gesture that I suppress a shudder.

'Have we met before?' he asks. 'You look familiar.'

'Miss Ward is new to London this week,' Edward replies quickly.

'Tell me,' asks Fitzroy, addressing me, though his eyes are moving quickly back and forth between us, 'what brings such a lovely lady into Edward's company?'

'I—'

'Elizabeth is a very fine horsewoman,' interrupts Edward, his eyes meeting mine. 'She was very taken with your thoroughbred.'

'Yes, I was,' I agree quickly. 'A magnificent animal.'

'Samson?' says Fitzroy, smiling at the compliment. 'He is a fine beast. That horse cost two hundred pounds,' he adds, scanning my face for a reaction.

'Oh,' I smile uncertainly, 'what an expensive horse.'

This seems to please him.

'Do you mean to trade in ships with Edward?' I add politely.

'Edward and I mean to buy a trading ship,' agrees Fitzroy, in the loud voice some men adopt when talking to a woman on business matters. 'We should take goods and sail them to Africa.'

'So Edward tells me,' I say. 'But do you not wish to explore, or find new wonders?'

Fitzroy gives a braying laugh.

'Exploration is for fanciful fools,' he says. 'Edward and I mean to make money.'

'So you take no risks,' I observe, sipping my wine. 'But you make no discoveries either?'

'Exactly right,' says Fitzroy. 'We take no risks.'

He pauses and I sense he is waiting for something. Perhaps to be given a glass of wine, or invited to join us.

There is a loud gong below and in the pit, musicians strike up. Though no one below seems to pay the slightest attention.

'Well,' says Fitzroy finally, 'I had better return to my companions.'

He casts his eyes over us both.

'You have caused quite the stir with your pretty companion,' he says to Edward, with a false casualness to his voice. 'People are already wondering.'

'Then let them wonder,' says Edward sharply. 'I am here to do business. Not to find a bride.'

'Of course,' says Fitzroy quickly, in a placating tone. His eyes drift to me.

'Be careful, my dear,' he says, with an affected smile. 'I am hopeful his lordship will wed my sister next year. Do not let him toy with you.'

I smile back.

'My heart is too hard to be toyed with,' I reply.

Fitzroy looks disconcerted.

'In any case,' he says to Edward, making his way to the curtain as the music sounds louder, 'Caroline is here tonight. Should I have her come greet you?'

Edward's face remains completely impassive.

'We should be delighted to receive her,' he says.

Fitzroy bows low and slides out from the curtain, leaving the two of us alone.

Edward takes a thoughtful sip of wine.

I move to the edge of the box and stare out into the dizzying crowd.

Fitzroy seems to have left a strange gloom in his wake.

'Your box is like an entertainment all of its own, is it not?' I ask. 'Watching the people.'

'I had not thought of it that way,' says Edward. 'Mostly I am occupied with knowing who is here and who is not.'

He sounds so heavy with it all. As though he truly hates this part of being wealthy.

Edward waves towards another box and I follow his gaze. A man waves back.

'A potential creditor of Mr Vanderbilt?' I guess.

'Something of that nature. You see my work is never done,' Edward says.

'Come,' I say brightly. 'Let us use this fine box of yours to best advantage. We shall find you a girl from the crowd.'

A flicker of a smile returns to his face.

'A girl?'

'Of course,' I say, taking his hand and leading him to the edge. 'I shall only be with you one week. You shall need some entertainment if you return to town, shall you not?'

I eye him mischievously.

'Perhaps you might even find a bride who suits you better than Fitzroy's sister.'

He laughs outright at this and I am pleased.

'Let us see,' I coax him, staring out carefully and pointing. 'What of her?'

'It is not polite to point,' says Edward, following my gaze. 'Ah. You mean the pretty girl with the mother by her side?'

'Yes,' I say, returning my hand to inside the box.

'She is married already,' says Edward. 'I should not want to duel her husband.'

'Married so young?' I exclaim. 'Very well. Who else might there be?'

I let my gaze drift. All the gentry look so very sour. You would think the aristocrats were here for a funeral. Especially when compared to the lively commoners in the penny pit.

'What of that girl?' suggests Edward, joining in the game. 'Opposite, with the green dress?'

'Oh, Edward,' I admonish. 'You should have no fun with her at all. See how high and tight her dress is laced? You should spend all night undressing her. Or you must put her skirts above her head and hide her face entirely.'

He laughs out loud.

'And see how she frowns,' I add. 'We are here to find you fun. Not give you the cares of a wife before your real one.'

'I suppose they do look very serious in that box,' he acknowledges. 'What of her then?' he asks, looking out. 'Surely she must meet your favour?'

'Which girl do you say?' I follow where his eyes go.

'That lady with diamonds in her hair,' says Edward. 'She might do for a wife, do you think? Her money might support a large estate such as I have.'

My eyes settle on the woman he points out and my heart skips a beat. For I recognise her. It is Harriet. But she is too immersed in her flirtations to notice us.

'She is a courtesan,' I say.

'That lady?' asks Edward. 'How can you be so certain?'

'I know her,' I say, peering closer now at the jet-black hair, the broad smiling mouth. 'That is Harriet. From Mrs Wilkes's house.'

Edward stares. 'That is Harriet? A courtesan?'

'Yes. See how she arranges all her jewels to face front,' I add. 'When she tilts her head you can see there is nothing behind. 'Tis a show for the theatre. Ladies do not style their jewels so.'

'She plays a lady very well,' observes Edward, taking in the expensive wines and sweetmeats that Harriet's box contains.

'That she does. And she looks to be jollier than most of the ladies here. Harriet is blessed with many advantages.'

I sigh to myself, remembering how Mrs Wilkes constantly commended Harriet's flawless figure, large green eyes and conspicuous charm.

We both look at the box as Harriet whirls and flirts and raps knuckles with her fan.

'Not all the advantages,' says Edward quietly, with a faint smile on his lips.

Chapter 21

*I*n the general din, no one seems to be watching the stage. Though it looks to me that the large chandeliers are being lowered.

'Is the play starting?' I ask, wondering why people bother to attend the theatre, if they do not wish to see the performance.

Edward is staring out into the crowd, presumably making some social observations of his own. He nods at my question, returning his attention to me. 'The actors have loud voices,' he assures me. 'And the theatre is shaped to carry sound. We should hear well enough once they begin.'

I move a little closer to the edge of the box. Two seats have been placed so we sit next to one another.

The curtain rises and I feel my spirits lift. Draped across the entire back of the stage is an enormous canvas, painted in oils to represent a strange foreign land.

I turn to Edward in delight.

'That is Egypt?' I ask, turning back to the yellow-hued scene of pyramid shapes and bizarre animals. On the stage itself are huge pillars that look to be made of stone, in the neo-classical way, but I guess must have been fashioned from some lighter stuff.

'Set design has become an art,' replies Edward. 'They make Egypt very well.'

I am entranced now, resting as far over the lip of the box as I can. I barely have time to take in all the stage works when two handsome young men step onto the stage, clothed in togas like Romans.

With the noise below, I strain to catch every word, as they discuss Mark Antony and his love for Cleopatra.

My eyes flick to Edward and I see he is gazing at my face, the ghost of a smile playing on his lips.

'Watch the play,' I laugh, his attention taking me by surprise.

'I should rather watch you, as you watch it,' he says.

I have a feeling, after his conversation with Fitzroy, Edward is enjoying the lighter atmosphere between the two of us.

'Well, I should rather you didn't watch me,' I retort. 'So turn your attention to the players.'

He smiles more to himself than to me and turns back to the stage.

After I've assured myself he is watching, I let myself fall into the engrossing world of the play.

Then, after a few minutes, I feel Edward's warm hand seek mine out and close on it. I allow my fingers to tighten on his. And with the performance taking my attention, I do not let myself think too much about what it means.

Chapter 22

*H*alfway through the performance, the curtain behind us ripples again and the same servant reappears with a tray of marzipan sweets and several paper twists containing hazelnuts.

Edward thanks him and drops coins into his hand.

'You remembered I liked the marzipan sweets!' I say, delighted.

Edward looks pleased. 'Of course,' he says. 'It is the least a gentleman can do for his lady companion.'

'Not a lady,' I grin back, eyeing the sweets with pleasure.

'Near enough,' he says, seeming touched at my reaction.

The servant waits before withdrawing and Edward turns to him questioningly.

'Miss Caroline Taylor asked me to deliver a card,' he says in answer to the unasked question. The servant bows and presents a perfectly white square of card, with the name *Mr Percival Brathwaite* on it.

Edward takes the card and considers it. His face is perfectly neutral.

'Please show her up,' he says.

I look at the card and back at Edward.

'She sends her brother-in-law's card,' he explains, seeing my confusion at the differing name. 'Society women announce themselves by way of their male companions. Caroline has perfect manners as ever,' Edward adds, his eyebrows raised.

'This Caroline . . .' I begin.

'Is suggested to be my wife one day,' he finishes. Edward is looking at the card. Then he raises his eyes to meet mine.

'She wishes to see her future husband?' I say, for want of another reply.

Edward shakes his head. 'I should have thought,' he says slowly, 'it is you she wants to see.'

'Why should she want to see me?' For some reason the thought of being sought out puts me in a high panic.

'She will have seen you in my box. That is its function, after all. To show all of London that Lord Hays is in town. And to showcase whatever company he might deign to have with him.' Edward smiles wryly at this last part and gives me an apologetic glance.

'Does she know anything about me?' I ask. Fitzroy's embittered face flashes before me.

'Only what the rest of the town knows,' says Edward. 'That I entertain a lovely female companion from the country. So it would be tactless to try and corral me into taking a bride.'

'Does Caroline not like to see the play?' I say in frustration. I had been mesmerised by the performance and am irritated at the disruption.

'Most come to the theatre to socialise,' he says regretfully.

The curtain is swept back before I can ask any more and a tall red-haired woman enters the box.

She looks so unlike Fitzroy that I find myself wondering how they can possibly be related. Though she, like he, is attractive.

Caroline has soft blue eyes, a pale pink pout and the kind of rounded cheeks you see on cherub angels.

My mouth twists. I can well understand why Edward should want her as a bride. She bears all the hallmarks of a 'society wife'. Her pale green dress is fashionable, yet cut modestly at the front, with long matching gloves. She wears her red hair swept high on her head, with sweeping ostrich feathers and enormous sapphires as ornaments.

More large jewels at her throat sparkle expensively in the candlelight and she seems to feel no discomfort from the weight of her high hair, or the wide dress.

Mrs Wilkes would have pointed out such a woman as a certain threat. Propriety and beauty combined.

I am suddenly acutely aware of my own lack of jewellery. Compared to Caroline's, my ribbons and lace must seem very poor. And my dress is not the latest fashionable shade or cut like hers.

As she approaches, I feel Edward move a little towards me. As though protecting me from something.

'Edward.' Caroline gives a broad bright smile, revealing small white teeth like her brother's. 'You have been hiding from me!'

She stays standing perfectly upright, but reaches her arm forward and dashes him with her gloved fingertips. Then her hand retreats as if uncertain how this flirtatious gesture should be resolved.

'Miss Taylor,' says Edward with a bow, 'how charming to see you. This is my companion, Miss Elizabeth Ward.'

Caroline's eyes sweep my figure and face as if trying to commit as much of me to memory as possible before decorum insist she look away.

I have the distinct feeling that Fitzroy has briefed her to find out more about me.

'Miss Ward,' she says after a moment, making me a curtsy.

We stand looking at one another.

Under her scrutiny, the weight of my hair seems to burn my neck and the cage beneath my dress digs at my hips.

'Will you not take a drink?' I suggest, eager to break the silence. 'We have red wine. Or the new foaming one. Champagne.'

Caroline looks at Edward uncertainly and I realise I have made some error of manners. Perhaps a lady should not offer drinks.

'Please do have wine,' he says quickly, stepping towards our little silver table. 'Take a glass with us.'

He pours her a glass of red wine. She takes it a little clumsily.

I'm noticing there seems to be something wholly uncomfortable in their interaction. It is hard to imagine they will one day be husband and wife and will have to bed one another.

I eye Caroline surreptitiously as she brings the glass to her mouth. I wonder if she has any idea what is expected of women when they marry. Rumour has it that some society girls know nothing until it happens.

Caroline takes the tiniest sip of wine and her little brow furrows.

'I never did get used to red wine,' she admits, lowering the glass.

'We have white,' I suggest. But she waves her hand politely.

'Please,' she says sweetly, 'I should not like to be a trouble.'

I smile at her uncertainly.

'Miss Ward,' says Caroline, 'you are new to London?'

I nod, opting for a half-truth. 'London society is quite new to me,' I say. 'I confess I find some parts of city life quite surprising.'

'Really?' Caroline is eyeing me carefully now and I finally see a shade of likeness to her brother. There is something vulpine in her gaze. As though she is turning me this way and that, trying to unravel me.

'You are from the country?' she asks cautiously.

I nod. 'From near Bristol.'

I am silently pleading she asks no more details about my background.

She considers my answer, shifting her weight onto one foot.

'How do you like the play?' she asks, surprising me with the abrupt change of topic.

'Very well,' I say, relieved to be telling the truth.

'You know it?' she asks. Her eyes are darting over me again. Assessing.

'A little. I read it as a girl.'

'I can hardly follow it,' says Caroline airily. 'It is hard to know what is happening. Besides, of course, Cleopatra is a woman without honour.'

Caroline's eyes narrow, sweeping the theatre beyond. They light on the courtesan I spied earlier, in her box.

'Like so many women in London,' she adds, her gaze settling back on me.

'But Cleopatra does have honour,' I blurt.

Realising I must justify my outburst, I continue speaking.

'I mean to say,' I begin, 'is this not what Shakespeare tells us? Antony and Cleopatra both have honour, but different kinds.'

Caroline looks confused.

'How can there be different kinds of honour?' she says. 'There is only one kind.'

I bite my lip. I may as well continue now.

'Antony has honour to his duty. To society,' I say. 'But Cleopatra has honour to herself. Hers is unchanging. His must waver wherever Rome goes.'

Caroline shrugs. 'It seems to me that Cleopatra is a wicked woman,' she says uncertainly. 'But I suppose that is the art of Shakespeare. To make us question.'

Her eyes light on Edward as she says this, as though sharing a joke. But he is looking thoughtfully back to the stage.

The tiniest glare of annoyance flickers in her features and is gone before I can be sure it was there.

She turns back to me with a polite smile and I wonder how she can be so civil. Truly, these society women are cold to the core. If a common girl were to meet with her betrothed's obvious mistress, there would be a catfight. But this woman is happy to accept her future husband's infidelity without a ripple. Perhaps that is how these arranged marriages are done. But it seems to me an empty kind of life. No wonder society men look to courtesans.

Caroline yawns, covering her mouth delicately.

'That dreadful Harriet girl is in one of the boxes,' she says. 'She styles herself a proper lady since she has managed to whore herself to a duke.'

Caroline toys with her heavy necklace as I peer out into the theatre. But I can no longer see Harriet. She has vanished among her huddle of men.

'Of course he will tire of her soon,' Caroline says. 'Already the duke must bore of being out of society. A lady will not receive a harlot into her parlour. So this Harriet creature must provide all his entertainment.'

Caroline shakes her head sadly. 'The duke perhaps flatters himself she loves him,' she sighs. 'But no girl who truly loved a man would condemn him to such a life. Such a marriage could never join society. The man must give up all polite company.'

I risk a glance at Edward as she talks.

I see something pass over his face and wish I hadn't. Because it is suddenly so clear to me how different we are.

Caroline's clever little eyes are darting back and forth now. Like she's working something out.

She gives an exaggerated sigh.

'What a fool I am,' she announces. 'I have left my fan with your servant, Edward.'

There's a split second pause, before he realises what's expected of him.

'Please,' he bows, 'allow me to bring it back for you.'

'Would you?' She gives him a delighted smile. 'You are so very kind. Are you sure it is not too much trouble?' she adds, as he shoots me an apologetic glance.

Edward's natural good manners swing into place.

'For you, nothing is too much trouble,' he assures her gallantly. And before I realise what is happening, Edward bows to us both and slips behind the curtain, leaving Caroline and me alone together.

Her cool blue eyes are on me now. Their warmth has entirely vanished, as though it were an act she affected with some effort for Edward's benefit. Her face looks almost cruel.

I realise she plays this game of social manners perfectly. Asking for the fan was a deliberate ruse to have me alone.

'So, Miss Ward,' she says archly, 'you hope to steal Edward for a husband. But your presumption is too great.'

The accusation is so preposterous I almost laugh out loud.

'I can assure you,' I say, struggling not to giggle, 'I have no wish to marry Edward.'

'But of course you do,' says Caroline dismissively. 'I do not blame you, of course. 'A simple country girl such as yourself must think she is close to a fine prize.'

She tilts her head, like a bird considering its prey. There's a long pause as she waits for her words to sink in. It seems they do not have the effect she hoped for, since she talks on.

'You couldn't honestly think you could pass for Edward's wife in polite society?' she says. 'You have not the refinement.'

Her eyes are taking in my dress and hair now.

'You may have a pretty face,' she adds, 'but you have no fashion. No manners. Your country charms will do you no good here.'

It occurs to me in a burst of incredulity that Caroline sees me as a genuine threat. It is too ridiculous. If only she knew.

'Perhaps vulgarity is prized more by certain men than you might think,' I reply, unable to resist goading her a little.

'Men toy with vulgarity,' she says in a light tone that doesn't mask her annoyance. 'They marry manners.'

Her hypocrisy is starting to rile me. She talks as though her love-less arranged marriage will be a noble thing.

'My vulgarity might be obvious to you,' I say, 'yet you must know how clear it is that you do not love Edward.'

Caroline frowns. 'Why should I love him? If we are to be allied, it will be for matters of family.'

I shake my head, pitying her.

'The life you desire holds no charms for me,' I say.

Caroline makes an ugly sort of noise.

'Marriage to Lord Hays has not charms for you?' she asks, eyebrows raised high. 'What, may I ask, do you imagine is a better life?'

'A life where I am not cast off to a lonely estate. While my husband romps in London.'

'Oh, you are not one of those romantics?' Caroline says, with a high peeling laugh. 'You read too many novels.'

'Perhaps I do,' I reply. 'But the only freedom your marriage will afford you is in choosing your dresses. You shall be locked in a gilded cage, seeking only to adorn your prison.'

Caroline blinks at me and I realise with amazement that she does not understand the reference.

So Edward's wife-to-be is not so clever with reading as she is with social machinations.

'That is Mary Wollstonecraft,' I add helpfully. 'Surely as a woman, you have read her writings?'

'I . . .' Caroline looks absolutely furious. 'I do not bother myself with such nonsense,' she manages.

Her eyes flash dangerously and I realise I may have underestimated her. Perhaps she has more fire than I thought. Certainly, my tutoring her on political writings has angered her greatly.

'There is some trick to you,' she hisses in a low voice. 'I know not what it is, or how you have insinuated yourself into Edward's company. But I mean to find you out. And when I do, you will be sorry.'

Before I can reply, the curtain twitches and Edward re-enters the box.

He's smiling broadly, proffering a fan. Then he glances at my face and his eyes dart between the two of us.

'All is well?' he asks.

We both nod and make pretend smiles.

'Very well,' says Caroline brightly, her acted warmth returning. 'Elizabeth and I were getting well acquainted.'

I find myself staring at her. The transformation is incredible. All at once she is sweet, likeable. It makes me wonder what monstrous girls society breeds.

Edward moves to my side, considering my face. He hands Caroline the fan, almost as an afterthought.

She takes it with a curtsy. Her eyes dart to Edward, sensing she is losing her audience.

'I must return to my companions,' she says. 'Though God knows I might have chosen better.'

Edward refocuses his attention on her at this last part.

'Fitzroy gives no thought to my safety,' she explains, a note of hurt creeping into her voice. 'He cares only that I might be seen at the theatre. Tonight I have only Percival and some silly girls to keep me company. And you well know he will afford me no protection should the crowd turn ugly.'

She frowns and Edward's eyebrows arch a little.

'You need not fear,' he says mildly. 'Were there any danger, I should be sure to protect you.'

Her eyes drop to the sword at his side and she gives a triumphant smile.

'You are most kind, Your Lordship,' she says, with a small curtsy. 'I hope to see you again, while you are in town.'

She flashes me a little look of victory and then retreats from the box, curtsying. Edward bows slightly, but his mind seems to be on other things.

'I enjoyed your ideas of the play,' he says, once the thick curtain has fallen back across the entrance to our box. 'Different kinds of honour. I had never thought of it that way before.'

'I do not think your future wife liked my notions.'

'Do not mind Caroline,' he says. 'She is only jealous.'

'She has no reason to be.'

Edward's dark eyes are full on mine.

'Women such as Caroline are uncertain as to their place in society,' he says. 'You must not mind it.'

'What does she have to be uncertain about?' I ask, surprised.

'Her family was not born to an estate. They acquired great wealth in the Indian colonies. Caroline must marry into the aristocracy before she is truly accepted as part of society.'

'Why does she not simply enjoy her money?' I suggest. 'If I had great wealth, I should not chain myself to a husband.'

To my surprise, Edward laughs. 'Not many women of my acquaintance share your view,' he says after a moment.

'You mean to marry her?' I ask, facing the players to hide my expression.

Edward glances at me.

'We are not formally betrothed. But it has been decided,' he replies. 'I owe Fitzroy a debt for his help in recovering my family estate.'

'You love his sister?'

'Not yet. But she brings a large enough fortune for us to make a fine home. I dare say we shall be happy. Once the children come.'

I take a careful sip of champagne.

'You sound like a courtesan,' I say. Perhaps it is the wine taking effect. Or maybe Caroline has riled me. But suddenly I do not care that I insult him.

He turns to me in surprise.

'That is what all the girls at Mrs Wilkes's house believe,' I add. 'That love can be bought for the right sum.'

I take another mouthful of champagne. I do not know why I am speaking like this. It is like a devil has got inside me, but I cannot stop.

'So for all your money, you aristocrats have no more freedom than us street girls. For you may not love who you choose,' I conclude.

Edward is quiet. I feel my stomach begin to tighten.

I am suddenly sure that this must be the end of our arrangement. Whores do not grow rich by speaking out of turn.

'Is that what you believe?' he asks softly. 'That love cannot be bought?'

I give a shaky smile. 'It does not matter what I believe.'

'It matters to me.'

I look up at him. His dark eyes are sincere.

'So what does a woman sell,' he asks softly, 'when she entertains a man?'

'She sells her company,' I say. 'She does not sell her soul.'

I turn my gaze straight ahead, not trusting myself to say anything more.

After a moment, I glance at Edward, out of the corner of my eye, and see he is staring at my chest.

I realise my fingers have automatically moved to the shape of my banknote. I move them away quickly.

Slowly, he moves so he is standing close.

My heart starts beating fast. I close my eyes.

'What of you and me?' he whispers.

'We have a business arrangement,' I say, working to fight the lump in my throat. 'That is no place for the heart.'

I open my eyes to see Edward has a tight little smile.

I feel tears prickle and look away.

'We are similar, you and I,' he says, gazing back out into the crowd. 'We have made ourselves so hard that no one can ever hurt us.'

I stare at the stage, waiting for a point when my emotions will not betray me.

I know what Edward says is true. Whether he thinks this a good or bad thing, it is impossible to tell.

Then he sighs as though women are a difficult mystery.

'For the time we have together,' he says, 'let us just enjoy one another.'

I stare at him for a long moment. Then we both turn back to the players.

Edward is quiet for the rest of the evening. His eyes are distant. And though we talk of the play, he does not seem his usual self.

When we return, by carriage, to his townhouse, he does not accompany me into the parlour. I fall asleep alone, cursing myself for speaking so freely. Tonight will likely be my last in this house.

Chapter 23

The next morning I wake alone and Sophie comes into the parlour to make my toilette.

'His lordship has asked if you might join him for breakfast,' she explains, as I allow myself to be layered in petticoats.

I take in this information. So Edward does not wish to end our arrangement as I feared. I wonder if he has forgiven me, or simply decided not to dwell on my outspokenness.

There is a knock on the door and two more maids glide in, one carrying the familiar accoutrements of the morning toilette, the other pulling a large trunk.

'Your clothes have arrived,' says Sophie, sounding pleased. 'I had the maids bring those that might be suitable for today. Should you like us to hold them out for you?'

'Oh yes!' I cry, betraying my excitement. 'Please do.'

'The dressmakers seemed to think them in very good taste,' confides Sophie, as she eases open the lid. 'They told us you had a very good eye for fashion and colours.'

'I have not much experience,' I admit. 'Besides watching fine ladies.

Let us hope I have a figure to match the dressmakers' art.'

I am hoping my bony frame has gained a little weight. Life in Edward's well-fed household means I have eaten three good meals a day. I flatter myself that my arms and legs begin to look rounder.

Sophie and the other maids carefully unpack the top three dresses, unfolding them reverently.

'They are lovely,' breathes Sophie, running her hand along the garment she holds – a light blue silk embroidered with tiny white peonies.

I stare at the dress, rendered speechless. Then I have crossed the room and am holding up the fabric, sliding my hand along the perfect stitching.

'You do not like the colour?' ventures Sophie uncertainly. 'The blue is too pale?'

'Oh no!' I gasp, finding my voice. 'No. It is just ... I simply cannot believe the loveliness.'

I look at her and we both smile.

'They are beautifully made, are they not?' she says. 'I think they will all look very well on you.'

My fingertips brush along the top of the dress. 'The stitches cannot even be seen,' I say admiringly. 'I have never worn such dressmaking.'

Sophie smiles as proudly as though she stitched the dresses herself.

'See how well the skirts are made,' she suggests, holding them out. 'Are they not fine?' The wide skirts fan out from the solidly constructed stays in a rippling expanse of flawless folds.

'Which should you like to wear?' she asks, as I admire the skirts.

My eyes flick across the other two dresses. Besides the blue dress, there is a light green silk, like the dew on morning grass. It is decorated with deep purple ribbons and stitched with gold trim.

The third dress is the softest dusky pink silk, ornamented with clouds of French lace at the bust.

'I think the blue peonies,' I say, after a moment, remembering Edward's blue carriage. 'What should you say, Sophie?'

'I think the blue is the nicest for today,' she agrees, hanging it over her arm. 'It is bound to be bright and you should put the sky to shame.'

I laugh at this.

'Shall we put it on you, Miss Lizzy?' she asks.

'Yes please.' I stand, hardly breathing in my excitement, as they fuss about me, unlacing and helping the dress on.

Sophie steps away as the other two maids lace my back in at high speed, tying, straightening and tugging with deft fingers.

Then she returns, wielding a large mirror.

'You are beauty itself,' she says admiringly.

When I am finally ready for breakfast, I abruptly remember Edward's silence last night. Now I know I will stay today, I realise how disappointed I would be to leave. But I wonder if he will reprimand me for my strong opinion.

The servants announce me and I walk into breakfast, keeping my posture tall as Mrs Tomkinson advised.

Edward is already seated, but he stands when he sees me enter.

'Elizabeth,' he says. And I feel as though he has said so much in that one word. He takes in my fine dress for a long moment.

'You seem to grow more beautiful by the day,' he concludes finally.

There is no false flattery in his tone and I feel myself blushing.

'Thank you,' I say, with a little curtsy.

'The dressmaker has done you credit,' he adds. 'And you have shown yourself refined in your choice.'

Sophie steps forward to whisk my chocolate and I wait for her to finish.

Edward nods that the servants leave us and considers me as I approach the table.

'You seem troubled,' he says, as I take a seat near him.

'I . . . I thought I might have offended you,' I admit. 'Last night. With my observations on your marriage plans.'

He eyes me keenly.

'You think you should not be allowed your view?' he asks. 'Because I pay for your company.'

I give a little half-smile at how well he has summarised things.

'Something like that,' I admit.

'Well, you must put your mind at ease,' he says. 'One of the things I pay for is your lively nature. The last thing I should wish would be for it to be subdued, like those tedious society girls.'

He pauses as though realising he has said too much and then smiles broadly.

I grin back and help myself to a bread roll from the table.

'What is your business for today?' I ask, imagining he will be gone during the daytime, as before.

Edward sits back in his chair and considers me.

'I am glad you asked,' he said, 'because I should like you to accompany me.'

I raise my eyebrows, halfway through a swallow of bread.

'On a business matter?'

He smiles, folding his napkin. 'Not exactly. Mr Vanderbilt made a clever delay,' he explains. 'I must travel to my country estate today to sign some documents in person. I wondered if you might accompany me.'

'To your country estate?' I am taken aback.

'My estate is fifteen miles outside London,' he says. 'It is tedious, for the journey is four hours in each direction. Ordinarily I might take a footman for company,' he adds, 'for it is a long journey to take alone. But I can spare no man today.'

'And you should like me to come in the carriage? For company?'

I am relieved this is the function he wishes me for. I had been a little frightened he should have wanted me for some greater purpose.

He smiles at me.

'I was hoping you would be kind enough to accompany me, yes.'

I take a sip of my chocolate.

'You hardly need to ask me,' I point out. 'You are paying for my company.'

'But the journey is long and over bumpy ground,' replies Edward. 'It will be arduous. I would not compel you if you should not wish it.'

He nods and then clarifies. 'You will also function as a witness while I sign the documents. But that is no task at all. Simply be present.'

'Then I should be happy to accompany you,' I reply.

Unexpectedly, Edward breaks into a wide smile.

'I am glad,' he says. 'The journey would be dull without you.'

He frowns slightly and reorders his words. 'Without company, I mean.'

I smile to myself and take another sip of chocolate.

'Might this delay stop you buying the ship?' I ask.

'No, no,' he assures me. 'It is a delay, nothing more.'

'So you will go and sign today? And the thing will be done?'

'Yes,' he says. 'Vanderbilt has done his best to inconvenience me. But aside from being out of London all day, it is nothing more than a feint. The business part will be over quickly,' he adds. 'I will conclude the rest in London as planned.'

I grin at him. 'If I keep you company,' I say, deciding to tease him, 'you must entertain me in your turn.'

'That is already taken care of,' he promises. 'I have packed the carriage with wine and cards. We shall have a little breakfast as we journey, and there will be fresh rolls and a joint of meat besides. So we shall be well fed and merry.'

'You already presumed that I should make the journey,' I accuse.

'I know how kind you are,' he says with a mischievous smile, 'where I am concerned. Besides, we do not have long together. I need to make the most of my money. I merely take steps to be sure our time together isn't tedious.'

'We shall have a merry time,' I promise.

We smile at each other.

'And I suppose you may buy a little presumption for fifty guineas,' I add, to mask my sudden sadness that the week seems to be going quickly.

Chapter 24

While Edward busies himself with business arrangements, I stand in the grand hallway, watching as servants race back and forth.

Mrs Tomkinson steps into view, armed with a covered wicker basket. She stops when she sees me, taking in my appearance with something like pride. I realise I have done well to choose the right clothing and have Sophie tie a pretty cap over my hair.

'Miss Elizabeth.' She curtsies.

'Hello, Bridget,' I grin. 'I hope you have strawberry jam in the basket. It is my favourite.'

She looks confusedly at the basket and then back at me.

'You are travelling to the country with his lordship?' she deduces.

I nod. 'Edward should need some conversation, else spend eight dull hours on the road.'

'But you wear your nice dress,' Mrs Tomkinson protests. 'You should need something different for the country.'

'What should I wear?' I ask, uncertain of country protocol.

'Something on your feet that will not mind the mud,' she says, eyeing my hand-stitched blue shoes. 'And I think I have a woollen cloak to cover your dress. If you go to his lordship's estate you shall be on foot for a part and you may be splashed from the carriage.'

She clucks her tongue in annoyance at this new task.

'I am already delayed in contacting the butcher,' she complains. 'I could not find his lordship to ask whether he would take a chicken fricassee or roast beef.'

'I think he should prefer roast beef,' I say, remembering Edward's choice of meat at the dinner with Vanderbilt.

Mrs Tomkinson nods gratefully. 'I shall return with your cloak and some clogs,' she promises. Then, as if she can't help herself, she reaches over and straightens my cap.

'You look quite the proper lady,' she says, nodding in a pleased way. Then she hurries off with her basket.

Mrs Tomkinson returns, as promised, with a thick wool cloak and clogs.

And once I am covered over for the journey, she allows Edward to lead me outside, to see a much larger carriage than the one we used previously.

'Should we need such a big vehicle?' I ask, rather overawed by the scale of it. 'There are only two of us.'

'The roads are very uneven,' he explains. 'The larger wheels will be more comfortable. You shall see.'

'This sounds like a fine journey to take a lady,' I tease.

'Mrs Tomkinson has already remonstrated with me,' Edward says, with an indulgent smile. 'I told her your kind heart would not see me travel alone.'

He hands me into the luxurious interior and steps up after. Inside are three baskets, which he opens to reveal a neatly packed picnic. There are loaves of fresh bread and dishes of butter, marmalade and jam.

'More breakfast?'

'I thought travel might make you hungry. And I like to see you eat.'

'Surely you are tired of watching women eat,' I laugh, 'with all your fine dinners?'

'Society ladies do not take pleasure in eating, like you do.'

I glance at him to see if there is mockery there. But his face is sincere.

Edward lifts out two covered china serving dishes and removes the lids.

'Veal pies, salmon and beef with horseradish,' he explains, showing me the contents. 'There is oatmeal with sweet cream,' he adds, 'and I have a bottle of fresh cider. Or French brandy to warm us.'

'We shall not be able to walk, once we have arrived,' I laugh, staring at all the food.

'I am determined to feed you up.' He picks up a plate and serves me a slice of bread, spreading it generously with jam. 'We shall have you chubby by the time you leave me,' he promises.

'You are accomplishing the work prodigiously,' I assure him, thinking that my stays already feel fuller at the front.

Edward knocks on the ceiling of the carriage and it lurches into motion.

'You were right,' I concede as the wheels roll beneath us. 'It is a very smooth journey. You might hardly know we are in a carriage.'

'Wait until we are out of the city, on the rutted tracks,' says Edward. 'You shall know then.'

'Then I had best eat quickly.'

Once we have eaten breakfast, we settle into the swaying motion of the carriage and fall into easy conversation.

Edward explains the sights of London as we leave the city and I talk about my farming upbringing as we start on the muddy country road.

'It broke my father's heart to give up the farm,' I explain. 'But the lord who owned the estate was greedy. We should have starved to make his rent.'

'That is how fools manage their estates,' says Edward. 'They squeeze from the peasants to offset their own laziness.'

The carriage rolls on a little further.

'Did you like farm life?' he asks.

I consider this. 'At times it was a hard life,' I say, 'but I liked it.'

I think back, struggling for memories. 'I spent much time with my grandmother. She was bred on a farm and she taught me all the ways. How to take honey, and use herbs and poultices and such. Those ways will be lost to our family now,' I add.

We are both silent, thinking of this, as the green English countryside rolls by outside.

'You did not think to stay in Bristol and marry some country boy?' asks Edward. His tone is casual, but I sense something behind it.

'I was not so popular with country boys,' I admit.

'I find that hard to believe,' he says, gazing into my face.

'Farmer husbands look for simple brides. I was too clever for my own good.'

We are silent again in the trundling carriage.

'Shall we play at cards?' I suggest, remembering he has brought a pack.

'What should you like to play?' he asks, removing a deck from the basket.

'Twenty-one?' I learned this game at Mrs Wilkes and I was good enough to beat everyone I played.

'Very well.' He shuffles the pack expertly.

'You shuffle well for a man who does not gamble,' I observe.

'One does not need to gamble to play.'

'So we shall play for no bets?'

'That sounds fair,' he says. 'I am not fool enough to bet one of Mrs Wilkes's girls at cards.'

I smile and Edward deals. And for all his humility, he goes on to play an expert hand. I stare at his winning cards. It is the first time I have been beaten at this game.

'You are good,' I observe, taking back the cards and shuffling them.

'Beginner's luck,' he replies. 'Another round?'

I nod. 'I have to win back some of my dignity,' I say. 'None at Mrs Wilkes's ever bested me at this game.'

I deal and this time around I vow to pay closer attention.

Picking up my cards, I examine them carefully. They are a good start.

'Why have you not yet married?' I ask, feeling suddenly able to pose the question that has been nagging at me for days. Edward is old to be a bachelor and seems in no rush to solidify his informal betrothal. 'Surely society finds it strange?' I add.

'I was married,' he says, looking at his cards. 'My wife is dead.'

'I am sorry.' This changes my idea of him. Somehow I cannot imagine Edward as a tragic widower.

'There is no need to be,' he says easily, taking a card. 'She was sixty when we wed. It was an arranged marriage. I only met her once.'

My eyes widen.

'But you were . . . There was no expectation that you should bed your wife?'

He shakes his head.

'The marriage was made when I was fourteen. The bride was a dowager with a large fortune. My father hoped to pay off his debts by selling his son.'

I take up a card in silent amazement. Surely even among aristocrats this is cold?

'Were you angry at your father?' I ask, counting my new hand.

He nods. 'Oh yes. Not only for the marriage. For his mismanagement of the family fortune. He nearly ruined us.'

Edward raises his eyes to mine.

'My father was famous for his gambling,' he says. 'And in London, you must imagine that made him a very bad gambler indeed.'

'I imagine it would,' I murmur.

Edward nods and then places his hand.

'Twenty-one.' He smiles.

I realise he has hustled me. He is a much better player than he acted.

'You did not tell me true!' I accuse. 'That is no beginner's luck. You play exceptionally.'

Edward smiles mischievously.

'It is how I used to win my passage and lodging,' he admits. 'When I went on my wild travels in Europe.'

'You must have played very well indeed. To fund your travel.'

'Certainly there are many in France and Italy who swore never to play me again,' he says. 'But I am sure there are many better card players than I.'

'You are too modest. Why do you not gamble now?' I ask, baffled. 'You are so good. You could win a fortune in the London clubs.'

'I do not like the London clubs.' Edward turns to stare out of the window.

In the silence that follows, I sense the talk of gambling and his father has woken some unhappy memory.

'Where is your father now?' I ask gently.

'He died a few years ago,' says Edward. 'I gave him an allowance.

And he lived out his days with a mistress. My father was … not a kind man,' he concludes. 'I did not see him in the years up to his death.'

I take Edward's hand and he glances at me gratefully. Then his gaze is back at the window.

Chapter 25

I expected Edward's estate to be large. But I am not prepared for how very large it is. It takes us half an hour to travel from the beginning of the grounds to the enormous country hall. And according to Edward, the land rolls on for many miles further in every direction.

'There we have a crop where there was nothing,' he says proudly, as we pass a field of waving wheat. 'And up ahead, I shall show you the new plough pattern that gives the farmers double yield.'

When he talks of his estate management there is a new energy to him that is infectious.

'I have never met a man with such a passion for farming,' I say, as he describes his plans to rotate crops to gain more nourishment from the earth.

'I find it a miracle,' he says. 'To see the new things grow from nothing but dirt. I never tire of it.'

The carriage pulls to a halt and Edward looks out.

'The ground is too rutted here to continue,' he says. 'We must go by foot. Do you mind?'

'You forget I am not a lady,' I grin at him, tugging off my shoes. 'I was raised barefoot with sheep and cows.'

'You will not wear the clogs Mrs Tomkinson gave you?'

'I should rather not, unless you mind very much.'

'I do not mind in the least,' he says, opening the door and helping me down. He smiles at my bare feet and I pick up my skirts, taking in the wide expanse of fields before us.

'We are trying this field out for cattle,' explains Edward, pointing to the mire of hoof-prints that have churned up the track. 'Though we have not had much success thus far,' he admits.

He takes my hand and leads me onto the grassier part of the field. I gaze at the cows in the distance.

'Is that where your cattle shelter?' I ask, pointing to an old hay barn. Edward nods.

'Then that is why your livestock does not fare so well,' I say.

He looks at me with interest.

'A barn like that is too damp for cows,' I explain. 'You should have a three-sided shelter, to let the air in.'

I glance at the lush ground beneath us. 'Your pasture is good,' I observe. 'Fix the barn and your herd should do very well.'

Edward is looking at me strangely.

'What?' I am suddenly self-conscious.

'It does not signify,' he says, with an enigmatic smile. 'Only, you are the most interesting girl I have had on my land.'

'I should prefer to be the most beautiful,' I say. 'But I suppose interesting will have to do.'

Edward closes my hand in his and walks me towards the barn. 'I have arranged to sign the papers here,' he explains. 'Vanderbilt found some arcane law forcing me to sign in situ.' He sounds admiring, rather than bitter.

We approach the barn and I instantly recognise the sound of a cow in labour.

'You are about to add another to your herd,' I say, pleased. I always liked the arrival of a calf.

Edward nods and frowns. Because another noise echoes forth. As though the animal were in distress.

We walk in silence to the large wooden barn. I can smell the fresh hay, as we step into the interior.

A hayloft is on one side and beneath it lies a brown cow, her eyes wide, her belly large. By her side kneels a farmer, in a white cotton shirt and simple woollen hose with gaiters to stop rats running up his legs. He has the thick muscles of a hard worker and brown hair bleached partly blond by the sun.

To the other side of the barn stands an incongruously fine table. I guess it must have been carried laboriously from the main house for the purpose of today's business.

By the table stands another man who is almost as unlike the farmer as it is possible to be. I take him to be a lawyer, or scribe, or some other employee of Edward's business arrangements. For he is old and wears the style of provincial dress favoured by formal clerks and lawyers, which I had forgotten existed outside London.

A dun-coloured waistcoat is stretched over his pronounced belly and matching breeches clad his skinny legs, with silver-buckled shoes on his feet. Atop his florid face, he wears a dusty wig that is starting to unroll on one side.

This man makes us a low bow as we enter. The farmer, occupied with his labouring cow, does not even notice we have arrived.

'My Lord,' says the lawyer-man, in the sober voice of one used to delivering bad news. 'Your Ladyship.'

Edward smiles politely, but does not correct him. 'Elizabeth,' he says, 'this is my lawyer, Mr Beckwith.'

The lawyer straightens from his bow to me and frowns.

'Your Lordship, I had asked for the animal to be removed,' he says, shaking his head in annoyance. 'But your farmer is stubborn on the point.' He frowns. 'Had I known there would be a lady present, I would have been more forceful.'

Mr Beckwith turns to include the farmer in this criticism, but the man has eyes only for his cow.

I turn to Edward, unsure how he will react to this. He is looking to the farmer, who has just noticed us and is now making to stand.

'Please, Robert,' says Edward, motioning he should stay down, 'there is no need. The cow needs you more than we do.'

Robert gives a relieved nod. 'I am sorry, Your Lordship,' he says. 'This one is having a difficult labour and we could not get her out in the field.'

He looks apologetically at the bewigged man, who is eyeing the scenario with obvious distaste.

'I petitioned in strong terms for the animal to be driven out,' Beckwith repeats to Edward in a low voice. 'But your farmer was afraid the calf would be lost.'

Edward waves his hand to signify this is not a concern and Robert returns his attention to the cow.

'Shall we see to the papers, Mr Beckwith?' says Edward. 'We may have this document signed and I can be back in London.'

Mr Beckwith makes another low bow and produces a large swathe of rolled paper.

'If I may, My Lord,' he says, 'I must draw your attention to these clauses.'

For a moment, I think Edward might change his mind. That he may have decided against Vanderbilt's ship as a bad business and will tell his lawyer he will not sign.

Then the two men begin talking in the language of property exchange. I turn my gaze to the cow.

I have not been on a farm in ten years. But I recognise the signs. From the position of the cow and her low noises, the calf has likely not turned.

Seeing Edward and the lawyer pay no attention to me, I step so I might examine the situation more closely.

The farmer is squatting at her side, apparently at a loss as to what to do next. The cow bellows suddenly, her nostrils flaring.

I drop down, so as to be on my haunches, level with the farmer. My feet settle easily into the soft earth of the barn floor.

'How long since she began?' I ask.

The farmer looks at me, his face sweating. For an instant, I think my fine appearance might decide him against answering. Then he seems to decide I am safe.

'She has laboured all night already,' he says, 'and I fear to lose them both.'

Checking that Edward and his lawyer are engrossed with papers, I slide my hand gently over the cow's belly.

'I think the calf has not turned,' I explain, keeping my voice down.

The farmer looks uncertain. 'This is the first year we have tried cattle,' he says.

I pause, to be sure I have things right. It has been a long time since I was on a farm. But the lessons do not leave you, when you are bred to it.

'I will show you,' I say, reaching under the cow's belly. 'See here?' I ask, gesturing he should put his hand in the same place.

'The hard part is the head,' I explain. 'The legs will be here.'

He nods apprehensively.

'You must reach inside and grasp higher up,' I add.

The cow makes another loud bellow, kicking her legs.

'I will hold her,' I say, recognising the need for fast action. 'You reach inside. Upwards, as I said.'

Quickly, I step around to the front of cow and lean on her shoulder, keeping her steady. I am greatly pleased that Mrs Tomkinson insisted I wear a thick wool cloak over my fine dress.

Robert reaches a burly forearm into the other end.

'I think I have it,' he gasps, after a moment.

'You feel the hard hooves? You are sure?'

He nods, grunting from the effort.

'Then pull,' I urge, using all my strength to keep the cow from rolling.

For a time I think nothing will come. Then there's a slopping kind of sound and I see a bloody calf hanging in Robert's grip.

The cow twists under me and I step up to allow her some room.

Robert places the calf on the straw, where it lies limp.

He looks at me and shakes his head sadly. The little body is blue and motionless.

'Rub the flank,' I say, moving quickly to show him. 'Here. Like this.'

I rub the calf vigorously, head to tail and back again. And after a moment, its little hooved feet kick. I feel a long-forgotten pulse of delight. There is a simple joy in farming that I always loved.

'There.' I pick up the calf proudly and place it by the mother's head. She begins licking it enthusiastically. The little creature makes a whinnying kind of sound.

Robert and I grin at each other, bonded by the shared moment.

Still smiling, I turn to see if Edward is finishing his papers.

Instead, I find he is staring at me in disbelief. The lawyer by his side is literally open-mouthed.

I look between them both, wondering how to explain myself. My cloak is streaked with birthing gore and my hands are covered in blood from the calf. Even I know that ladies do not help birth cattle. It is Robert who finally breaks the silence.

'Reckon that's a fine match for you, My Lord,' he says, nodding towards me. 'The husband does the fields and the wife does the livestock.' He gives me a broad wink of appreciation.

Edward eyes my bloodied hands.

146

'Another hidden talent?' he asks mildly.

I am caught between pride and embarrassment.

'It is something that comes natural, when you are brought up to it,' I say, wiping my hands on the cloak. I move to a water trough in the corner of the barn and begin rinsing away the blood with enthusiastic strokes.

'And I shouldn't have liked to see the calf and mother die,' I call over my shoulder, still feeling the need to explain myself. The birthing residue comes away easily, making me feel less self-conscious.

Once clean, I look back to see Edward smiling as though he is proud of me.

'Come,' he says after a moment, 'let us get back to the carriage. There is someone I should like you to meet.'

Chapter 26

The carriage draws closer to a large country hall, of the Tudor kind. It is fashioned from imposing redbrick, towering to several storeys, with enormous latticed windows on the ground floor. Two grand wings sweep out either side of the main building, approaching a small moat, which stretches around and out of sight.

Undoubtedly it is a grand ancestral building, but I think it would be a cold place to actually live in.

It is only after the carriage rolls over the moat bridge that I realise Edward truly intends to take me inside.

'We are going into your house?' Panic makes my words sound strangely high-pitched.

'Inside the manor, yes.' He is smiling at my obvious nerves. He takes my hand. 'Do not concern yourself,' he says kindly. 'There is nothing to fear.'

'But who is it you wish me to meet?'

'My mother,' says Edward. 'I think she should be charmed by you. And she has few enough visitors.'

'Your mother?' Now I truly am afraid.

'She will like you,' he says, squeezing my hand. 'Just as I do.'

'Are you very sure of that?' I ask, as he helps me out of the carriage.

He stops in front of me and straightens my cap.

'Very sure,' he says. 'Take off your cloak, so she might see your dress. For she likes pretty things.'

I do as he asks, still wrought with anxiety.

Edward considers me with a sweeping gaze.

'Lovely,' he decides. Then he frowns, moves forward and gently smooths my frowning forehead with his fingers. 'Better,' he says approvingly.

'I do not know if this is wise, to meet your mother,' I am saying, as he takes my hand and pulls me unwillingly towards the house. 'You may make a mistake on my charms.'

'If my mother likes you half as much as I do,' says Edward, in answer, moving me towards the main door, 'she will like you a great deal indeed.'

I barely take in the huge hallway and stairwell as we enter the house. The interior is very grand, but unlike Edward's townhouse, it is not in the lighter contemporary style. Overall it is larger with a lot of dark wood panelling.

I follow uncertainly behind him, growing more and more nervous as he leads me through the house.

'Should not a footman announce us?' I ask, thinking it strange we make our own way to greet his mother with no servant to take us.

Edward shakes his head.

'I know where my mother will be,' he says. 'There is no need for formality.'

Nevertheless, we do encounter a neatly dressed maid as we move through the house. But rather than seeming surprised, or perturbed at the unexpected arrival of her master, she gives us a delighted smile.

'Lord Hays!' she beams. 'We did not know you would be returning so soon.'

'I am not returned quite yet, Tabitha,' Edward replies apologetically. 'I had some business that needed to be signed on the estate. This is my companion, Elizabeth,' he adds.

The maid curtsies to me, with a little smile. The lines around her eyes suggest she is middle-aged, but her cheerful temperament makes her seem younger.

'Should I prepare a meal?' she asks. 'There is plenty of rabbit, for the gamekeeper sends us a steady supply.'

Edward turns to me and back to the maid.

'We shall be returning to London rather quickly,' he explains. 'But perhaps you might prepare us something good to take in the carriage.'

The maid curtsies again. 'It will be done. Do you still mean to return to us by the end of the week?'

Edward nods and the maid beams once more.

'We shall be sure to have something fine prepared,' she promises. 'Your mother is by her fire as usual,' the maid adds, and for the first time her face looks sad. 'She slept long this morning, but I believe she woke this past hour.'

'Thank you,' says Edward, with a sad smile of his own. 'We go to her now.'

'Your mother is unwell?' I ask, my uncertainty heightening, as the maid scuttles away.

'No,' replies Edward. 'But she takes laudanum for her nerves. It makes her sleepy.'

I make no reply, but I am beginning to understand why Edward has no fear of introducing me to his mother. If she is one of those who makes daily use of opium, she likely remembers little from one hour to the next.

'You are very easy with your servants here,' I observe, thinking him a lot more natural than in London.

'They are like family to me,' he replies. 'I grew up with many. Or they are relations of servants I grew up with. I hold them very dear, for a household is made by all its people.'

Edward leads me through a large door into the belly of an immense wood-panelled room. A huge fire burns in a medieval-sized grate, the thick logs sending their smoke up a wide chimney.

The only furniture in the room is a hard-looking sofa, a large easy chair and a rug, all of which have been arranged close to the hearth. As though someone were trying to make a small fireside room out of an enormous wood-panelled expanse.

As we move closer to the fire, I realise that the large chair is occupied. A small woman sits inside it, shielded from view by the size of the chair back. But evident now we step around the front.

She wears formal dress, though it is of an old-fashioned style, with a less rigid structure than my attire. Even so, it must make her uncomfortable to dress so properly. Her snow-white hair is made in careful ringlets, and the neatness of it is in contrast to the frail papery skin of her face and the sleepiness of her blue eyes.

I see Edward's likeness in her face, in the finely made cheekbones and the high sweep of the brows. But where he has a solid kind of handsomeness, his mother's features are more delicate. I can imagine her as a young beauty, looking almost ethereal.

When she sees us, her smile is so kind I forget to be afraid.

'Edward!' she says, her thin voice rusted with age. 'You are kind to visit your mother.'

He stoops to kneel by his mother's chair, taking her hand and kissing it.

'You are well?' he asks. 'Not in pain?'

She shakes her head.

'No,' she assures him. 'The tincture takes care of it.'

Her eyes sweep up to me.

'Who is your lovely companion?'

'This is Elizabeth,' says Edward, standing. 'I thought you might like to see something bright.'

'You are right in that,' his mother says. 'How delightful to see such young beauty. Come closer, child, so I might admire you better.'

I step forward and she clasps my hand. Her grip is surprisingly warm and firm.

'So very pretty,' she says, nodding her head. 'And I can see from your eyes that you are lively and good-natured.'

She looks to Edward in approval.

'What a fine companion for you,' she decides, turning to me with a wink. 'For Edward is often dull and serious.'

I laugh.

'Not so much these past few days,' I assure her.

Edward's mother nods at me thoughtfully.

'I am glad to hear it,' she says.

I glance at Edward, who looks a little abashed. Then his eyes stray to his mother's birdlike arms.

'Have you taken any food today?' he asks.

'Oh yes,' she assures him. 'Tabitha takes very good care of me.'

'Yet you seem frail,' he admonishes. 'Do you eat that good broth I ordered for you? From the doctor?'

His mother waves her arm vaguely.

'It is hard to remember.'

Edward frowns. 'Elizabeth, would you mind keeping my mother company, while I fetch a dish of broth from the kitchen?'

'I should be delighted to,' I promise. 'I shall find out all your secrets while you are gone.'

He rolls his eyes, touches my shoulder and retreats from us.

'I was blessed with Edward,' says his mother, watching him go. 'He was the most clever boy, even from a very small child. God made me a mercy in giving me a son who was nothing like his father.'

'You must tell me more about Edward,' I encourage her. 'What was he like as a boy?'

His mother shuffles slightly upright and then winces as though her clothes hurt her.

I move to help but she raises a hand.

'It is well, it is well,' she murmurs. 'Us women are used to our restraints, are we not?'

'We are indeed,' I agree, thinking of my own tight stays. 'But surely a venerable lady may dress as she chooses?'

Edward's mother laughs at this.

'Maybe so, child,' she concedes, 'but when you are as old as I, you gain habits. Edward's father was a tyrant for dress and I learned under his authority.'

Her knotted fingers stroke her skirts thoughtfully.

'Edward was the most caring boy,' she says. 'I often wonder if his situation made him that way.'

She leans forward, her eyes glistening.

'He was made to take on many responsibilities that should have fallen to his father.' She shakes her head. 'He rose to the challenge beautifully. But I fear it has made him preoccupied with estate business. Though he always had an eye for pretty girls,' she adds, considering me with a sparkle to her eye.

'I do my best to keep his mind from business,' I promise, smiling.

She takes my hand gently, but her grip is firm.

'I have always prayed,' she continues, 'that he would find a woman to watch over him. For Edward was denied the proper frivolities of childhood. And his disposition grew more serious than it should have done. He deserves love and laughter more than most.'

Her hold on my hand tightens. I nod, not certain of what role she imagines I have at her son's side.

'I am sure Edward will make a fine marriage and bring his family great pride,' I say carefully.

'A girl to make him merry,' she replies with a wink, and I smile gratefully.

'I can certainly do that.'

'Be sure you do.' She pats my hand approvingly.

There is the sound of a door opening and I turn to see Edward has returned, carrying a plate of broth.

'For there is nothing worse than a dull man,' concludes his mother, raising her voice for his benefit.

Edward smiles a little.

His mother releases my hand.

'I was telling your lovely companion how she must make you lively,' she explains.

He reaches us and kneels to place the broth on the small table next to his mother.

'She is accomplished in that business,' he says.

'Good,' replies his mother. 'It is about time you found a spirited girl, rather than those simpering society creatures.'

Her eyes droop a little, as though she grows tired.

'Today, my son looks as well as I ever saw him,' she murmurs, pleased. 'Edward, you have a sparkle to your eyes, which warms my heart to see.'

'Will you not take some broth?' he urges. 'I should like to see you eat a few spoons before we leave.'

'At my age it is not so easy to swallow such foods,' she replies. 'For they make the broth very rich.'

Edward drops to her side.

'Yet you must take rich foods for your sustenance,' he says gently, stroking her thin arm. 'Promise me you shall try the broth, if not now, then later today.'

She nods, but her eyes are closing. And as her lips move to make a reply, she is falling into sleep.

Edward stands, watching her sleeping form, and turns to me.

'She sleeps most of the time,' he explains. 'We were fortunate to have so much conversation from her. I think she liked you very much.'

He studies his mother again. She is breathing gently.

'I try and have her eat,' he says. 'But she forgets and the laudanum numbs her appetite. I do not think she has eaten yet today, though Tabitha will have done her best.'

'Has she taken the laudanum for a long time?' I ask.

Edward nods.

'Since I was a boy. I think it was her way of escaping the brutalities of my father.'

There is something heartbreaking in his face. Automatically, I reach for his hand. He smiles.

'Come,' he says. 'Our business is done. And you have greatly cheered my mother. I suppose we must return to the city.'

But he hesitates, as though perhaps he would rather not.

Chapter 27

'm sad to see the beauty of Edward's country estate roll away. Though I'm enjoying being back in the carriage.

Edward and I have our own cosy little world in here. We're wrapped in blankets against the slight evening chill, and sharing our abundance of food and wine.

As promised, Tabitha packed us a further basket of jugged rabbit, with fresh bread and another bottle of wine.

'I enjoyed meeting your mother,' I say, as Edward fills my glass with wine.

'You did not expect to enjoy it?' he asks, catching my tone.

'No,' I admit. 'I was in terror of it. I am nervous around fine folk. And your mother is very fine.'

'There is no need to be nervous,' he says. 'Your manners do you credit.'

'Thank you.' I hesitate, before plunging on. 'Your mother was very frightened of your father? His shadow seems to haunt her still.'

Edward nods slowly. His face is pained and for a moment I think he won't reply. I almost regret asking him. Then he speaks.

'He was a terror, my father,' Edward says quietly. 'A gambler and a philanderer and a brute.'

I take his hand.

'We lived in fear of him,' he says. 'My mother particularly. I always thought ... I still think ... If only I could have protected her better.'

I keep the pressure of my hand steady.

'You were just a boy,' I say quietly.

He shakes his head, with a strange kind of smile.

'I take it back through my mind often,' he says. 'What I could have done. What I should have done. When I began to manage the family estate, it gave me something to free my mind from it all. Something to occupy my thoughts.'

I nod, understanding this. Street girls know all about pushing away the bad thoughts. It is how we survive.

'When I was old enough, I went to London,' continues Edward. 'I met Fitzroy. And between us, we found a way in law to discredit my father and have me declared heir before his death.'

I stroke his fingers, thinking how terrible his father must have been to force his son to such an act.

'My father never forgave me,' adds Edward. 'And I never forgave him.'

'Did you speak to him before he died?'

He shakes his head. 'Perhaps I should have done. I heard afterwards that he asked for me. Perhaps he wanted to ask my forgiveness. But I do not know if I could have given it.'

We sit for a while, the steady motion of the carriage rocking us.

'It is a lovely estate,' I say eventually. 'I can understand why it is so important to you that it prospers.'

'I am glad you think so.'

'And you mean to marry well and grow it even larger,' I say.

'You do not agree with this notion?' determines Edward, pouring me more wine.

'I did not say that.'

'You did not need to. I could hear it in your voice.' He re-corks the bottle and toasts his refilled glass against mine.

I laugh. 'I had forgotten you aristocrats were so well trained in social nuances.'

The carriage reels sideways through a heavy rut and Edward pulls me tight against his body.

'Why is it so important,' I say, as the carriage rights itself, 'to grow the estate? You have made it profitable. Why not let it be?'

'If I grow the estate, I can secure it for future generations.'

'But what of you?' I ask. 'Surely you do not mean to give your whole life for this? To be a conduit for your family's legacy?'

Edward's eyes are on mine suddenly, searching.

'And what would you propose?' he asks. 'How would you suggest I live my life?'

His words sound like a rebuke, but his face is anything but.

I look back at him for a moment and then turn my eyes away.

'I only mean . . .' I say hesitatingly, 'that you should be permitted a happy marriage. At least with a woman you have a liking for.'

'Ah.' He smiles, leaning back. 'You are talking about Caroline. You see we do not love one another.'

Edward strokes his chin, considering.

'If we were to marry, it would be a union of convenience,' he admits. 'But perhaps you are overlooking just how convenient it would be. Caroline's family comes with trading links. Shipping. I could establish a profitable trade with great ease.'

I frown. 'May you not find some nice society girl?' I suggest. 'Some pretty personable young thing. Retire here with her and make a happy family? Certainly, your mother thinks you deserve such happiness.'

Edward smiles at this.

'Some aristocrats have gone that route,' he says. 'From what I have seen, their marriages are no happier in the long run. After a few years, they spend their days in London, avoiding their wives, with all the other lords. The only difference is they have no financial advantage from the arrangement.'

'Are no aristocrats happily married?' I press, strangely dismayed at the thought.

'Perhaps a few,' concedes Edward. 'Are common marriages always happy?'

'No,' I admit. 'But there are many happy marriages. Where the man and woman are a comfort and companion to one another.'

I am thinking of my village near Bristol. The old couples sitting out the dances holding hands. Or running their humble smallholdings in mutual respect and liking.

'Then perhaps we should all have been born commoners,' Edward says. 'So we might be happier.'

I smile at this. 'I do not think you are formed for poverty.'

'And you neither,' he observes.

I move a little closer against him. Edward is so easy to be with.

'It is so nice,' I say, 'to have you all to myself in the carriage. I cannot think of a better way to travel.'

The movement of his body against mine suggests I have surprised him.

He hesitates. Then he kisses my hair. As a lover might.

'And what of our short marriage?' he murmurs. His voice is thick and dark. 'Are we all of convenience?'

I smile a little against the warmth of his body.

'If we are,' I reply, my eyes drifting closed, 'then we are the most convenient arrangement that ever was.'

Chapter 28

I awake to the rocking motion of the carriage. Edward is smiling down at me.

'How long was I asleep?' I ask.

'A few hours.'

I shake myself awake.

'I am sorry,' I apologise, 'for I was supposed to be your entertainment.'

'You were entertaining enough in your slumber,' he assures me. 'It is rather charming to watch how deeply you sleep.'

London is already coming into view. I blink, wondering if perhaps I have mistaken it.

'We are back already?' I say.

Edward nods.

'What shall we do this evening?' I ask, as the stalls and lanterns of King's Cross twinkle in the dusk light.

'There are many different entertainments we might be seen at,' says Edward.

'You are not tired?' I ask, thinking he has not slept, while I did.

'A little.'

'But still you must go?'

Edward nods again.

'What of you?' he asks. 'Are you not weary? It was a long journey today.'

I shake my head. 'I have slept. And besides, I am never tired when I am with you.'

I realise I have said more than I meant to. But Edward's face does not show he has perceived it.

'Well then,' he says, sitting up a little, 'it grows late, but we can have the carriage leave us straight at some entertainment. What shall we do?'

I turn to him, surprised. I was not expecting to be consulted.

'Surely you must know the delights of the city?' he presses. 'We shall go wherever you like.'

I smile at him uncertainly. 'The truth is,' I admit, 'I know hardly anything of London. I stayed mostly inside the house at Mrs Wilkes's. And in Piccadilly I stay in a few streets where there is likely trade.'

Edward's eyebrows arch.

'You do not know much of London? But there is so much to see. There are all kinds of entertainments.' He takes my hands. 'Shall we see the exotic animals on the Strand? Or go to a gambling house?'

He seems more animated now and it occurs to me that I afford a rather greater social freedom than a true lady might.

'Are women allowed in gambling houses?'

He waves his hand in disdain. 'Money decides the rules. You will see.'

I smile at the thought of visiting a fine gaming house with Edward. Like all street girls I have heard magical rumours of the large houses. That their walls are lined with sweetmeats and fine wines flow freely.

Then I remember. My dress is for daytime.

'This dress is not suitable for evening,' I say.

'Does that concern you?'

'It does not concern me,' I say slowly, 'but others will not like it. If I go to fine places in this dress, I will be chased out as a whore the moment you step away from my side. People will think I do not know how to dress at night. They will think I stole the dress.'

'I did not realise that,' he says quietly.

I shrug. 'It is how things are. I do not mind.'

Edward frowns. Then his face breaks into a smile.

'I have thought of a fine entertainment,' he says.

I look at him in smiling puzzlement. I like him in this mood. He seems to have a boyish energy that I did not see before.

'A place where it matters not what either of us wear,' he adds.

I look at him waiting for enlightenment.

'We are going,' he announces, 'to a masquerade ball.'

Chapter 29

'*I* have always wanted to attend a masquerade,' I admit, once Edward has given his driver instructions. 'Is it as wild as they say?'

'It is a very popular entertainment,' he says. 'And many aristocrats are quite brazen in their costumes.'

'Do their masks offer true concealment?'

'Yes.'

'So that is why people might dress however they wish?' I deduce, imagining anonymity must be a rare treat among the small world of London nobility.

'That is so,' says Edward. 'They dress as anything at all. You will see milkmaids, highwaymen, kings and queens. It is quite a spectacular sight.'

I ponder this.

'Then I understand why it is so popular,' I decide.

'Oh?' He looks at me questioningly.

'Aristocrats have so many formal rules,' I say, remembering how strange I found all the customs at Mrs Wilkes's. 'Wearing disguise must be like a freedom.'

Edward laughs softly. His eyes look thoughtful. 'Yes,' he says, 'I suppose it is. Although,' he adds, 'society ladies have a way of taking their formality wherever they go.' He's looking at me admiringly as he says this.

I squeeze his hand and stare out of the carriage.

This is a rich part of town. I am worrying again and my hand falls to stroke my blue skirt.

'The masquerade is on Oxford Street?' I add, repeating what he has already told me. 'You are sure I will not be chastised for my day dress?'

Edward gently stops the movement.

'At a masquerade, a girl who looks like you might wear a sack and be celebrated,' he promises. 'Everyone is in costume. No one should mind. You will see.'

I smile uncertainly.

'What of masks?' I ask, my voice rising in slight panic. 'We have no masks to wear.'

'Look out of the window. What do you see there?'

I have been so lost in Edward's company that I have not been paying attention to the carriage's bumpy journey over the London mud and cobbles.

I recognise Regent Street from seeing it the first time I arrived in the city. But unlike the wide expanse that receives public coaches in the daytime, the night-time route is decked in red lanterns announcing masquerades.

I peer closer. The streets are full of vendors selling flimsy masks and costumes.

'They sell masks here?' I say, turning to Edward in delight and then pressing my nose back to the carriage window. 'Costumes too!'

Now I am excited. So long as we have costumes and masks, no one will know me for a whore. I could be anyone.

I grin at Edward.

He smiles back, then knocks on the top of the carriage. The vehicle slows to a halt. Almost immediately, vendors swarm towards the door.

Edward opens it and jumps down, but I hang back a little, intimidated by the rush of sales people. This is what gentry folk experience all the time, I realise. When their fine carriages are recognised for the vast wealth they carry.

Edward hands me down into the milieu of shouting voices and I cling close to him.

'A mask, Your Lordship!' shouts a gravelly voice. 'I sell the best. And for the best price!'

'Come with me, Your Lordship!' presses another seller, pushing close. One tugs at my dress and I squeal in alarm, pushing tight against Edward. He looks down and his hand falls to the sword at his hip.

Instantly the crowd of vendors shuffles back, though not far enough to give up a possible sale.

Edward's eyes are on mine and I nod to show I am not frightened. He takes my arm firmly and guides me directly to a small shop, pressed back behind the rows of street stalls.

'We will buy masks and costumes here,' he says.

The mask sellers slip away disappointedly, realising Edward already has a place to buy.

I take in the building. It's a low wooden half-timbered house. The kind London is packed full of. A swinging shop sign shows a picture of a costume and a mask. Edward knocks at the door, then opens it and hands me through.

I step into a musty-smelling paradise of strange garments, masks and veils.

'It is like a conjurer's shop,' I say, as Edward comes in behind me.

'That it is!' announces a creaky old voice. 'A conjurer's shop, my dear! For lovely creatures such as yourself to cast their spells.'

'Hello, Peters,' says Edward, stepping forward to greet the man warmly.

'Your Lordship,' says the man, bowing.

'You must call me Edward,' he says, pressing the old man's hand tightly in his.

'Edward then,' agrees the man. 'I knew him since a boy,' he adds, gesturing the remark at me. 'You'll never find a gentler character or a kinder master.'

'Peters used to work as our tailor,' says Edward. 'And for other families nearby.'

'I was always the Hayses' tailor,' says Peters, setting his lip stubbornly. 'Never did as good work as I did for the Hayses.'

'And now you are a costumer?' I ask, surveying his shop. I like the old man.

'That I am, young miss,' he says, scrutinising me. 'Where did you find this lovely girl?' he asks Edward. 'I know all the society ladies and she has none of that mean cast about her.'

Edward laughs.

'Can you find her a costume that will do her beauty justice?'

The old man eyes me thoughtfully. 'No,' he decides. 'Best you clothe her as a nun. Else you will spend your night fighting off other men.'

I laugh at his flattery.

'There you have it,' says Edward. 'A nun, we will dress you as.' He is trying not to smile.

I shake my head. 'I should have no fun at all.'

'Well then,' says Peters, 'if it is fun you are after, then perhaps a nymph, or an angel.' He draws out a very flimsy looking skein of material that hardly resembles a dress.

'Do you wish to get me killed?' says Edward, stepping forward and replacing the garment. 'I will spend the night duelling if she wears that.'

166

'A queen then,' decides Peters. 'She has a regal nature to her, do you not think?'

'A queen of olden times?' suggests Edward. 'That would mean modest clothing,' he adds approvingly.

But I am only half listening. I have spied a garment tucked in among a row of silk dresses. I dart forward and pull it out.

'What of this?'

'A shepherdess?' asks Edward.

I nod, holding up the dress delightedly. I know how well it will look. It is not so flimsy as an angel or nymph, but I know it will flatter me.

'It should remind me of my country origins,' I say.

'Very well,' he says. 'What costume should I choose?'

I frown thoughtfully. 'Something very low,' I say. 'That is the fun of it, is it not? Lord Hays dressed as an ostler, or a footman. You will find out how the poor people are treated.'

'That would be very dull,' protests Edward.

'Then you must be a shepherd,' I decide. 'To match me.'

He smiles at this. 'Very well. We shall be a country couple together.'

'It should be very different from your usual smart dress,' I tease. 'What should you do without your boots and buttons?'

'The same as any country shepherd,' he says. 'I shall wave my crook around.'

Peters is already rummaging through his clothing and he produces another costume. A shepherd and a shepherdess. Easy garments for a country life.

Edward's attire consists of rough brown breeches, a matching jerkin and a loose blue tunic to wear over the top. There are a pair of grey wool gaiters and a jaunty brown hat.

'You will look very handsome,' I say, looking at the clothes approvingly.

Peters hands me my shepherdess costume – a loose blue bodice splitting into four panels at my waist, a basic matching skirt and a white shift with long loose sleeves.

'You may dress behind the curtain at the back,' he says, pointing over my shoulder. 'Your young lord will not mind dressing in front of me.'

I smile at them and head towards a thick curtain hanging at the end of the small shop. I duck behind it, and see a little stool and an arrangement of dried flowers – obviously Peters's way of making his dressing area fitting for lords and ladies.

Quickly, I shed my clothes and put on the looser shift, the soft bodice and the skirt. I tie the ribbons at the back, thinking how much more comfortable I feel without the bones of my rigid stays keeping me upright.

I emerge to see Edward and clap my hands to my mouth in delight.

'You look so ... handsome!' I exclaim, taking in the open shirt and his bare calves.

I walk nearer, taking his shoulders in my hands and turning him this way and that.

'What a fine shepherd you make,' I say, marvelling at the transformation.

Edward's muscular arms and chest are prominent. And without his usual shoes and stockings he seems much younger. In peasant dress, his striking features seem even more captivating. The broad arch of his dark eyebrows and the sculpted height of his cheekbones catch the candlelight.

'You remind me of a pastoral portrait,' I say. 'The kind painters make to show idyllic country life. With impossibly handsome men. Here,' I add, reaching to pull the ribbon from his brown hair. It falls in a thick curtain around his jaw and I tuck it back over his ears. 'Now you are truly a shepherd,' I say.

There is a mischievous glint in Edward's eye and I realise Peters is looking at us with a sentimental smile.

I take a hasty step away and smooth out my dress.

'I like you very well as a shepherdess also,' says Edward, his hand moving to my soft-fitting bodice. 'Though you will have to stay close at my side. I do not want some jealous man kidnapping you.'

I laugh, remembering when we first met. How he didn't believe my story of being seduced at a masquerade.

'I should not be fooled for a second time, My Lord,' I promise. 'I can assure you I am most wary of men in masks.'

Peters is manhandling a large mirror and we both turn to see.

For the briefest of moments, I think I am looking at a painting. A country idyll with a happy husband and wife in their farming clothes.

Unexpectedly it gives me a stab of pain. This was once a dream of mine. Long before Mrs Wilkes. Before Kitty and Rose and Belle and Harriet.

It is as though someone is mocking me. Holding up my girlish fantasy now I am a whore.

'I think I might give up the estate and take to herding sheep,' announces Edward. 'If this is how well my wife would look, it should not be such a bad life, should it, Peters?'

Edward looks to include me in the joke. But as he catches my eye, his smile falters.

I realise I have not taken care to hide my feelings. With difficulty I manoeuvre a practised smile into place.

'We are missing only our flock of sheep,' I say, laughing lightly. Edward is puzzled for a moment and then his gaze returns to the mirror.

I take in my reflection anew, twisting my thoughts away from memories and into the present.

Without rigid stays and petticoats, the true shape of my body is unavoidably on display. I have never felt so naked. My street girl clothes are designed to show as much of my breasts as possible. But they conceal other aspects of my figure.

In contrast my shepherdess skirt ends mid-calf, showing a great deal of leg, and my feet are bare, adding to the effect of partial dress. I rather like it, I decide, for all the indecency. The costume has a simple loveliness. From a time before women wore wigs and gloves and seven petticoats to fan their skirts out wide.

'You must have a hat,' decides Edward, selecting one from a wooden crate on the floor. It is an old style shepherdess hat – far smaller than the one I usually wear and tied with a jaunty blue ribbon.

Edward places it on my head and gently fastens the ribbon in a large bow under my chin.

'There,' he says, taking a step back to admire. 'Now we might see your lovely face, with all those curls around.'

I smile, looking in the mirror uncertainly.

'I need a mask,' I say.

'I had forgotten,' says Edward. 'What a shame to cover you up. Might we have two masks?' he asks Peters. 'And veils too. We shall go in absolute disguise,' he adds to me. 'You will see the fun of it.'

Peters produces two plain black masks, with hanging veils, and we secure them on our faces. Now the pastoral scene in the mirror has turned dark. The shepherds have a devilish look.

'You see how no one will know you?' asks Edward.

I nod, taking in my reflection.

'See how her brown eyes sparkle behind the mask,' observes Peters, sounding pleased. 'It is a very pretty shepherdess you have by your side, Lord Hays.'

Ordinarily I might blush at such a compliment. And in a rush I understand why masquerading is such a popular activity. To be so completely disguised is liberating.

'Are you ready?' asks Edward, assessing my costume with pleasure. 'I am going to show you what London entertaining is all about.'

I nod, a slow thrill creeping through me. Tonight, I can be anyone I want to be.

Chapter 30

O n Oxford Street two solitary giant torches flame as beacons. The Pantheon rears white against the dancing light. Its many large rectangular windows have thick damask curtains concealing the intrigue of the interior.

I have only seen the building once in the daytime, when a public coach carried me into London. Since the Great Fire, brick and stone buildings have sprung up all over the city. In stark contrast to the wooden buildings of my country birthplace. And while I admire the swagger of an entire street of brick and stone, the enormous Pantheon looks a little forbidding with its unyielding columns and straight walls.

'It is styled to look like a Roman temple,' explains Edward, noticing me staring. 'I saw many like it as a younger man.'

'You were in Rome?' I am impressed.

'Many young lords make a tour of Europe,' he says. 'So they can sow their wild oats.'

'I cannot quite imagine you as a libertine.'

Edward smiles slightly.

'I had my moments,' he says. 'In France and Italy I also learned

172

more about farming methods. When I returned, I applied what I had discovered and our family estate made a profit for the first time in years.'

I nod at this. From what I know of him, this is typically Edward.

'Should you like to travel there again?' I ask.

He thinks about his.

'Perhaps one day. I enjoyed travelling very much. But now I am older, I am less inclined to venture overseas.'

'Why?'

Edward frowns.

'Travel can be unpredictable,' he says. 'Managing the family estate made a business man of me. I learned what my father did not. That unnecessary risk is to be avoided.'

'I had forgotten,' I reply, 'that you do not like risk.'

'No,' he says. 'Not in business.'

'It sounds as though making money has become a habit that precedes all else.'

'Perhaps,' he says mildly, looking towards the entrance. A mass of people form an untidy queue of costumed revellers. It is too dark to easily see their outfits. But a thicket of sticks, staffs, crooks and tridents wave above the throng.

'Looks like we shall have to get ready to push the crowd,' I sigh, knowing all too well the mob mentality that forms whenever Londoners gather en masse.

But Edward takes my hand and leads me to the front of the queue. When he arrives in front of the two smartly dressed doormen, he takes off his mask.

The effect is immediate. The men bow and the crowd parts.

'I see,' I say, turning to Edward in surprise. 'So a lordship comes with benefits besides a country estate.'

'Some are more useful than others,' he says with a smile, leading me on.

The masquerade has two more entrances, each with progressively stricter entrance criteria. I hold Edward's hand uncertainly. But the instant staff see his face, we are ushered through as honoured guests.

Edward buys two hand-illustrated tickets for five guineas each and hands them to me.

'Five guineas?' I say, taking the ticket.

'It helps keep undesirables out,' he says with a little smile. 'Although they cannot account for such factions entirely of course. That is part of the fun.'

I grin at him.

'This must be the only place in London where people are judged solely on how much money is in their pockets,' I say, wishing it were so elsewhere.

'I suppose it is.' Edward replaces his mask. 'Are you ready to masquerade?'

'With you, always,' I reply, realising only as I say the words how true this is. I will be sad to leave the fantasy life I am living with Edward.

A curtain is held back for us and then we are in the huge domed ballroom of the Pantheon.

My mouth falls open in wonder.

Thousands of candles sit atop countless mighty chandeliers, and every table and surface around the room is decked in sparkling candelabras. Rippling flames play out as far as the eye can see, while the sides of the hall are decked with sweets, bread, cheeses and enormous bowls of fruit. Towards the back I make out a crowded wine service area.

'It is like daylight!' I whisper under the glare of the illuminations. 'And the *noise*!' I add, giddy with delight at the experience. A wave of high-pitched squeaking sweeps over us – the sound of the masqueraders enjoying frantic dialogue in disguised voices.

'Edward, look!' I can barely contain my excitement.

The masqueraders are a whirling mass of black featureless faces set against the most elaborate and incredible costumes. High hair pieces tower several feet in the air, their bizarre ornaments and jewels making a bobbing dance of their own above the crowd.

My eyes light on some of the more outlandishly dressed female guests.

'Who is *that*?' I ask, pointing to a near-transparent outfit.

A curvaceous young woman is draped in diaphanous materials that barely cloak her nudity. And she has not troubled herself with a mask.

'That is Iphigenia,' says Edward. 'A sacrificial victim of Greek myth, undressed and ready for sacrifice.'

'I do not mean her costume,' I whisper. 'Do you know who she is?'

'Elizabeth Chudleigh. She is married and a lady. But it will be a scandal if the journals report her.'

I stare at the woman, mesmerised.

'Should not her husband mind?' I manage.

Edward shakes his head.

'She has produced an heir. Her husband does not much care for her company. So she is free to take a lover as she wishes.'

I let my eyes rove the rest of the room. Aside from Elizabeth Chudleigh, most guests wear masks. And the majority are masquerading from the lower social hemisphere.

With the masquerade mask a solid disguise to the upper face and a black veil hanging over the mouth, the physical camouflage is impressive. Particularly as many attendees also wear heavy hoods, wigs or the headgear of their various professions.

Milkmaids and gardeners, footmen and flower girls, ostlers and pastoral nymphs tramp the thick wooden floorboards.

But dotted in among them are the occasional guests covered in spectacular jewels.

'Those guests cheat,' I protest, pointing to a lady draped head to toe in diamonds. 'She shows she can be nothing less than a duchess.'

'Yes,' agrees Edward, his mouth close to my ear so as to share his thoughts with me alone. 'Some cannot bear to be poor, even for fun. It is a little sad, is it not?'

I nod slowly.

'Shall we have some wine?' he asks. 'I can have some brought to us.'

But over the din of the masquerade, I make out the first chords of a violin.

'Music!' I cry in delight. 'Edward, we must dance before we drink.' I take his hand and drag him towards an eddying huddle of guests who are arranging themselves into a circle.

He shakes his head and pulls back, but I press forward, unwilling to take no for an answer.

'No one will know you,' I protest, inching him towards the music. 'And even you must know this song, Edward. It is a country dance.'

He is laughing and allowing me to coax him now.

'Very well,' he says. 'You are sure it is a shepherdess you came as? And not a cattle prodder?'

I beam back at him. 'I will be anything you like, so long as you dance with me,' I reply, as we take our places among the other guests.

I am almost skipping on the spot from excitement and Edward is looking at me in amusement.

'I love dancing,' I say. 'This is one of my favourites.'

It is a lively country melody. Completely different to the complex steps of fashionable French dancing.

I take in the other dancers. They are poised rigidly. In the way of aristocrats who have it ingrained not to make a show of themselves. I can already imagine how they will dance. Like puppets on a route march.

I frown, promising to enjoy myself in any case. The stuffy ladies can go hang, I decide. I am masked. No one knows me. I shall dance as enthusiastically as if I were at a country fair in Bristol.

The first dancing chord strikes out. As predicted, the other dancers begin a precise, measured step. Only just meeting the lively beat.

I break into a wide smile, letting the music wash over me and my body follow. Masquerading truly is liberating, I realise, as I plunge full force into the dance.

At first Edward is a little out of time. But when the part comes for us to lock arms, I pull him back into the rhythm.

'You see!' I cry, as we spin to the music. 'This one is easy. You step only on the third and then swing.'

I pull him into the same fast step, flinging myself wholeheartedly into the dance, letting my skirts whirl out wide.

Edward has something approaching a smile now and as we break into the second verse, he has mastered the rhythm.

By the time we are on the third, we are both laughing aloud as we skip and spin. Edward looks the happiest I have ever seen him. As though he hasn't a care in the world.

We press close and then swing apart, looping and reeling as the music drums in our ears. Our hedonism has even rubbed off a little on the other dancers. I notice a few have picked up the beat. Others smile in approval as Edward and I whirl like mad things.

'Are you not glad I made you dance?' I grin, as we bounce around one another. 'You are enjoying it hugely, I can see it.'

'I would enjoy it more had not all those men gathered,' observes Edward wryly.

In the heat of the dance I had forgotten the loose shepherdess costume. I take a hasty glance around, to see the dance floor has attracted a little ring of male spectators. Many of whom seem to have their eyes glued to my bodice, which barely disguises the motion of my breasts as I dance.

'You must use your crook on them,' I decide, breathless as the song comes to the end. 'That is what a good shepherd would do.'

'Maybe I should use it on you,' he says. 'To keep you from dancing.'

I give him my widest, most beatific smile.

'Never, Your Lordship,' I say. 'Now we know how much you love to dance, you must partner me every time.'

Chapter 31

We wander away from the dance, breathless and happy. Edward steers us to the wine service area, where he orders a bottle of wine.

'Do you like the masquerade?' he asks, pouring me a cup.

'Very much,' I decide, taking a long sip. 'I love it.'

He seems pleased. 'I hoped you would.'

'Everywhere you take me is better than the last,' I admit.

We are beaming at one another, lost to the world.

'You are so different,' I say, in a flush of honesty, 'from the lords I met at Mrs Wilkes's.'

Edward considers this.

'How did you find yourself with Mrs Wilkes?' he asks.

'I was ruined,' I say easily. For I suddenly feel I may tell Edward everything. 'The story is a cliché. My seducer took me to Mrs Wilkes. And since my fine plans had been broken, I let Mrs Wilkes lead me to a life of sin with hardly a protest.'

'Your seducer was the man who gave you the banknote?' Edward guesses.

His perception is unexpected. I nod and frown, not wanting to say anything more. My easy admission has become complicated in the reality of painful memories.

Edward stays silent.

'What of you?' I ask, to break the suddenly charged atmosphere. 'Who was your first?'

He laughs. 'A servant girl. Like every young lord.'

'Oh Edward,' I tease, 'how terribly commonplace. To seduce a poor servant.'

'She seduced me,' he replies. 'My lover was a thirty-year-old widow who polished the silver. I was sixteen and giddy with lust. She used me mercilessly for profit.' His tone is amused, as though he respects such behaviour.

'Am I to take it you enjoyed the seduction?'

'Every moment of it,' he says. 'Though my father did not like how much money I gave her. He dismissed her in the end. But I think she had enough by then to do very well for herself.'

I smile at this.

There's a cough behind us.

'Edward?' says a familiar voice.

We both turn in alarm, to see a man dressed as King Henry the Eighth. He only wears a half-mask and I recognise his lower face immediately. It is Fitzroy.

I feel myself drawing close to Edward. As though my heart has been squeezed. I am hoping Caroline is not here.

In the high spirits of the masquerade, I had forgotten that Edward is a high lord with an arranged marriage.

'Fitzroy,' says Edward, but he doesn't sound pleased.

'I recognised your voice,' replies Fitzroy. 'I can always tell the timbre of true gentry.'

'What a magnificent costume,' says Edward politely.

'I had extra diamonds stitched,' says Fitzroy, stroking his fur-lined chest. 'All kinds of low folk slip into the masquerade. It's as well for them to know who is their better.'

He seems to consider Edward and me fully for the first time.

'I did not know you were attending the masq,' he says pointedly. 'Had you informed me—'

Edward holds up a hand, cutting him off.

'There is nothing to concern yourself with, Fitzroy,' he says. 'The business on the estate was done today. Vanderbilt can have no more objections. We will sign at the Exchange on Friday, as arranged.'

Fitzroy's face looks as though he is searching for some objection.

'I could have come with you,' he says finally. 'Born witness to the signature. So we could be sure Vanderbilt could have no other recourse.'

'Elizabeth witnessed the signature,' says Edward.

Fitzroy's eyebrows shoot up. His eyes flick quickly to mine and I see something jealous there.

'A shepherdess tonight,' he murmurs, looking at my loose shift.

I feel my hand lift to my mask, assuring myself of its comforting presence.

'You are privileged indeed,' he continues, 'to spend so much time with Edward.'

I glance at Edward, uncertain of how to respond.

'And your costume is certainly beguiling,' adds Fitzroy, his gaze openly roaming my figure now. 'A king can admire such country purity.'

I smile rigidly and make a curtsy.

'I am grateful for your royal favour,' I reply.

'I saw you both dance,' says Fitzroy. 'You were well spoken of to be sure, Miss Shepherdess. I think you will be besieged by admirers if you leave Edward's side for an instant.'

He stares at me for a long moment, as though he suspects me of something. Then he turns his attention back to Edward.

'I thought you did not dance,' he says, letting the observation hang on the air like an accusation.

'This lady found the dancer in me.' Edward is looking at me warmly.

Fitzroy frowns.

'Be watchful, Edward,' he says, with a meaningful glance at my loose dress, 'that you do not lose sight of your purpose in town.'

'You forget yourself, Fitzroy,' says Edward, his voice suddenly cold, 'if you think to tell a lord how to conduct himself.'

Fitzroy blinks as though he has been slapped.

He gives a low bow.

'Of course, Your Lordship,' he murmurs.

He straightens, his eyes shifting to a point over Edward's shoulder, and he gives us both a short bow.

'Do excuse me,' he says. 'I believe I see Lord Grey with his mistress. He means to debate on slavery next week and I must hear his view.'

He glances at Edward, seeming to recover his early self-assurance. 'This will influence our business,' he adds. 'Your trade could be assured for another two years at least.'

Fitzroy pauses and regards us both. 'I shall send Lady Stafford to speak with you,' he adds. 'She will influence his lordship badly if she overhears us speak. You might distract her.' He yawns affectedly. 'Her ladyship likes to take on pet charitable issues. Slavery is her latest.'

Fitzroy darts away and I bring my wine glass close to my mouth, looking out into the crowd.

I can't forget the look on his face when Edward chastised him. Something tells me Fitzroy is the kind of man who would make me pay for it if he could.

'Who is Lady Stafford?' I ask as Fitzroy retreats.

'She is Lord Grey's mistress,' says Edward.

'Oh.' I take a sip of wine. 'Do any aristocrats stay faithful?'

Edward laughs easily. 'Not many. But I mean to,' he says. 'Once I have a wife.'

He is looking into the crowd, in the direction of Fitzroy. And I am suddenly very grateful that Caroline doesn't seem to be in attendance.

Chapter 32

*L*ady Stafford comes to greet us dressed as an orange girl.
She has teamed the simple costume with a striking diamond necklace and silk gloves. And despite her towering hair, it's
almost impossible not to stare at her enormous bosom spilling from
the low dress. But somehow Edward manages.

'This is Elizabeth,' he says, bowing by way of introduction.

'A pleasure to meet you,' I say, politely curtsying. Since Lady
Montfort, I am a little wary of older ladies. But Lady Stafford gives
me a warm smile.

'How lovely to make your acquaintance,' she says sincerely.
'Edward, you have a beautiful girl there. What a charming smile she
has! What a tumble of curling hair! Why you are like a little elfin
thing, with those sparkling eyes.'

She leans closer. 'You should beware of him, my dear. Lord Hays
is easily friended but impossible to wed. Many girls have been disappointed.'

'Oh,' I say, smiling back, 'I have no wish to marry. Besides,

Edward spends his whole time making money. Being his wife would be a lonely thing indeed.'

Lady Stafford gives a pleased laugh. 'That is what London is for,' she says, touching my arm. 'So us poor women can avoid our dull husbands.'

Even Edward laughs at this.

A diamond-clad woman walks past and as my eyes follow her, Lady Stafford lowers her voice disapprovingly.

'That's Nancy Fisher,' she says. 'She's the most celebrated woman in the *demi-monde*. Until the next favourite takes her place.'

I cannot stop staring. I have heard tales of Nancy Fisher, the famous courtesan. She moves with such ease and grace that I can well see why she is famed.

'What's the *demi-monde*?' I ask, watching as a cloud of men light around Nancy, pouring her drinks and fawning over her.

Lady Stafford's eyebrows go up. 'Oh Edward, you have brought a little country mouse to the masquerade.' She lowers her voice dramatically. 'The *demi-monde* is the other world, the half world. Where women of a certain kind are condemned to live – not in society, but not quite out of it. Once a woman enters that world, she can never be respected again.' She gives a grand flick of her fan to signal the scandalous nature of the intelligence.

The demi-monde. I turn the phrase around in my mind. The half world. I guess that's where Harriet and Belle must be now. Successful lovers, but never respected wives.

'Are you new to London?' Lady Stafford asks me.

I turn to Edward, unsure of how to reply.

'Elizabeth is from the country,' he says.

Lady Stafford clasps my hand in her gloved ones.

'You must join my parliamentary cause,' she says.

'Elizabeth is only in town for a few days—' begins Edward.

'Nonsense!' announces Lady Stafford. 'You only wish to influence the girl, because it is against your business interests.'

She taps Edward's arm disapprovingly with her fan.

'Do not think I haven't heard, Edward, that your next venture is trading ships. Nothing gets past me.'

He gives a little smile. 'I do not doubt it, Your Ladyship.'

'Slavery is an awful business,' she continues. 'You may fool yourself you trade only in commodities. But you are responsible for what they are used to buy.'

She glowers at Edward for a moment. Then she turns back to me.

'Tell me, my dear,' she says, 'what is your view on the slave trade?'

There is a long pause and I feel suddenly that Edward is eager to know my answer.

'I am from the country,' I begin slowly. 'From near Bristol. Which, as you know, is a large port.'

Lady Stafford nods encouragingly.

'So I sometimes saw slaves,' I continue. 'Not many, you understand. Since we do not employ a great deal in England.'

'And what did you think to see them?' prompts Lady Stafford.

'I thought . . .' I hesitate before stumbling on. 'I thought their faces were so resigned that slave advocates must be right. Negroes are not really people.'

Lady Stafford looks disappointed. I take a breath.

'They seemed to accept their fate so dumbly, with so little emotion . . . It seemed to me the Negroes must be more like cattle,' I explain, remembering my thoughts at the time.

Lady Stafford opens her mouth to reply, but I swallow and charge on.

'Then I came to London,' I say, 'and I . . . I saw women. Women who had been sold into bawdy houses.'

I look quickly at Edward.

'Those women had that same look,' I continue. 'That same dumb, scared look. And I realised then' – my eyes are on Edward's – 'that the expression is not that of someone lower than human. It is that of a person who has been beaten so low that they dare not lift their head, for fear of where the next blow will come from. It is an expression a face should never hold.'

I take a shaky sip of wine and look down, realising I have said too much.

'So I do not think it a good business,' I whisper. 'This slavery.'

'Oh my dear,' Lady Stafford is wiping her eyes, 'how wonderfully you speak of it.'

She turns to Edward.

'I refuse to let you keep this lovely girl to yourself,' she says. 'Where have you been hiding her?'

'She has only been in town a few days,' he says, with a smile. 'And already she has met Lady Montfort and Charlotte Montfort, and attended the theatre.'

'Well then, that explains it,' decides Lady Stafford. 'You have taken her out in the worst company in London. She must think us city women are joyless creatures.'

Lady Stafford smiles warmly at me.

'We are not all cold devils like Lady Montfort and those theatre-harpies, you know. Some of us can see the fun in life.' She winks at me. 'You must come to one of our meetings.'

I give her a little smile.

'I am afraid I am only in London for a few more days,' I admit, collecting myself.

Lady Stafford looks first at me and then Edward. Then she tactfully changes the subject.

Chapter 33

*E*dward and I have two more dances before he suggests we make our way home in the carriage.

'It is still early,' I point out. 'Hardly past midnight. Surely you would like to be seen here a little longer?'

'I should,' he says. 'But I should also like to make the most of my time with you.'

The way he says it makes his meaning clear. And quite unexpectedly, a pulse of pleased anticipation passes through me. The truth is, I am looking forward to being alone with him.

I do not dwell so much on what this might mean, but let him lead me out to the carriage, which awaits us in front of the Pantheon.

Edward's hand tightens on mine and there is that little flutter again. The reality is inescapable. I have feelings for him. But following the heady thrill of the masquerade, this does not frighten me as much as it should.

He hands me into the carriage and as the door shuts, it is just the two of us inside the velvet-lined walls. It feels close, intimate, and the atmosphere is charged.

Edward knocks on the roof of the carriage and the horses lurch to a start. Without taking his eyes off me, he puts out an arm and draws shut the curtains, so we are completely concealed inside.

Then he leans forward and rests his hands lightly on my waist. The warmth of the contact radiates through my thin dress.

'It has been a torture to watch you dancing in this dress,' he murmurs.

'Shall I take it off for you?' I reply, in a dreamy kind of state.

He is silent. Then his hands begin to unlace my costume. The top half falls away and I shiver as the cool night air hits my naked skin.

Edward's fingers glide softly over me, raising a trail of goose bumps. Then he pulls me slowly forward against his body.

Until now, there had been something restrained in his movements. But when our lips touch it's as though a charge has erupted between us.

I respond to his kiss eagerly, wrapping my arms around his broad back, pulling him close.

His hands roam my body and I tip my head back as his mouth seeks out the sensitive skin on my neck. I am pushed back against the seat of the carriage. Edward moves so his weight is over me, pulling up my skirts. My hands move to tug away his clothing. It is powerful, this sudden desire for him. I can barely think, but that I want him.

I open my eyes to see his dark gaze on me and suddenly I am uncertain what is happening between us. To hide my confusion, I pull him to me in another deep kiss, wrapping my legs around him, drawing him in.

I had meant to regain control. That the act I am so accustomed to will reorder my strangely disarrayed thoughts. But this time it is different between us.

As he moves inside me, my body arcs into his of its own accord and a sigh of pleasure tumbles from my lips. Edward moves softly, never taking his eyes from mine, and though I am shamed by it, the lust for him threatens to overwhelm me.

I am pinned by his gaze. As though he sees all of me.

'Elizabeth,' he whispers, and it is only then that the true terror of my vulnerability hits me.

It is as if I have awoken sharply from a dream and I press my body tight against him, clawing his back with my fingers. I can see in his face that he knows. I am using every trick to reclaim myself and change the dynamic between us.

I drop my hands, driving him deeper. Forcing him to surrender.

Edward gasps and then his arms wrap tight around me as he collapses forward.

He buries his head against my neck. I stare up at the jolting ceiling of the carriage.

Relief is washing over me like a great golden wave.

For a moment, locked in Edward's embrace, I had a terrible feeling.

I was falling deep and far away. Into a place of no return.

Chapter 34

'There!' announces Sophie, holding the glass. 'I have never seen such a fine lady. Not in all my days.'

She says this with a sense of ownership. As though I were her own lady.

I gaze back at my reflection in wonder. Today Edward and I will visit Vauxhall Gardens. I have chosen the dusky pink silk dress for the occasion, with soft clouds of lace at the neck.

'You are fairer, even, than the Duchess of Devonshire as a debutante,' Sophie adds. 'And she was the best beauty London has ever seen.'

I take in my reflection, hardly recognising the fine lady looking back. The dress is art itself, fitting to every curve of my body at the top and emphasising my small waist with the flare of the skirts.

The silken sleeves are turned at the elbow in a delicate froth of French lace, making my arms look beautiful. Even my long fingers seem elegant.

Something about the pink silk makes my skin appear even more flawless than usual. The square of exposed bust line looks invitingly plump – perhaps a combination of the impeccably made dress and the extra meals of the last few days.

'We shall make your toilette to match,' says Sophie.

I am becoming more used to being dressed and coiffed now, and sit easily as she begins washing my face.

'You like the dress very much?' she observes, since my eyes are glued to my reflection.

'I cannot stop gazing at myself,' I admit. 'I can hardly believe it is me.'

I wonder if Kitty would even recognise me. She might mistake me for a real lady and catcall.

Sophie laughs and begins stacking my chestnut curls high onto my head. She offers an assortment of hair ornaments, and I choose pink ribbons and feathers to match the dress.

'You shall look like a summer's day,' she announces happily, as the three girls work to arrange my hair.

I eye myself while my curls are woven high. My brown eyes are alive with pleasure and my mischievous look is even more evident than usual. I threaten to split my face with the wideness of my smile.

'There's a flush about you too,' observes Sophie. 'A felicity to your manner this morning.'

'What woman wouldn't flush to wear such a dress?' I reply lightly, averting my gaze from the glass. 'For you know, Sophie, dresses make women happier than men ever could.' But even to my ears, the nonchalance sounds acted.

When my hair is finished with, the maids return with a pair of matching shoes and I am given a final view of the glass.

'I think I need a flower,' I say, remembering some of the finer fashions I have seen. 'I saw some lovely pink roses in the garden. Might I have one of those?'

Sophie nods admiringly. 'I think that would be a fine choice, Miss Lizzy. I shall fetch you one at once.'

I arrive at breakfast and Edward's eyes grow wide.

'You look breathtakingly beautiful,' he says, as I take my seat.

I smile at the compliment. I take up a bread roll and pick at it.

'I have no jewelled hair ornaments like the fine ladies do,' I say apologetically. 'But Sophie did her best with laces and feathers, as you can see.'

'I think Sophie did very well. And I should be so proud,' he adds, 'to have you at my side. I think there will be no lovelier lady in Vauxhall.'

I swallow down the bread. 'I ... Thank you,' I say. 'You are most kind.'

I search for something to change the subject.

'Your business is nearly concluded?'

'Quite so,' says Edward. 'Soon it will all be concluded,' he adds, taking a roll and biting into it. It occurs to me it is the first time I have seen him eat breakfast.

'You are hungry today?' I ask, taking a sip of chocolate.

'I find I have a greater appetite than usual. These past few days.'

He looks up at me, a glint in his eye.

'You know, it was unwise to wear such a lovely dress,' he adds.

I take another sip of chocolate.

'Why is that, Your Lordship?'

'Because I imagine it will take me some time to lace back up,' he says softly. 'Before we leave for Vauxhall.'

Chapter 35

Vauxhall Gardens are just outside the city, to the south. And the dirt track route is packed with coaches, carriages, horses and riders as we arrive.

'Why are so many people here?' I ask in bewilderment, staring out of the window of the carriage.

I have heard of the pleasure gardens, of course. And Edward explained Vauxhall to me during the journey. But I am yet to understand the appeal.

'If it is just a garden,' I ask, leaning bodily out to see past the crowds, 'what is there to do?'

Edward draws me back inside the carriage.

'Take care,' he says. 'Horses can come by fast.'

I smile at his concern. 'Will we just be strolling around?' I press, sitting back beside him.

'That is part of it.'

'Aristocrats must be bored indeed to find that entertaining. Walking in nature is something us common folk try our best to avoid.'

This draws a loud laugh from Edward. The carriage jolts to a bumpy stop.

'Come on,' he says, opening the door to hand me out. 'You will see.'

'Is there anything inside?' I ask, as I drop down by his side. 'Besides trees and grass?'

'Many entertainments,' he says, offering me his arm. 'We may see a hot air balloon. Famous singers and musicians attend.'

This sounds better. I nod approvingly.

'And towards that side are Spring Gardens,' says Edward. 'They are closed walks. Famously romantic.'

'But we are not here for romance?'

'No.'

'Then why are we here?'

'Purposes of business,' he says. 'Some of Mr Vanderbilt's creditors will be here today. It is good to meet with them. Remind them I am of fine family and can help them in their endeavours.'

We join the milling crowds paying their entrance fee and I catch my first glimpse of several huge white-stone buildings – like high-pillared temples thronging with people.

'What are they?' I ask, taking in the gazebo-like structures and their unusual hexagonal shape.

'Those are the rotundas,' explains Edward, speaking with his mouth close to my ear. 'They serve tea and sweets.'

'I like them,' I decide, as he pays over our shillings for entry. 'Why are they open like that?'

Edward smiles. 'So the aristocratic ladies might show off their fine dresses. And the men their fine coats.'

'I should have guessed.' So much of gentry living seems to be about display.

As we move through the crowds, I look up and see a magnificent archway of trees, shaped to form a closed green corridor high above our heads.

'Look at that!' I cry, pointing. 'How very beautiful.'

'It is lovely, is it not?' agrees Edward.

I nod. 'You will need to hold my tall hair,' I joke, 'for all the staring upwards I shall do.'

He smiles.

'You did not tell me true, Edward,' I admonish. 'For this is not really a garden.'

My gaze is stretching up and around, taking in the huge tree-lined walkways and the impeccably landscaped beds that are all around.

He laughs. 'It is a little grander than the average garden.'

As we move towards the rotundas we pass entertainers performing on tightropes and breathing fire for pennies.

'Can we pay a penny?' I beg Edward, as we pass a falconer. 'I should love to see the bird.'

'Very well,' he says, with a smile. 'Have you ever held one?'

'No,' I say, as we get closer.

'I will show you,' Edward says, walking me to stand beside the falconer.

'The lady should like to hold the bird,' he says, handing the man a coin. The bird-handler accepts it with a surprised smile and produces a strip of meat from a leather pouch.

Edward holds me close as the falconer dangles the meat near my hand. And I give a little shriek of delight when the bird hops across onto my wrist.

'Shhh,' advises Edward, holding me tighter, his face next to mine. 'Do not scare her.'

'She is heavier than I thought,' I whisper, my eyes soaking in every part of the bird's shining feathers and curved beak. 'Isn't she magnificent?'

'She certainly is,' says Edward, but his eyes are fixed on my face, rather than the bird.

I look away and back to the bird. She sits so tamely on my wrist. My thoughts go to the bird market and the creatures in cages.

This falcon can fly where she chooses. But she returns to a master. I turn this idea over, for consideration, as I watch her rip at the meat. I had not thought it possible that such a creature should not prefer always to fly free.

We surrender the falcon back to its handler and continue the journey down Vauxhall's busy avenue.

'You like birds?' asks Edward.

'Oh yes,' I say. 'Though I should not like to keep one caged. When I am sad, I like to buy a bird from the market and set it free.'

He looks at me with interest.

'You are sad? I cannot imagine it.'

'You cannot imagine that a street girl could be sad?' I return. 'I thought you were a man of the world.'

He stops walking and holds me still, his hands on my waist.

'I should not like to think of you sad,' he says. I am staring into his finely featured face now, falling into those dark eyes.

He is so handsome.

'I . . .' I am not sure how to respond. In my experience, men find it easy to say things of this nature, but rarely match their words with action.

'It is not for you to concern yourself,' I say gently. 'This is the life I chose. They are my mistakes. Not yours.'

He leans in close and makes the gentlest of kisses on my mouth.

I feel myself breathing him in, falling into him.

It is a heady confusion and somehow I cannot fix the muddle he is creating in me.

I close my eyes, unresisting, letting my lips move deeply against his.

Then, with my heart pounding, I press my hands to his chest and break the kiss.

His eyes are on mine, questioning.

He has paid for my person. So why does this feel like something more?

Perhaps Edward finds the answer in my face. For without saying a word, he takes my hand, leading me onwards.

I follow, too dazed to ask where we are going.

I fear that perhaps he is angry. But his expression does not look so.

He is peering towards one of the grander rotundas. The stone pillars are festooned with colourful banners of fabric, and it houses men and women in incredibly rich dress.

'I see Fitzroy,' says Edward, his voice giving no hint that something just passed between us. 'He is with a few of Vanderbilt's creditors.'

Just hearing Fitzroy's name makes my stomach twist.

'We shall not go to them just yet,' decides Edward. 'Let us take a little walk in Spring Gardens first.'

'The romantic gardens?' I ask, in a teasing tone. 'Surely you need no such arts to seduce me.' I am thinking of the kiss we just shared and my humour is an attempt to bring back a semblance of control.

He smiles. 'I merely aid your education,' he says. 'Even a Piccadilly girl might be shocked at the brazenness of some aristocrats in Vauxhall.'

I raise an eyebrow. 'I find that hard to believe.'

'We shall see.'

Edward guides me into a close maze of hedges, guarded and secret walkways. As we turn inside, it seems as if we are completely alone. But every so often we catch a sigh or a gasp from another closed section, reminding us that clandestine amours are all around.

Edward was not exaggerating. It really is quite shocking. Some people are indulging in relatively innocent caresses. But others are rutting like animals in the shrubbery, their fine clothes hanging loose, or discarded on the grass.

'You see?' he says, as we glimpse a couple. 'Something about the gardens makes people quite brazen.'

'It is not so different to Piccadilly at midnight,' I say, thinking of the alleyways and backstreets. 'Though the people here are better dressed, of course.'

Edward steers me onwards. 'I will show you my favourite part,' he says.

I feel my heart pick up a little.

He leads me into a long walkway and there's an ardency about him as we reach the end. I wonder if he means to resume our kiss. And whether I should feel the same dual tugs. To give myself to him or to draw away.

We are standing in an enclosed space, hidden by hedges, facing one another. And Edward takes me in his arms and kisses me. This time he is even harder to resist. My body is betraying me.

He slides his fingers down my waist and I feel myself shiver with anticipation.

'Elizabeth,' he whispers, moving his hand under the hem of my skirt, 'have you ever taken any pleasure? From being with a man?'

The question takes me by surprise and my practised expression does not manoeuvre fast enough.

'Of course,' I say, with a flirtatious laugh, pulling him close. 'I enjoy men more than most women.'

'You do not have to lie to me,' he says. His fingers are moving smoothly up my thighs now. 'I want you to ... It would give me greater pleasure. If I knew that you liked your time with me.'

'I do.' I'm confused by the sensations he's stirring in me.

Edward still looks troubled.

'When you lay with a man, do you ever ...?' he asks, leaving the question hanging.

I feel my face begin to heat.

Of all the things men have asked me to do. I never thought I could be embarrassed again. But here I am, blushing like a young girl.

'No,' I admit. Because he seems to be able to tell when I am lying.

'That is what I thought,' he says.

He pauses and then his hands begin softly roaming under my skirts again. Now I am afraid. Because I have no intention of letting *that* happen. Not with anyone. And his kisses seem to have earned some unexpected power over me.

'I do not wish for it,' I say, panic rising up. 'I have no desire for it. I am here for your pleasure.'

Edward smiles. 'I will not try, if you do not wish,' he says. My face must show my relief, for he looks sad.

'But I would like something else,' he says.

'What?' I am anxious again.

'Let me take you as I wish to take you,' he says. 'Do not use your seductions.'

'I . . . I am not certain . . .'

'Please,' he says.

I find myself nodding nervously. Falling into his dark eyes.

He unlaces the top of my dress, loosening, caressing.

Then his hands stroke my breasts beneath my clothing and his mouth moves to kiss my neck. I tip my head back, my skin tingling with pleasure.

His mouth drops lower to my breasts, planting gentle kisses. It is delicious. I feel my breath tightening. My body growing warm.

Edward hitches up my skirts and his fingers slide softly up my legs. And then his hand is higher, moving gently. It feels so good I accidentally gasp.

'This is how I want you,' he whispers. 'Like you are now.'

I can barely speak.

'Just like this,' he whispers. His fingers dance lightly over me. 'I want you to take the same pleasure I do,' he murmurs, his hand moving softly. I feel my whole body lifting, as though my soul is rising up to meet his fingers.

'Please,' I gasp. 'Please stop.'

He pauses and I sense he would like to continue his tantalising stroking. But seeing the pleading in my face, he moves his hand away so it rests between my thighs.

My body sinks slowly back to a reassuring reality.

He kisses my mouth. 'I liked you that way,' he whispers.

'I liked it too,' I admit, still hazy with the feelings rioting in my body. 'But I cannot . . . ' I struggle for the words and fall silent.

I stare into his eyes uncertainly. I want him, I realise with a jolt of shock. It is the first I have felt such feelings in a long, long time.

Then we hear the movement of skirts and a loud female voice echoing along the walkway.

I open my eyes to see Edward's gaze and I feel a stab of pain. Because I wish he would look at me that way forever.

But there is relief too. For we both know what he nearly got from me.

We both stand still, our faces inches apart, neither wanting to be the one to move away. Then the voice sounds again, coming nearer now. And I tear my gaze from his and step back, pulling the laces of my dress tight again.

When I look up again I see hurt in his face. He must see that I shall not be so easily seduced again.

I look away from him guiltily, pretending to consider the source of the sound that disturbed us.

Walking towards us are a richly dressed couple. An ageing lord and a woman who is unmistakably a courtesan.

She clings to the man's arm, her face tipped up to his flirtatiously, in a gesture that wives do not make to elderly husbands.

Her bodice dress is similar to mine, with wide skirts. Though hers is deep green and has an affected little cloak at the back, in the French style. She wears a choker of perfect pearls and a matching bracelet. Expensive gifts rather than inherited estate gems. And her curling black hair is styled high with a jaunty little ship perched in the top of it.

There is something strangely familiar about her walk and I peer closer as they close in. She is laughing in a high false trill and neither is paying any attention to the path ahead.

Then I recognise her.

Harriet.

She sees us, in our broken *tryst*. Her face sets in surprised recognition.

'Lizzy?'

I can hardly believe it. The green eyes. The smattering of girlish freckles across her perfect little nose. The pale perfect skin. Most mornings, at Mrs Wilkes's house, I woke to see her heart-shaped face slumbering next to me.

'Harriet!' I cry, overwhelmed to see her.

I take the excuse to force myself away from Edward's side.

I run at her and hug her tightly, knowing that she will not care that we have not made the proper greeting. Harriet never minded for aristocratic manners.

She hugs me back and I marvel at her familiar perfumed smell, pressing against her rigid scratchy dress.

We pull back, regarding each other.

'What a wonder, to see *you*, Lizzy,' she says, taking in my dress and hair with a practised eye. 'I am surprised to find you so well dressed,' she adds, with her usual bluntness. 'I heard you were in Piccadilly.'

'I was,' I admit, my eyes sliding to Edward, who is hanging back. 'I have a ... short arrangement. This is Lord Hays,' I add uncertainly, turning to Edward. He steps to my side and bows to Harriet. His expression is unreadable.

'Lord Hays,' she says airily, nodding at me as though in appreciation of a game well played.

She makes Edward a curtsy that is so half-hearted it borders on impudent. But all the while, her eyes rest tightly on his, considering what indecent acts they might enjoy together.

I had forgotten this about Harriet. She is a master at making men desperate for her.

I frown at her and she gives me a casual shrug.

You cannot blame me for trying my luck, she seems to say.

I suddenly regret Harriet's presence. She is not beautiful in the conventional fashion, but charisma radiates out of her, sweeping along anyone in her path. Her large green eyes were much talked about by men at Mrs Wilkes's. As was her tumult of glossy black curls, which she would encourage men to plunge their fingers into.

I have a dread that she will ask Edward to tumble her curls.

'I have heard of your fame,' replies Edward politely, moving a little closer to my side. Just in that moment, I feel my affections soar for him. Had he fallen for Harriet's charms so soon after what just passed between us ... I don't know how I should have felt.

Harriet gives a feminine little peal of laughter, which echoes out from the closed hedges. 'Of course you have,' she says, delighted. 'I am *quite* famous. Do you hear that, Teddy?' she adds, addressing the remark to her beau. 'You are fortunate to have snared my affections this afternoon. I do hope you shall reward me accordingly.'

The man at her side nods uncertainly. He is a short man, with dark hair turning to grey. He is in his sixties, but in that vigorous way in which aristocrats age.

Harriet hugs me again, then releases me still holding my arm, as if unwilling to relinquish physical contact.

Her eyes flick vaguely back to the man at her side.

'This is the Duke of Buckingham,' she says, taking his hand and patting it, while still holding mine. 'He is my little pet for today.'

She turns to stare the duke full in the face and he seems to melt under her gaze. Harriet has always had this effect on men. She could make anyone want her.

'Teddy, this is Lizzy, my old bedfellow,' she announces. 'We shared a tiny cot, if you can imagine such a thing. To see me now, in my grand bed and sheets.'

'Did Lizzy tell you of me?' asks Harriet, directing her attention back to Edward. 'She and I were very close. *Very* close,' she adds, sliding her hand suggestively up my arm.

I shake my head a little at her.

This is one of Harriet's tricks. To pretend she takes girls as lovers.

Edward's face is perfectly neutral, so I cannot tell what he makes of her behaviour. Harriet drops her hand as though she meant nothing at all by the gesture.

She pats the arm of her duke again, coming to a conclusion.

'You must see Denny,' she says to me. 'I have hired him as my footman.'

'Denny?' I ask in disbelief. 'From Mrs Wilkes's? I can hardly believe she would let him go. Denny was her best servant.'

Harriet gives a catlike smile. 'Wilkes will give me anything I wish,' she says. 'I still send some men to her house, so she does not dare refuse me.'

This is typical Harriet. While the rest of us struggled to avoid Mrs Wilkes's wrath, she knew how to keep the old woman wrapped around her finger.

'Come,' she says. 'You shall see Denny.' She turns to her companion again. 'Teddy and I were to enjoy ourselves in the gardens. But he should not mind waiting a little, should you, Teddy?' She presses his arm. 'I shall make it *very* much better for you later on.'

The duke seems to lean into her, his lips slightly parted. As though he almost pants for her.

Having assured herself of his submission, Harriet turns to me. 'Come,' she says. 'Denny is by the rotunda.'

I turn to Edward uncertainly.

'I have some business in the rotunda,' he says easily. 'I might attend to that while you meet your old friend. Do not be very long,' he adds, eyeing Harriet.

'No,' I agree, trying to signal with my eyes that I do not want him to leave me for long. Harriet always had a way of making you do things you regret.

We walk out of Spring Gardens together and I have the uneasy feeling that Edward is unhappy. He leaves us with a polite bow and I watch him as he walks towards Fitzroy, whose showy wig can be easily seen in the crowd.

'So tell me, Lizzy,' says Harriet dramatically, as my eyes follow Edward. 'You have been foolish and fallen in love?'

'I ...' I drag my eyes away distractedly. 'No,' I reply, without really thinking. Then her question registers with more weight. 'No, of course not,' I add.

Harriet's face has wound into a knowing smile.

'He is very handsome,' she says. 'You must be careful, Lizzy. For a girl could easily end up loving such a man. And that is no way to keep him.'

She turns an indulgent smile to her duke.

'That is how we keep you men generous, is it not?' she purrs, running her hand down his chest. 'We make it a game for you to win our hearts.'

The duke stands motionless with lust as her hand wanders downwards. Then, just before her fingers skirt the top of his breeches, she whips it smartly away and turns back to me.

'There is Denny,' she announces, pointing. 'Denny!'

A familiar face turns and lights up when it lands on mine.

'Denny!' I call, equally delighted.

Denny was my favourite servant at Mrs Wilkes's. He was always ready to eject customers who proved brutish and never judged us girls.

'Bring the wine,' Harriet calls to Denny. 'We shall all take a drink.'

Denny approaches holding a hamper. He is richly dressed as a footman. And the blue eyes and blond curls of his youth have settled into a decided handsomeness.

'Look at you!' I announce, hugging him tight. 'I left you a boy. You are now a handsome man!'

He blushes and looks pleased.

'You look very well, Lizzy,' he grins.

'Doesn't she?' agrees Harriet in a strange little voice. 'Such a fine dress. And a lord for a gallant, no less. Who would have thought she might have done so well?'

Her green eyes flash at this last remark and once again I regret chancing upon Harriet. She always was prone to jealousy.

'Pour the bottle, Denny,' she orders. 'Let us help Lizzy forget her fine clothes and remember we might still enjoy ourselves.'

Denny uncorks a bottle of red wine and fills four glasses, passing one to each of us and taking one himself.

'A toast,' announces Harriet loudly. 'To wealthy men!'

The volume of her voice causes a number of people to turn their heads. A nearby husband and wife start, and the woman tuts loudly, glaring at Harriet.

'Be sure to please your husband,' coos Harriet, with an evil smile. 'Or I shall come to claim him. And once he has sampled my charms, he shall have none of you.'

The lady looks away with a frightened expression, tugging at her husband, who seems unable to take his eyes off Harriet.

She gives a triumphant laugh, holding her glass high.

'To wives,' she cries, 'for their dullness, we owe all our income!'

She chinks her glass against the duke's and Denny's.

I feel my eyes drift to the far distance, where Edward is standing in the rotunda.

I start a little to see him looking directly at me. His eyes meet mine and then he looks away.

I drink a heavy sip of my wine. It is strong.

'Drink it all down, Lizzy,' says Harriet. 'We shall have some more.'

She turns to her duke. 'I am so thirsty,' she says, chewing her lip. 'Should we have some burgundy? Do you think? White wine is so very good for slaking thirst.'

The duke nods indulgently. 'You shall have the best,' he promises.

'I shall send Denny,' says Harriet. 'He shall be sure to take the finest they have. Should we ask for the prestige vintage?' she adds, with an odd simper at the duke.

He looks about to contradict her, but she carries on speaking.

'How should I reward you?' she ponders, intercepting his refusal. 'I believe I know.' She gives an affected laugh and then takes my arm once more, drawing me close.

'It is so very good to see *you* again, Lizzy,' she says. And then she moves forward, holding my arms and bringing her mouth to mine in a deep kiss.

I have been away from Harriet for so long that I have forgotten to be on my guard for things of this kind. She thinks nothing of using her friends to drive up her profit. In my surprise, and with the strong wine, it takes me a moment to collect myself and pull back.

Harriet leans towards the duke, tapping his nose with her finger.

'I hope you are not thinking wicked things,' she scolds, moving her face close to his. 'For I still have a horsewhip.'

The duke's face has darkened with some unreadable expression and Harriet smiles victoriously.

'Perhaps one day Lizzy may visit my house while you are there,' she adds airily.

I know she has no intention of arranging this. It is all part of her cat and mouse. I can imagine how she will play it.

If only you had been here before. You might have found Lizzy and me in a very happy situation. Maybe one day ...

In any case, Harriet has achieved her desired effect. Denny comes back with a thirty-pound bottle of burgundy and the Duke is only too happy to fill both our glasses.

'That is *so* much better,' says Harriet, draining her glass. 'It is so difficult to think when I am thirsty.'

She flutters her eyelashes and turns the bottle so as many people as possible will see the expensive motif etched on the glass.

A group of young lords is passing by and I notice every one of them turn their head, taking in the luxurious package, which is Harriet.

She beams at them and sips prettily.

I am looking over to Edward again now, wondering when he will come and rescue me. If Harriet drinks much more wine, she might do anything.

To my surprise, I see Fitzroy look towards us. He and Edward talk for a moment. Then Fitzroy begins walking out of the rotunda, heading in my direction.

I take a nervous sip of wine as he approaches.

Harriet follows my gaze and watches with interest.

'He comes for you?' she whispers.

'He is a friend of Edward's,' I reply, ignoring her insinuation.

Why does Edward not collect you himself?

I try to reason with myself not to be offended. I am well paid to be Edward's companion after all. There is no need for him to personally attend me as though I were a society lady. But something about the situation feels wrong. After what just passed between us in the garden I expected ...

208

You are being a fool Lizzy. Be grateful for what you have.

Fitzroy approaches and Harriet takes in his expensive clothing and greets him with a wide smile. He returns it with a snakelike leer of his own.

'Harriet,' Fitzroy makes her a low bow. 'Lord Hays requested I give you his card.'

The words hit me like a lightning bolt.

Edward gives Harriet his card?

I feel it like an actual physical pain.

How could he?

Harriet takes it in her little white fingers and I feel something harden inside me.

'Does he?' Harriet says in a delighted voice. 'How very charming.' She shoots me a victorious glance. 'I had thought he was all eyes for Lizzy.'

'Oh no,' I say, my voice leaden. 'There is nothing of that kind between Lord Hays and I.'

Fitzroy is taking this all in, revelling in my humiliation. No doubt he will return this information to Caroline.

'I must call on Lord Hays,' says Harriet, rolling the words around with pleasure. 'After you have parted company of course Lizzy.'

I cannot look at her. The thoughts in my mind are whirling like fire. I know I have no right to expect Edward's loyalty. In the gardens I made it clear to him I did not want a lover's intimacy. So why do I feel so hurt?

Fitzroy's attention is back on me now. I do my best to compose my features.

'Edward asked that I bring you to the rotunda,' he says, his eyes skirting over me curiously.

'Does he?' I say, handing back my glass to Denny. 'Then I shall come. I loved seeing you,' I say to Harriet. 'We should meet again.'

My false smile is almost faultless, though doubtless Harriet sees it flicker.

We hug. 'Take care, Lizzy,' she whispers, kinder now.

I nod into her shoulder.

'And you, Harriet,' I say sincerely. I am not angry with her. Men are a game to Harriet, nothing more. It is Edward who has shown himself heartless.

Her eyes rest on me for a moment. Full of warning. She gives a little shake of her head I know what she is telling me.

Do not fall in love.

Then we are back to our masquerades. Hers as seductress, mine as a lady.

Chapter 36

*F*itzroy walks me unhurriedly across the grass, towards the rotunda. I am wracked with humiliation. I still cannot believe that Edward would court Harriet so openly.

'I am glad of the chance to speak with you privately,' Fitzroy is saying.

'Oh.' I cannot think of how else to reply. This does not feel like the kind of remark a man would make to a lady. But I do not know enough to be sure.

'Caroline and I had wondered about you,' he says. 'You were quite the mystery to us.'

I make no reply, but keep my gaze on the rotunda. It seems far away.

'Caroline was sure you were about to steal Edward away,' Fitzroy continues, not deterred by my silence. 'But I reassured her, for I know Edward well.'

'Perhaps you had hopes he might marry you,' he continues sympathetically. 'You poor girl. I wish I could have warned you.'

Unexpectedly, Fitzroy places a solicitous hand on my arm.

I turn to him in quick outrage. But he makes no move to retract his arm and I do not wish to make a scene by removing it.

Waves of betrayal are coursing through me.

Why did Edward give Harriet his card in the gardens? He could have easily waited for a time when I would not be openly humiliated.

'I only hope,' breathes Fitzroy, 'that you have not allowed Edward to seduce you.'

Were it not for the pain in my heart, I should laugh at this. But all I feel is hurt.

'Edward will marry my sister soon,' continues Fitzroy. 'Did he tell you so?'

I nod my head dumbly.

He waits as I make no reply. I am barely following what he says.

'I cannot imagine Edward plans to see you again, once his business in London is concluded,' Fitzroy observes.

I keep my eyes straight ahead, but the rotunda has blurred.

'Edward is a bachelor,' I say easily. 'He may go where he wishes.'

I feel sick to my stomach.

We are at the rotunda steps now and Edward is visible near the front of the crowd. I feel a tight burst of rage at him as he turns to greet us. Forcing back an unexpected urge to cry, I set my practised smile.

Not for the first time, I am grateful for my training with Mrs Wilkes, which taught me to hide the deepest hurts. But I never thought I would use this particular skill with Edward. The pain of it is unexpectedly strong.

I allow Fitzroy to lead me through the crowd of people in total mortification. In these fine clothes, my whore's bravado has vanished. I feel as bad as if I were a genuine lady whose honour had been violated.

A single thought is tunnelling through my mind.

Edward. Edward has betrayed me.

The idea pierces my heart. That he brought me here. He made me dress this way. And he made me a mockery among his friends.

For a moment, I hate Edward. Then I catch sight of his face, lit up with such genuine pleasure to see me, and my fury wavers.

He pushes through the crowd and holds me by either shoulder – as near as unmarried aristocrats dare to embrace in public. Then, as if unable to help himself, he kisses me quickly on the lips.

I stand rigidly, still caught in my anger. Edward pulls back, confused. His eyes hold a question.

'Are you feeling quite well?' he asks, full of concern.

'No, I . . .' I raise my hand to my head. 'I think the sun . . . I seem to have a headache.'

Edward's eyes move between me and Fitzroy. He is about to ask a question when Fitzroy speaks.

'Elizabeth introduced me to Harriet as I hoped,' he says. 'A lovely girl and quite famed.'

'Yes,' says Edward, his eyes moving to Harriet's flirtatious stance in the Vauxhall crowd. 'We met.'

'Elizabeth and I are becoming quite good friends, are we not?' adds Fitzroy, with a smirk.

'Yes,' I say, forcing the word. 'Good friends.'

'Well, Edward,' he says. 'I have many people to talk with. The creditors are all for us. You will own the ship. As soon as the Naval Office signs.'

Edward gives a tight smile, but his eyes flick back to my face in concern.

'Then you and I will trade together,' adds Fitzroy, reaching towards Edward and touching his arm. When Edward does not respond, he makes a rapid smile at both of us and then steps into the crowd.

As he disappears, Edward looks at me. I look away.

Chapter 37

I sit silently in the carriage as it rolls back to Edward's townhouse. Despite all Mrs Wilkes's teachings, I cannot summon the coquettish girl who men pay for company. And when we arrive, I get out without waiting to be handed and make straight for the parlour.

When I get there, I stride to my cheap linen dress, which is folded neatly behind the screen.

I stoop down, letting my hand run over the fabric, and tears tumble onto the blue material.

Things were so much simpler when I wore this dress. I should never have tried for higher.

Wiping away my tears, I rise to see Edward is at the door.

'Elizabeth,' he says softly, 'what is the matter?'

'Nothing is the matter,' I retort, turning my face away. 'A street girl such as I does not feel as a lady might. You should know that.'

Within a second he is at my side.

'You are angry?'

I open and shut my mouth again. Affront washes over me in a dangerous tide of anger. How can he not know?

I begin unlacing the pink silk I wear.

'You overestimate what your money buys,' I say, moving away and working to take off the dress. A lump is rising in my throat.

'Elizabeth,' Edward begins.

'Lizzy,' I spit, 'My name is Lizzy.'

'You are angry about what happened in the gardens,' he says, though he sounds confused rather than apologetic. His eyes swing up to mine. 'I am sorry you were offended,' he adds in a strangely formal tone. 'I did not think the usual ... protocols applied with you.'

'You humiliated me,' I accuse, 'in front of Harriet, in front of *Fitzroy*.' Remembering Fitzroy's smugness fires up a new rage in me.

'I did not think you would mind,' says Edward bluntly. 'Given your background.'

How dare he!

I turn away from him and continue working on my laces.

'Elizabeth –' Edward stops as if realising something for the first time. 'Why are you holding your old dress?'

'I am returning to Piccadilly,' I say, amazed he could think there might be another end to this conversation.

For a moment I think he will try and persuade me to stay. Then his face sets in resignation.

'If you leave, then you may wear the dress you are in,' he says finally.

My mouth is open in shock.

'You think I should wish to go back to Piccadilly in *your* dress?'

'It is a great deal more valuable than the garment you came in,' he says, sounding confused.

'I do not want *anything* from you.' My words come out as an angry hiss.

He raises his arm to stop my frantic unlacing.

'Keep the dress,' he says. 'I have no use for it. Do not be so proud.'

I push his hand away.

'My pride is all I have,' I snap. 'You may not take it from me. Not for all the silken dresses in England.'

'Elizabeth. Lizzy.' He sounds exasperated. 'I do not understand why you are behaving this way.'

The top of the dress is open now and I cannot remove it without him seeing me in my shift.

'Look away,' I demand.

He makes to speak, and then stops and turns slowly around.

'You do not have to go,' he says, standing with his back to me.

I ignore him, heaving away the skirts and tugging loose the wide petticoats. Then I pull up my old cheap linen dress. It feels strange to be that girl again.

I drag the laces tightly closed, forcing myself to stand more upright.

'I will send your money to Piccadilly,' says Edward, still facing away.

'There is no need,' I say. 'I have not fulfilled my side of the bargain. I do not expect you to fulfil yours.'

I know my pride will hurt me in the long run. But right at this moment, it tempers my anguish with stubborn satisfaction.

For all the heaviness in my heart, I will walk out of here with my head held high.

You see, Lord Hays. No money can buy my free will.

This thought salves the deep pain in my heart.

As I move to walk past Edward, he turns to bar my way. There is something different in his face now, as though his earlier haughtiness were an act that has crumbled.

'Please,' he says. 'Please stay.'

He moves his arm to my shoulder. I look down at it and up into his eyes. There is an earnestness there that confuses me.

He catches both my shoulders.

'I am truly sorry,' he says. 'I should not have sent Fitzroy to collect you.'

What?

I blink at him.

'You think that is why I am leaving?' I manage, open-mouthed.

Edward looks confused. 'It is not the reason? Why then?'

'You gave Harriet your card!' I accuse. 'In front of *everyone*. Must you make it so clear I am nothing to you?'

In my anger I am mixing my words up. But I am so hurt I cannot help myself.

Edward is looking at me in disbelief. Then to my amazement he laughs.

I push his hands away from my shoulders angrily and make to push past him. He catches me easily and I struggle.

'Wait. Elizabeth. *Wait.*'

Something in the force of his voice stops me.

'I did not give Harriet my card,' says Edward.

I stare at him. Does he think me a fool?

'I *saw* Fitzroy give it,' I retort.

He shakes his head.

'Elizabeth. Think. Fitzroy wants me to marry his sister. He plays games with you. I did not give Harriet my card.'

It takes me a full few seconds for this to sink in.

'You did not?' I manage. Some traitorous part of me is singing with relief.

'No.' Edward is fighting back a smile. 'I have no wish to ever meet with Harriet again.'

The ice in my heart melts away. But some stubborn part of me is still angry at appearing such a fool.

'You might have told me,' I say haughtily. 'To be careful of Fitzroy's lies.'

'I had no idea he could be so devious.' Edward looks thoughtful. 'I imagine Fitzroy was relying on your society manners not to confront me.'

'He had no such luck,' I retort hotly.

Edward laughs again and I bat at his chest in annoyance.

'I am sorry,' he says, regaining his composure. 'I just ... You were jealous? Of Harriet?'

'No,' I falter. 'Not a bit.'

I can tell he doesn't believe a word of it. Edward is appraising me now, as if seeing something new for the first time.

'I did not realise,' he says quietly. 'I would never have sent Fitzroy to collect you. I should have come myself.'

'Why did you send Fitzroy?' I ask, suddenly curious. I had thought something was amiss.

Now it is Edward's turn to look uncomfortable.

'I ... I did not like how you were with Harriet,' he admits, his eyes cast down. 'I saw her kiss you.'

My eyes widen.

'You and I got so close in Vauxhall,' he says. 'Then you pulled away from me. I did not know the reason. When I saw you with Harriet, I thought perhaps she was your lover.'

'You thought Harriet ... and I?' I almost laugh aloud. 'You think I prefer the company of women to men?'

Edward looks embarrassed.

'That is Harriet's way,' I say. 'It is just an act. For foolish men,' I add, in a tone that suggests he is in this category. 'Whores play at being lovers for sport,' I add. 'All us girls do. You must know that,' I add, thinking he cannot be so naive.

'I did know that,' he admits. 'But I thought I saw something different in how you looked at her.'

'*You* were jealous?' I say, hardly able to believe it.

He smiles slightly. 'No more than you were.'

'There is nothing between Harriet and me,' I say shortly. 'You were a fool to think it.'

'I am truly sorry,' Edward says. His voice is soft and this time I believe his apology. 'I should have better protected you from Fitzroy's machinations.'

I close my eyes, trying to pick a single thought out of all the confusion. His need for me to stay has brought another dimension to our liaison. What I can't decide is why it frightens me.

I open my eyes again, settling them on his.

'What does it mean, that you were jealous?' I ask. My voice trembles, though I do not mean it to.

'The same as it did for you,' he replies, his eyes on mine.

I take a little shuddering breath.

Edward holds out the silken dress folded over his arm.

Slowly, my fingers close on it.

Chapter 38

The next morning, Edward has more business planned at the Royal Exchange. I had been expecting to stay in the house, awaiting his return. But instead he sends Sophie to dress me to accompany him.

I have persuaded Edward that I only need one servant to dress me, so now Sophie arrives alone to style me in companionable privacy.

With no other servants to listen in, I feel easy with her. And she in turn seems happier to reveal her true opinions to me.

'His lordship is in a strange temper,' she confesses, as the warm washcloth makes its last pass over my face. 'One moment he is in high spirits and the next he is thoughtful.'

I absorb this information, wondering if perhaps I am something to do with it. Last night Edward stayed with me in the parlour. But we were in a sober kind of mood. As though something between us had shifted. When he took me in his arms, it felt more intense, somehow. As if part of our masquerade had become real.

'I imagine he is awaiting the closing of his affairs,' I reply, thinking of what I know. 'He goes to the Exchange to sign the final contracts. For the thing will be done tomorrow.'

Sophie nods and moves to my trunks.

'Have you been to the Exchange before, Miss Lizzy?' she asks.

I shake my head.

'Not inside,' I admit. 'Though I have passed by. It looks very large and fine,' I add, thinking of the huge stone construction. 'Like the world's finest open air market, but for business and trade, rather than vegetables and meat.'

Sophie smiles at the description.

'Shall you wear a more sober dress?' she asks. 'For it is mostly men inside, is it not?'

'Yes,' I agree. 'Perhaps the green and gold dress. That looks like commerce, does it not?'

'I think it a good choice, Miss Lizzy. But you should be careful,' she adds. 'I do not think it wise for women to be seen there.'

Sophie has begun giving me these snippets of advice. And I suspect they come via Mrs Tomkinson. They are both colluding to help me act like a lady and I am grateful.

'Ladies are not seen where men do business?' I clarify, turning the information in my mind and wondering what damage I could feasibly do my 'reputation'.

'Not so far as I know,' says Sophie. 'But you are so beautiful,' she adds loyally, 'I cannot imagine any man would complain.'

Once my outfit is complete, I descend the stairs to meet with Edward. He is giving orders to servants in the hallway and stops to watch as I come down.

'Very lovely,' he says approvingly. 'A perfect dress for the Exchange.'

I smile and a hand goes up to my hair, which has been styled semi-formally with grey and green ribbons and feathers.

'You see I have filled my hair with pretend emeralds and silver,' I reply. 'So I might be seen to have some value of my own.'

Edward grins. Then he notices the servants are staring up at me and looks at them admonishingly. Immediately, the staff return to their duties and I walk down the rest of the stair to only Edward.

'You look a picture,' he murmurs into my ear, as I reach him. 'It will be hard for me to do business, knowing you are waiting nearby.'

'I am not to enter the Exchange?' I ask.

He shakes his head, smiling.

'Not the business part,' he says. 'That is no place for ladies. There is talk of riots, with the recent slavery protests.'

Ironically I feel a little put out. Despite this apparent care for me to be treated like an aristocrat. I should have liked to see inside the Exchange. And I have no fear for my reputation, after all.

'Then where shall I be?' I am wondering where a finely dressed woman might wait alone in London.

'You shall see presently,' he says, with a mysterious smile. 'But I think you should like it.'

'Will Fitzroy be at the Exchange?' I ask, thinking I should not like to see him.

'Fitzroy will be there and Caroline as well. But you shall not need to meet either of them.'

'Why is Caroline there, if women are not allowed?' I protest.

'She will not be in the Exchange building either,' he replies. 'Caroline wishes to buy some silks imported by Exchange traders. They are kept in a different place, for ladies to buy.'

'But that is not where I shall be?' I am confused now.

Edward smiles. 'No,' he replies, kissing my forehead. 'You shall be in a special place. Because you are special.'

*

The Exchange is even larger than I remember when we arrive.

It is a huge building, with neo-classical pillars and a frontage inspired by a classical temple. Inside is a wide courtyard, ringed with fine shops selling the spoils of the colonies. Beyond the courtyard is a sealed walkway of smaller rooms, where business is conducted.

As we step into the Exchange courtyard, finely dressed men rush to and fro, alongside the more ruggedly attired admirals, captains and buccaneers.

'What business do they do?' I ask, watching two boys heave a money chest into the inner business confines.

'Seafaring trade,' says Edward. 'Men come to buy and sell goods from ships, or to fund shipping missions in the hope of making their money and more. Sailors come to beg funds for voyages and make a case for a trading venture.'

'It sounds exciting,' I say, taking in the rush of adventure that seems to surround the Exchange.

'It is an incredible place,' agrees Edward. 'It quite took my breath away when I first stepped inside. Fortunes are made and lost within these walls.'

'And you will have your ship for trade,' I murmur.

'Yes,' he agrees. 'Once the ship is secured, Fitzroy has trading contacts. He will set up on known routes and we will trade for goods.'

We both watch as a captain and lordly dressed man make their way out arm in arm. They seem to have settled on some happy agreement and the exhilaration is evident in both their faces.

We push forward into a group of people petitioning for charity and funds. And a man dressed in government clothes is suddenly at our side.

'Would you give to the district purse, Your Ladyship?' he asks, bowing low.

I turn in surprise. For I recognise the man. It is the beadle who chased me out of Mayfair as a whore, when I was searching for dressmakers.

My eyes widen.

'I know you,' I say.

The beadle bows lower, doffing his hat almost to the floor.

'Perhaps from the Montfort ball?' he suggests. 'Her ladyship was kind enough to give funds for Mayfair street work.'

'Did your work clear the streets of whores?' I ask. 'For I was one of those you threatened with a horsewhip.'

The man frowns and when he sees I am not joking, his face sets in horrified recognition.

'I . . .' he stutters.

'I would not give funds for such an uncharitable business,' I say, cutting him off. 'You should focus your efforts on helping fallen women, not bullying them.'

The beadle's face is a picture. His eyes skirt to Edward and back to me.

'If I caused offence I am truly sorry . . .' he begins.

'I am not offended,' I reply. 'But you should be more careful to be kind in future.'

'Of course, Your Ladyship.' The beadle bows again – apparently his default gesture for aristocracy – and scuttles away.

Edward raises an eyebrow at me.

'Someone from your past life?'

'Not so past as you might imagine,' I reply. My eyes sweep the rest of the Exchange and go back to Edward.

He is watching a shipment of colourful goods. Strange-shaped fruits and bright cloths. Discoveries from the New World, I deduce, taking in the interest that follows the arrival.

Edward is observing the unpacking of the medley with something wistful in his face.

'I always found the exploring ships most thrilling,' I say, following his gaze.

'Yes,' he says, still entranced by the cargo. 'It is a heady kind of business.'

'So where would you have me wait?' I ask, after a moment. 'If not with you?'

He breaks out of his reverie and his face lights up.

'Ah,' he says, in a pleased way. 'I had forgotten. I have chosen a good place for you. Come with me.'

And he takes me by the hand as easily as if I were his real wife.

Edward leads me around the far side of the Exchange and through the high stone pillars.

'The far side is the trading market,' he explains. 'For contracts and promises. This is the actual market. Where many fine things may be bought.'

My eyes open wide in wonder as he leads me in.

'I never knew this existed,' I say, taking in the stalls heaped with spices and jewels.

'It is a fine place, is it not?' says Edward, smiling at my amazement. 'All the wealth of the colonies is here.'

I am so in wonder of it all that I have not stopped to think what purpose he might have for bringing me.

We pass a stall that sells dishes of clotted cream for a penny and then we're at the back, with a few closed shops.

They are rich-looking, with little glass fronts and real gold leaf painting out their purpose. I read the window.

'SR Oaks. Fine jewellers.'

I turn to Edward in confusion. 'A jewellers?'

He nods, looking pleased at my reaction.

'Shall we go inside?'

I clutch onto his hand tightly as he pushes the door of the shop, causing a thick iron bell to jangle. I look up at it in alarm. Edward gives me a reassuring squeeze.

A tall woman in sumptuous silk ascends from a hidden cellar to greet us.

'Lord Hays!' She sounds both shocked and delighted.

Edward bows.

'I have some business in the Exchange,' he explains. 'I will be gone around an hour. Would you attend to this lovely young lady? She is a relative of my mother's.'

The woman steps forward as if to claim me.

'Of course, Your Lordship,' she says.

'She would like some ornament for her hair,' he says. 'I think something with sapphires. But she must choose what she likes.'

'Sapphires?' I cannot believe he would be so generous.

Part of me is delighted. But another part feels that this is wrong. Like a clumsy seduction. A week ago I should have been thrilled to be bought fine jewels. But after what has passed between Edward and me . . . Something seems a little amiss. He is treating me like a courtesan and I realise with a shock that I do not like it.

'Perhaps,' he says quietly, 'you might wear them for me, after our week is over. For I might return to London after my business is done.'

I make him a pretend smile. Because I cannot bring myself to answer.

It is the first time in our arrangement he has sought to induce me with gifts. A week ago this was what I wanted. So why is the gesture turning me cold?

I think of Caroline, waiting somewhere nearby. I try to imagine being a mistress to her wife and find I cannot.

The shop-woman is moving her lips silently, committing the request to memory, and passing a solicitous arm around my waist.

'Should you like to sit?' she asks. I nod dumbly, looking at Edward who has an encouraging expression.

I have never been inside a fine shop of brick and glass before, and I wonder if there is an expected way to behave. My scant accessories were bought from the open stalls on London Bridge – Mrs Wilkes's cost-cutting measure.

'Will you take a dish of cream?' the shop-woman asks, as I place myself on a comfortable chair to the side of the small shop.

I look at Edward uncertainly.

He nods.

'Yes. Please,' I agree.

The woman walks quickly to the door, opens it and then bellows out into the wider Exchange beyond.

'Emily! Bring a dish of cream!'

She shuts the door and her face reverts to quiet solicitude.

'Hair ornaments,' she says, half to herself. Then she vanishes into the back of the shop.

'You have often mentioned that you lack the right ornament for your hair,' explains Edward.

'Yes,' I reply, my voice sounding strangely formal. 'It is delightful that you thought of it.'

The woman returns, waddling under the weight of a huge stack of trays. Carefully, she places them down and selects the first, holding it out in a flourish.

'Oh!' I am charmed despite myself and turn to Edward to include him in my delight.

The tray is filled with the most exquisitely wrought hair ornaments. They are delicately fashioned from silver and gold, with artistically laid jewels.

My hand reaches to touch them, mesmerised.

'They are beautiful,' I say.

The ornaments are many different shapes. Birds and butterflies, flowers and leaves, and all kinds of arrangements of gems.

I pick out a dainty silver comb with pearls dripping from it.

'I cannot believe they are so lovely,' I say.

'Finest silver, with the silversmith stamp, as you see,' says the shop-woman, adopting a pleased-sounding sales patter. 'And the jewels are bought here, direct from the ships. So you can be assured we have the best colours and the best price.'

She is talking to Edward rather than me.

'What do you think?' I ask him, gazing at the jewels.

He eyes the selection. Then he picks out a lovely bird of paradise, its wings spread wide, with sapphires and rubies detailing the feathers.

'I think this should suit you very well,' he says. 'A bird flying free. That is how I think of you. A wild creature who must always have her freedom.'

I look at him, touched. I had not known he thought of me that way. Perhaps I have misjudged his intention. Carefully I take the jewelled bird from his hands, my eyes fixed on his.

'Yes,' I say softly. 'I think this would do very well.'

Edward breaks the gaze first, looking back at the box.

'What of some butterflies as well?' he suggests, picking out two smaller pieces, with ornately jewelled wings. 'They would look very pretty with your curls.'

They are lovely, the butterflies. I am also conscious they are so much more expensive than anything I have ever owned.

The door clangs and a girl enters, holding a dish of cream that she presents to me.

'Thank you,' I say, taking the china dish. There is a little silver spoon and I take a polite mouthful.

'Mmmmm!' I announce, louder than I mean to. 'This is delicious.'

Edward is smiling at me.

'Try some,' I say, holding out a spoon.

He hesitates and then takes an obliging bite.

228

'That is good,' he acknowledges, sounding almost surprised. 'Very good.'

'Emily,' says the shop-woman, turning to the girl, 'fetch the best wine from downstairs.'

She turns to me. 'Should you like Chablis or Bordeaux?'

'Chablis please,' I reply, realising less than a week ago I should I have been confused by both terms. My time with Edward has educated me more than I realised.

'Should you take a glass, Your Lordship?' asks the jeweller.

He raises a hand.

'No. Thank you. I have business to attend to.'

He glances out of the window at a large clock in the Exchange.

'I must go attend to my affairs,' he says to the shop-woman.

'Yes, Your Lordship.' The woman curtsies and her eyes flick to me. 'Should you like to set a figure for the jewels?'

'Put everything on my account,' says Edward. 'Let her spend whatever she likes.'

He winks at me. 'There is no limit. So long as she is smiling when I return.'

'Of *course*, Your Lordship,' agrees the shop-woman.

Edward turns to me.

'I shall only be gone an hour,' he says apologetically.

'I shall be very bored spending your money,' I tease.

He hesitates and then takes my hand, speaking low.

'Stay inside the shop. There has been talk of riots these last few days.'

His eyes shift to the shop-woman, clearly not wanting to concern her. 'Do not wander out into the Exchange,' he concludes.

'I have no reason to,' I point out.

He smiles and kisses my hand. Then he makes us both a low bow, lingering on me last, before turning on his heel and exiting the shop.

The shop-woman turns to her assistant who has arrived back with a silver tray and wine.

'Lord Hays is the most handsome of them all, is he not?' she asks, taking a glass and pouring it to the brim with white wine. She is studying me, clearly wondering what our true relationship is.

'I am not his relative,' I admit. 'We have a ... a short arrangement.'

She hands the wine to me with an approving nod at my honesty.

'Well, my dear,' she breathes, 'you have certainly done well for yourself. Very well,' she adds, sounding pleased. 'From what I hear, every girl in London had hopes of winning him,' she continues, her eyes following his retreating figure through the shop glass. 'And here he is, all eyes for you.'

She pours her own modest glass of wine and takes a sip.

'Perhaps he will take a place for you in the city?' she suggests.

'He has been kind,' I say. 'But I am not sure I should like to be his kept mistress.'

A week ago to be Edward's courtesan would have been my dearest wish. But our time together seems to have awoken something in me. Something that refuses to be cheapened.

The jeweller breaks into a great wide grin and clasps my hand.

'Very good, very good, my dear,' she agrees. 'For there is little enough freedom for us women, is there not? You take your life while you are young and beautiful. Surrender your liberty to a man when you are too old to do else.'

She straightens up.

'Shall we look at some of the hairpins?' she asks. 'We have some beautiful jewels among them. We may select the brightest and set them how you choose.'

I nod, taking a deep sip of wine. This seems like it will be merry.

'We shall be sure you have the latest fashion,' she adds. 'No other lady shall have it. And no one should wonder why you have Lord Hays and they do not. For they shall blame their jeweller.'

I laugh and the shop-woman begins sorting through her various trays of jewels.

'They are so very lovely,' I say, gazing at the elaborate silverwork.

'Perhaps you are hungry for more than cream?' asks the woman as she lays out the jewels. 'We may send the girl for beef cuts. There is a good tavern nearby.'

'I am a little hungry,' I say cautiously. 'But I have been eating rich food for days. I should very much like a plain hot sausage.'

'Such as the street stalls sell?'

I nod, wondering if I have committed some dire misdeed, but the shop-woman smiles broadly and pats my arm.

'I should like a sausage myself,' she says, beaming. 'Emily will fetch us some. There are many sellers on London Bridge. She should be back in ten minutes.' The woman thinks for a moment. 'I shall have her bring some good ale back. For that goes better with a sausage than wine.'

'I know of the best stall on London Bridge,' I say. 'I shall step out and point your girl the right way.'

I step out into the Exchange to show Emily how she might find the stall I mean. And she scurries off in the direction of London Bridge.

I take a moment to stare into the whirling mass of the Exchange, with all its colourful characters. And suddenly I spot a familiar plumed hat in the crowds of traders.

Mr Vanderbilt.

My eyes follow him as he walks across the Exchange, his sword bobbing at his hip, his riotous buccaneer dress looking more in keeping in this part of town.

I am so delighted to see him, I cry out his name, running towards him without thinking if I am proper.

He turns, frowning, and then his weathered face creases deeply with pleasure. I pick through the crowd until I am close enough to clasp his hand warmly.

'It is good to see you,' I say. 'Do you come to finish your business?'

'Miss Elizabeth,' he says, grinning at me. 'Yes, I am here to make some arrangements. Why, you look even more beautiful every time I see you.'

I smile. 'Thank you.'

'Gold and green,' he adds, taking a pinch of my skirt fabric admiringly. 'Your dress alone should be enough to buy a fine ship. Are you here with Lord Hays?' he adds in confusion.

'Yes and no,' I admit. 'He is here for business. I am in the jewellers.'

'Be sure his lordship buys you sapphires,' he says. 'You'll find no finer than in the Exchange.'

'I will . . .' I pause and take a breath before ploughing on. 'I wondered if I might ask a favour?'

His wiry eyebrows go up. 'Anything within my power.'

I chew my lip, trying to think of how best to phrase my confession.

'I will not be in Lord Hays's company beyond this week,' I admit, letting the inference sink in. 'Our . . . arrangement will come to an end.'

Mr Vanderbilt's wise blue eyes seem to take my meaning.

'Is that so?' he says slowly. 'Well, you made him a fine lady, my dear.'

I give a half-smile.

'You are kind,' I say. 'In my . . . my other life, I had a friend. A girl who worked at Mrs Wilkes's house. By the name of Rose.'

Mr Vanderbilt nods patiently, taking the information in.

'She was taken up by a suitor,' I say. 'His plans were to go overseas. Might there be some way of finding where they went? I should love to get a letter to her.'

Mr Vanderbilt rocks back on his heels, assessing the situation.

'Do you have a name?' he says finally. 'Full name? For him or her?'

I nod. 'Rose Savoir. And his last name was Stewart. He titled himself a captain.'

Mr Vanderbilt sucks his teeth. 'If he told you his true name, then there may be a way,' he says. 'Those that travel sign their names with customs. I could take a look at the records for you,' he adds.

I clasp his hand in gratitude. 'Thank you,' I say. 'I should only like to know where she went. So I might have a picture of her in my mind.'

He nods sadly at this and I wonder how many friends he has lost to far-flung places.

'So you will not marry Lord Hays?' he says after a pause.

I shake my head.

'It is the talk of the Exchange, you know. London society is small. And there has been much said of Edward's beautiful new friend. They have seen you together and think you have stolen his heart.'

'No,' I say determinedly. 'Edward should not wish to give up the world for a girl such as me. And I should not wish the restrictions of his society. We are only together for a few days more.'

Mr Vanderbilt looks thoughtful.

'Then he is a fool,' he says roundly, patting my shoulder. 'To have so little time with you. For you are a fine girl and worth ten of those society sneerers.'

He thinks for a time.

'Do you have plans for when you part ways?'

'I shall find a better place to rent,' I say. 'I live in Piccadilly for now. I should like to try my luck in Mayfair.'

'Hmmm.' Mr Vanderbilt considers this in his gravelly voice. 'So you shall have a little capital?'

'Yes,' I nod. 'His lordship is very generous.'

Mr Vanderbilt pauses. 'In my voyages, I have been to America,' he says slowly. 'And it strikes me as a fine place for a woman to start anew.'

His old eyes meet mine.

'It is a young country,' he adds. 'A good country, perhaps, for a widow travelling with a little inheritance. America is a place where England's old society holds no sway.'

Mr Vanderbilt winks at me and I understand his meaning. That I could start fresh in America. None should know me a whore. I could be respectable again. The thought thrills me more than I should have thought.

'I should be happy to find you a good ship to sail on,' he adds. 'You should need forty guineas for the passage.'

The reality of his suggestion is buzzing around me. I will have fifty guineas after I part Edward's company.

America.

'That sounds very interesting,' I say, thinking how far ten guineas might last me after my fare is paid. 'Thank you.'

'Think of it,' continues Mr Vanderbilt. 'You can always find Percy and me if you come to the Exchange. If you choose to take a ship, we would be sure you got the best price and were taken care of on-board.'

'I am most grateful for the suggestion,' I say. 'Though I confess, the idea of a new country is frightening for a woman alone.'

Mr Vanderbilt takes both of my hands in his and squeezes.

'And yet,' he says, 'it strikes me that a woman such as you must have been very brave in her past. Very brave indeed.'

For some reason I feel tears rise up. Mr Vanderbilt gives my hands a final paternal press and then releases them.

'Good day, Miss Elizabeth,' he says, making me a low bow.

'Good day, Mr Vanderbilt,' I say curtsying. 'I am sorry for your ship,' I add, not knowing what else to say.

He winks at me. 'You need not worry yourself about an old seadog such as me,' he says. 'Life is always an adventure.'

And with that he vanishes into the main quadrant.

Chapter 39

I remain staring out after Mr Vanderbilt for some time. Until it occurs to me the jeweller might be wondering where I have got to. I turn, making my way back through the press of the crowd. In the past few minutes, the mass of people has suddenly thickened. And it is only then I realise that there are shouts coming from the main Exchange. They are rough cries, which put me in mind of when the mob rises in Piccadilly.

My heart begins to beat faster and I turn in alarm. The crowd around me seems to swell and charge, sweeping me towards the sound of men's ugly shouts. In my fine clothes it is difficult to manoeuvre away easily.

A surge of movement strikes, like a wave of people has hit the crowd, and I am pinioned in among the bodies. A few moments ago people were milling. Now they are a thick eddy.

I swing around desperately, looking for the jewellers, but it has vanished in the crush.

A loud crash sounds, like a window breaking, and then all hell breaks loose. Missiles are being thrown across the crowd. Rocks and stones hit the shop fronts.

I cannot believe how quickly it has turned. The source of the discord is not easily seen, but I am in true terror now. For I am in no doubt it is a riot. Gasping with the effort, I push myself out of the swell and towards the fine shops.

If I cannot make it back, Edward will not find me. He expects me to wait in the jewellers. And besides, Caroline is nearby. First he must go to assure himself of his wife-to-be's safety. To come to me first would be to insult her unthinkably.

I take in the other shops. Perhaps one will shelter me until the mob has passed. For I am finely dressed, after all.

But as I watch, I realise several shops are already being looted. In the middle distance, a pack of men, roughly dressed, are smashing the glass front of an ivory shop. Its owner has grabbed up a hunk of wood and is waving it at the looters, but he is brought down by a heavy fist to the jaw.

With the owner down, the pack becomes a torrent. Ragged men are clambering hand over fist to loot from the broken frontage.

Other shopkeepers are grabbing up their wares and racing indoors, pulling down wooden shutters. My eyes scan desperately for an open shop. Perhaps there is still one that can house me safely.

I see one, a small dressmakers, with a clutch of pretty shop girls fluttering like panicked chickens to protect their stuffs.

I head gratefully for them, thinking they will come to my aid. But I am too late. Two men have made it ahead of me. They grab at the girls indiscriminately, pulling them to the floor. I catch only a flash of skirts and screams, and my hands fly to my mouth in horror.

Kitty warned me of riots. Of what men are capable of. But I can scarce believe the pack has descended so quickly.

Blind terror sends me racing in the other direction. I dismiss the hope of the jewellers. For having seen the other shops, I am no safer there than in the crowd. I spot a slim alley, which I think to be an exit, and hurtle towards it.

The alley runs between two shops and is mercifully empty. I plunge down it at a run. But instead of leading out of the Exchange, it splits into a warren of dirt tracks, which the shop staff use to relieve themselves and dump their refuse.

I am faced with two possible directions, so I pick the alley with a lesser stink to it. But as I run towards the end I realise I've made the wrong choice. Barring my way is a little pack of unkempt men, and I freeze.

'Well well,' says one, moving closer, 'what have we here? A fine lady to have some fun with.'

He eyes his companions. 'What sport we shall have.'

The other men close at his sides, like a pack of wolves advancing. I back away wishing I had some sort of weapon.

'I am no lady,' I retort, 'and you could not afford what you seek from me.'

'Seems to me, we do not need to afford you,' says the leader.

His arm shoots out, grabbing me by the wrist.

'Let me go!' I shout, pulling my arm. But his fingers close tighter. I can see his face up close now. He smells of brandy and his nose is a network of broken veins. His eyes have the rheumy motion of a drunkard.

'Get her on the floor,' he advises his companions. 'I'll pull her skirt up.'

He looks around him to assure himself there are no witnesses. And in that moment I kick him squarely between the legs.

Since this is unexpected from a lady, my action takes him wholly by surprise.

He doubles over moaning and I push him bodily into his companions. They were drunker than I thought and the impact throws them off balance.

My eyes fall on the opening between them and I charge through, running along the urine-soaked alley. When I reach the end, I realise all I have done is double back on myself. Ahead of me is the boiling riot of the wider Exchange.

I glance behind, to see the men are giving chase at a rambling drunken speed. And so I plunge back into the crowd.

I'm greeted by a mayhem of noise and missiles. The tumult has reached fever pitch and the crowd is a boiling mix of screaming shoppers and shouting rioters. Almost immediately, the crowd shifts and I'm transported deep into the centre, like a ship on a strong tide.

The force of people on either side squeezes all the breath from my body and I cry out in pain. Then there's a wave of falling bodies and I'm dragged down beneath a crush of people.

My face slams into the floor and I feel the weight of twenty people on top of me. In the tangle of waving limbs it's impossible for any to stand and I am paralysed beneath the mass.

I try to take a breath but my chest is held tight. My eyes swim and black circles swirl in my vision. A vague awareness that my dress is being trampled drifts in my dimming consciousness.

Then I feel strong arms pull at me. And I'm wrenched slowly but surely out of the fallen mass, like a cork from a bottle. I gasp as my lungs are freed, and kick with my feet to try and establish firm ground.

'Elizabeth!' cries a voice.

I look up at the sound of my name and see Edward's face. I suddenly realise that his strong arms are securely grasping mine.

'Edward!' I am so overjoyed to see him I can hardly speak.

'Are you hurt?' he cries, shouting above the crowd.

I shake my head. 'I couldn't breathe,' I croak, my hand to my chest, feeling as though I will cry.

With one sure movement he lifts me bodily into his arms. Then he carries me through the crowd, surefootedly pushing his way.

I press my face into his strong chest and start to sob. Frightened racking gasps shake me. I push into him like a child and his arms tighten.

We break out into the street and in a few moments Edward is loading me into the carriage. I open my eyes.

His dark hair is hanging free and there is a line of blood on his face.

'You are injured,' I say, my fingertips brushing his cheek.

He shakes his head. 'I told you to stay in the shop,' he says. But his tone is not angry.

'I stepped outside for a moment and the crowd took me,' I admit. 'I was frightened to go back to the jewellers. Men were looting the shops.'

He shakes his head. 'I paid some men to stand guard on the jewellers. I was gone but a moment. You should have trusted I would come back for you.'

'You paid men to watch over the shop?'

He nods. 'I did not want to alarm you by telling you there was a guard. But you were always safe. So long as you stayed inside.'

'I did not think you would find me in the crowd.'

His fingers trace the line of my chin.

'I would never have left you.'

I nod, feeling tears well up again.

'Did you find Caroline?' I ask, remembering he must have gone to her first.

Edward shakes his head, as if remembering his future wife for the first time. 'I will go back now, to be sure she got to safety.'

He pauses fractionally and then he moves forward, kissing me on the lips.

'I am glad you are safe,' he says, pulling back. And an expression flashes across his face of fear and relief all at once. 'I thought I might have lost you.'

Then he's out of the carriage and I hear him issuing orders to protect its contents at all costs.

As men bearing swords come to stand outside either door, I wonder to myself.

Why didn't Edward save Caroline first?

Chapter 40

In the carriage on the way home, I forget myself. I cling to Edward, not caring that I have no right to expect his comfort. I circle my arms around him as though I would never let him go. He strokes my hair and holds me close.

It is only when the carriage breaks from the busier streets, into the sanctuary of Mayfair, that I loosen my grip on him a little.

The day has moved to afternoon already and it occurs to me there will likely be some last entertainment to be endured this evening. This will be our final night together. I need to collect myself, for I owe Edward a merry evening.

The carriage pulls up in front of the large doors of the town-house. He opens the door, steps out, but to my surprise, he doesn't hand me out. Instead, he scoops me up and carries me into the house, like a bride over the threshold.

Mrs Tomkinson, who has opened the door for us, makes an uncharacteristic flutter when she sees us, clucking around me like a mother hen.

'What happened to Miss Lizzy?' she demands, taking in my ripped and dirtied dress. 'Is she hurt?'

'Elizabeth was caught in a mob at the Exchange,' says Edward, walking past Mrs Tomkinson with me in his arms. 'She was greatly frighted and needs rest. I will take her up to the parlour now.'

'I will send a glass of wine,' promises Mrs Tomkinson. She peers into my face anxiously.

'You were not hurt? Those brutes did not hurt you?' she asks.

I shake my head, overwhelmed by their kindness. I cannot remember the last time people were so solicitous of my feelings. They are treating me as though I have the sensibilities of a lady and not the hardened nature of a street girl.

Edward carries me gently up to the parlour and lays me on the bed.

He touches my face, looking into my eyes.

'Do you have pain anywhere? In your body?'

I shake my head, a lump rising in my throat. I cannot think I would have been so shaken by a mob before. It is as though something in me has crossed over.

Very carefully, Edward unlaces my stays. I wince as they fall open.

'You are bruised,' he says, running his hands along my ribs, inside my stays.

'Maybe a little,' I admit. 'I did not feel it when my stays were tight.'

'You do not complain,' he says, more to himself than me. 'Most ladies faint for the slightest bruise.'

He takes my face in his hands.

'You should make a greater fuss,' he admonishes. 'Or how am I to know you are hurt?'

I give him a small smile. 'I was more frightened than hurt. And farm girls are not raised to make a hue and cry for a small bruise.'

Edward makes a grim smile in return.

'Well, you should,' he decides. 'You are much more than a farm girl now.'

For some reason my eyes fill with tears. Why am I so emotional? It is as though my feelings have been painted on the outside of my body.

'Shall I send for a doctor?' he asks.

I shake my head.

'It is just a few bruises,' I say. 'Mostly my pride is hurt that you had to come and rescue me.'

To my relief, Edward laughs at the joke.

'I would rescue you a thousand times,' he promises. 'You need not be so prideful.'

There is a knock at the door and he distractedly gives permission to enter.

I am expecting Sophie, but it is Mrs Tomkinson herself who enters, carrying a tray bearing a decanter of red wine.

'I wanted to be sure the right wine was brought,' she says primly to Edward, as if daring him to question why she is doing maids' work.

'Of course,' he says, 'you were right to come yourself.'

Mrs Tomkinson curtsies and hurries over to deliver the tray. She places it in Edward's hand and pours the wine into a glass.

'I discussed with the cook and we thought Italian wine was best for calming the nerves,' she says, lifting the glass and pushing it into my hands.

'Drink it all down,' she insists. 'It will do you good.'

I sip the wine gratefully and when I see Mrs Tomkinson means to stand over me until it is drunk, I upend the glass and finish it in a few gulps. It warms my stomach through.

'Very good,' she says approvingly. 'You will feel the benefit of it presently.'

She stands, brushing down her skirts, as if suddenly abashed at her interest in my health.

'Well,' she says, 'I have to supervise the silver polishing. I will make sure Sophie is on hand to bring you anything you might need.'

Mrs Tomkinson curtsies to both of us and scuttles out.

Edward smiles at me.

'My housekeeper seems taken with your good health,' he observes.

I smile back. The wine is doing its job and I am feeling more like my old self.

'I feel better now,' I say, a little embarrassed to be cosseted for a few bruises.

'Yes,' he says. 'The colour has returned to your cheeks.'

Edward reaches forward and toys with a fallen curl of my hair.

'Tomorrow my business in London will be concluded,' he says, looking at the tendril rather than me. 'It will be our last day together.'

'So it will.' The same thought had just been in my head.

There's a long pause. 'Elizabeth,' he whispers, 'I feel something for you.'

It is a strange half-finished admission. But somehow I know exactly what he means. I feel the same.

He seems to be waiting for an answer and it takes all my strength not to reply. Because the truth is, I do not know if I can give him what he wants.

But in that moment, as he stares into my eyes, I am overcome with a rush of longing for him.

He must see something in my face, because he moves forward, so our lips are almost touching. And suddenly it is me kissing him passionately. I do not know what has affected me. Whether the danger of the mob, or the gentleness of Edward's care. All I know is in this moment, I want him with every facet of my being. It is like there is a hunger in my heart which must be fed.

His arms wrap tight around my waist as he responds to my kiss. My armour is falling away completely, in the torrent of desire for him. When he breaks away I am dizzy with him.

He reaches forward, lifting me towards him on the bed. My eyes close as I breathe him in. There is something about this kiss. It seems to take my soul with it. I open my eyes, to see Edward gazing at me.

He doesn't speak, but I can see in his face that he knows. I am all open to him.

'Elizabeth,' he murmurs. His hand moves to caress my collar bone and along the top of my open stays.

I close my eyes, knowing what he is asking.

He wants me to give him all of myself. Not just what can be bought.

His mouth is at my neck. My skin shivers. I am pressed against him, burning for him. His lips move back to mine and I feel as though I am falling.

As his hands move down, pulling away my stays, there is no resistance left in me.

I move to let my skirts fall away and my hands pull at his shirt.

We hesitate, breathless, half dressed, both knowing this is the point of no return. And with his eyes on mine, Edward gently takes off my last piece of clothing.

Then the thing is done. My boundaries are all gone now. I am his, body and soul. As we move together, everything is changed.

I feel myself rise up to meet him, breathing into him, tumbling into his eyes. I can no longer tell where I end and he begins. My body flutters in exquisite tension, knowing this is different from before. Waiting for when everything will change. And when the moment comes, it is a white-hot wave, sweeping over me, forcing my head back, making me cry aloud.

I gasp, pulling him close as my breathing slows again. His arms wrap me tighter and then we are floating, entangled with one another, sighing back into the bed.

Later, as we sit in bed drinking wine, something has shifted between us. It makes me sad. The best I can expect from Edward is to be his mistress. But the idea is a leaden cold in my heart.

'I suppose,' he is saying, 'we should ready ourselves for one last evening together. We might attend a social dinner, or take a ferry-boat to the entertainments on the South Bank.'

'You must be seen tonight?' I ask.

He looks at me, slightly puzzled.

'I mean to say,' I clarify, 'might you not be absent? You have almost completed your business, after all.'

Edward's face is a picture. As though this possibility never occurred to him.

'I suppose the matter is in hand,' he says slowly. 'One night's absence would do no harm. Though Fitzroy will expect me to be seen. I have never missed a night when I am in London.'

'You do not need to be seen every night,' I urge. 'You must rest and have some fun for yourself. Else what is all the money about?'

He smiles at this.

'What would we do instead?' he asks.

I smile back at him, liking the 'we'.

'We could have a simple dinner here in your parlour,' I suggest. 'And I will read to you. Or we could play at cards.'

There is a boyishness in Edward's face. As though the prospect of baulking his social engagement is a heady thrill.

'I would like that very much,' he says.

'Good,' I return. 'You may wait here and relax. I will order us a simple dinner from Mrs Tomkinson.'

*

We eat roasted chicken, with thick slices of bread. And afterwards, I read Edward some writings by Alexander Pope. And after a few rounds of cards, he undertakes to teach me chess. I am a bad pupil, but he is patient.

'How easy life would be,' sighs Edward, placing his pawn with a rueful smile, 'if this were all that was expected of us.'

'What do you mean?' I ask, frowning as I study the squares on the board.

'If this was our life,' he says, 'and we had no other obligations of family, or income.'

'That it would,' I agree, selecting the queen and moving to take his pawn.

'You cannot do that,' he says, moving the pieces back. 'Your queen cannot act like a horse.'

'I thought she could move any way,' I protest.

'That is typical of you,' smiles Edward. 'You must have freedom complete.'

There is something in his eye as he says it. And I realise what he is hinting at. Though it has not been said out loud, we both know what he will likely suggest tomorrow. That I become his mistress in London.

'Oh Edward,' I say, 'have you not learned yet? It is not freedom women seek.'

'Then what is it?'

'Control over their men,' I reply, taking his knight with a deft movement.

Chapter 41

As the night draws on, we lie on the bed, sheets draped over us, with Edward stroking my hair.

I am drugged for him, heady with a feeling I should not feel. I have given him something which can never be taken back. I know I should be more frightened than I am. But I feel so warm and safe. As though nothing can hurt me.

'Tell me,' whispers Edward, 'about when you first came to London.'

I relax a little deeper into his arms.

'When I first came to London,' I say, 'I was a country fool.'

'I cannot see that about you,' he replies.

'Well, it is true. I hoped to find work and fell into the trap of the first handsome man who said he could help me.'

I pause, remembering how it was. The sudden crowds and dirt of London. The dawning realisation that it was much harder to find a place than I thought.

'My seducer saw what easy prey I was,' I say. 'And he told me he would find me a place to stay.' I look down. 'I was so foolish. I believed him when he said he had fallen in love with me.'

'And he abandoned you?'

'He told me we would marry afterwards. A few days passed and he never took me to Fleet Street as he promised. I think I knew then,' I add.

Edward says nothing, only carries on stroking my hair.

'After a week, he had tired of me,' I say. 'He told me he could not afford to have me for a wife, for I had no work. Then he took me to Mrs Wilkes. Said I would do very well there. My beauty would make me rich.'

I look at Edward.

'He made it sound as though he had helped me, rather than ruined me,' I say. 'When I saw Mrs Wilkes I was frightened. But she made my seducer pay me, for my week with him, and I liked her a little more.'

I smile at the memory.

'But you did not spend his banknote?' asks Edward.

'No,' I say, shaking my head. 'I have carried it since.'

I give him a sad smile. 'It was the very last of my country pride. If I did not spend his banknote, then I had not sold my virtue.'

I close my eyes and swallow.

'I still had hopes of being a wife one day. Then things happened,' I whisper, 'that made me realise I would never be that girl again.'

Edward hugs me to him.

'Once I was in Mrs Wilkes's house . . . I was destitute and homeless. There was no question I could refuse what was asked of me.'

'Did they hurt you?' he whispers.

I nod and the tears come.

'New girls are sold as virgins on their first night,' I explain. 'And again and again until every dupe has had them.' Words are spilling out now. I cannot stop them.

Edward says nothing, but his arm tightens around my chest. Somehow, this makes me feel better than any words ever could.

'It was worse in the beginning,' I add. 'It became better.'

'And now?' he asks gently.

'Men lie,' I sigh. 'It hardens the heart. Divining the true opportunities from the deceivers is an art I struggle to learn.'

'Your ambition is for a rich protector then?'

'It is a means to an end,' I say. 'I work to earn my own independence.'

'Your own independence?'

'What every courtesan wishes for,' I say. 'Enough money for a house and a lifelong salary.'

Edward is gazing deep into my eyes.

'You do not think you are worth more than that?' he whispers.

'I have learned the hard way that life is hard. I should not be tricked again, by dreams.'

He strokes a line along my jaw.

'You are such a truly beautiful thing,' he says. 'You should have more faith in your dreams.'

I give him a sad smile. 'Outer beauty fades fast,' I say, 'and inner beauty does not buy bread.'

He kisses me very gently on the lips. 'You have more value than you know, Elizabeth.'

I smile, thinking how hollow his words are. We both know I have not enough value to be his wife.

Chapter 42

$\mathcal{J}$ awake to a high commotion. The whole house seems in uproar and I sit up in bed, trying to take in what is happening.

It is still early. Barely past dawn by my best reckoning. What can all the noise be about?

Since the dressmakers' visit, I have all kinds of garments at my disposal. I slept in a lace-edged shift, which can be readily accessorised to make a dressing room outfit. The kind a lady might wear while entertaining female relatives in her chamber.

So I pull on a loose silk skirt and drape a fine muslin around my shoulders, covering the upper part of my bust.

I am about to make for the door, when I remember that ladies cover their hair indoors. I hastily grab a frilled cap and tie it under my chin, pushing up my chestnut curls the best I can.

As I break out into the hallway, I see a procession of footmen and servants carrying trunks and baskets back and forth along the hallway.

A few nod to me, as they see me begin to descend the stair.

I see Edward stride in from the front door, issuing instructions in a rapid low voice. Then he sees me high on the stair and stops.

'Elizabeth.' He smiles up at me.

'Edward.' I gesture to my partial dress. 'You see I come in dishabille just to see your face.'

He seems pleased at this.

'You are like the rising sun,' he says, 'at the top of my stairwell.'

I laugh, coming down two stairs at a time.

'If you must rob Shakespeare,' I laugh, 'you should make the right words.'

I arrive slightly breathless before him and unexpectedly Edward catches me up in his arms. He spins me around and I laugh aloud.

'There are no right words for you,' he says, kissing my head and placing me back on my feet.

'You are packing to leave?' I ask, nodding towards the convoy of loading servants.

Edward nods and a spike of pain stabs my heart. A foolish part of me thought . . . I am ashamed to admit what.

He catches the expression on my face and pulls me into his arms.

'I have it all arranged,' he says. 'You may stay here until you find a house you like. I will be back in London within the month and we may arrange your own servants and carriage then.'

I smile at him. The first courtesan smile I have ever given him. Edward has handed me the dream of every street girl. The very thing I have wished for since my ruin. And how cold and empty it is now I have it.

'You will complete your business today?' I ask, studying my fingers so I don't have to look at his face.

'Yes.'

'When?'

'Twelve noon,' he says. 'That is when titles to the ship are handed over. I will meet with Vanderbilt for one last time. Shall we take our midday meal together?' he suggests. 'When I am finished? I do not know how long it will be until we see each other, after today.'

'I should like that,' I reply. 'Shall we take a walk in the park before you go to the Exchange?' I add, thinking this a nice way to spend the last few hours. 'Mrs Tomkinson can make a picnic of our breakfast.'

'Is there a park near here?'

I laugh. 'Edward, there is a park only a few streets away. Hyde Park. It is famed.'

'I never did go to Hyde Park,' he admits. 'Perhaps it would be nice to see it before concluding my business.'

Edward seems uncharacteristically uncertain as we wander into Hyde Park. As though the function of parkland is not quite clear to him.

'We will sit here,' I direct, pointing to a springy patch of grass. 'I shall take us a cup of milk.'

Edward sits, arranging our breakfast, while I walk over to a milk-maid and a tethered cow. I hand her my penny and she pumps warm fresh milk into my cup.

I return to Edward, who has assembled our breakfast picnic on the grass.

'Try it,' I say, handing him the cup. 'It is fresh.'

He takes a long draught and his eyebrows arch.

'It is good,' he says. 'I did not know you could get fresh milk in London.'

I sit next to him, stretching out my legs and enjoying the sun on my face.

Edward sits as though he is unsure how to place himself and I draw him back, so his head rests on my lap.

'There,' I say, 'now you can see the sky.'

'I never saw the sky from this angle before,' he says.

'You never lay on grass?'

His head turns in my lap to indicate he hasn't.

'Not even on your estate?' I am rather shocked.

'I work on my estate,' he says. 'I do not use it for leisure.'

'Maybe you should,' I say, reaching into the picnic basket and drawing out the book I have packed. 'Come,' I add, 'I shall read you one last poem before you go.'

He nods his assent and I open *The Faerie Queene*, selecting the poem carefully. As I start to read, Edward closes his eyes.

> *'One day I wrote her name upon the strand,*
> *But came the waves and washed it away:*
> *Vain man, said she, that does in vain assay*
> *A mortal thing to immortalise;*
> *For I myself shall decay,*
> *And my name be wiped out likewise.'*

I shut the book and Edward's eyes open.

'You do not read the whole?' he protests.

I shake my head.

'The sun gets high,' I say. 'You must be going.'

He nods his assent and sits up a little.

I turn, so he cannot see the sadness in my face. For he did not realise, in the poem, I was telling him goodbye.

Chapter 43

It is a strange thing to be in Edward's house, knowing I am leaving. I have ordered the midday meal from Mrs Tomkinson, taking care to select Edward's favourites. And Sophie has helped dress me in something I hope will please him best.

For the most part, I have spent these few hours distracting myself by reading. But the minutes seem to crawl by.

I have thought about my situation from every angle. But I still cannot make the idea of being Edward's mistress fit. The world is open to me in a way it wasn't before. It is not just the money. I feel different in myself.

As a younger woman, I allowed myself to be debased. Now, it is as though I have been given a second chance to be fresh and free.

There is a sound at the parlour door and I am startled out of my thoughts. I did not expect Edward back so soon. And when the door finally opens I jump out of my seat.

But to my great shock, it is not Edward who walks through, but Caroline.

I freeze and my heart begins to beat faster. Even with my low background, I know that people do not just let themselves in to visit fine houses unannounced.

'Elizabeth,' she says, with the smallest of nods.

Her tone seems to hold an accusatory edge and I feel my breathing constrict. What does she mean by coming here?

'Did something happen to Edward?' I ask, immediately fearful for him.

Caroline doesn't reply. Instead she walks into the room and removes her gloves. She is wearing a sumptuously embroidered green dress which fits her neat figure perfectly. Her hair is swept under a jaunty little hand-crafted hat. She looks around the room and her eyes settle on a decanter and glasses.

'Will you not offer me wine?' she says. Her voice is tight.

'I ... Yes of course.' I am awash with nerves, and unthinkingly move towards the decanter to pour her wine. She nods in satisfaction as I hand her the glass and the gesture jolts me out of my confusion.

'Edward,' I demand. 'Did something happen?'

Caroline takes a deeper sip of wine than I would expect of a lady, and fixes me with her mean little eyes.

'Yes,' she says finally. 'Something happened with Edward.'

My heart lurches.

Caroline's finger traces the rim of her glass.

'Edward,' she says slowly. 'Has called an end to our marriage prospects.'

The room seems to whirl around me.

Edward has ended their engagement?

A tiny hopeful part of me whispers that I am the reason.

Anger is rolling from Caroline in waves. But for all my unease and shock at her presence a quiet joy is dancing beneath the storm.

257

Edward will not marry her!

Caroline is scrutinising my face. There is so much tightly wound rage in her that my stomach starts to pound,

'Edward has also cut his trading ties with my brother,' she spits punctuating this with a furious swig of wine. 'There is some nonsense talk that he will fund Vanderbilt's fool exploration voyage. To the New World.'

Caroline makes me a humourless smile so packed with hatred that I take an involuntary step back.

'And do you know what I think?' she asks, her voice low and dangerous.

I shake my head.

'I think,' he says, 'that you have beguiled Edward. Bewitched him. Convinced him to throw my family aside.'

I shake my head. 'I never asked Edward not to marry you,' I say quietly.

She eyes me for a moment and sips more wine. Fury flashes in her eyes.

'I found out about you,' she says, carefully articulating each word.

I feel the blush hot in my face.

Caroline nods. 'I made enquiries,' she continues. 'No-one in London society had heard of you.'

She eyes me triumphantly.

'But servants will always talk,' she says. 'A few shillings to Edward's ostler was all it took to discover your secret. How you appeared in tawdry street clothes with your face cheaply painted.'

Her face has settled into a sneer now.

'You are not even a courtesan,' she continues, shaking her head as if she can scarce believe it herself. 'A common Piccadilly gutterwhore.'

For the first time in a long time the word makes me flinch.

'Edward will return soon,' I say shakily. 'I would like you to leave.'

Loathing animates Caroline's features.

'You low girl,' she hisses. 'How dare you use his name to threaten me. I have worked all my life to earn myself a chance in the aristocracy.'

She takes two fast steps towards me and grabs hold of my arm. 'You think you can earn yourself the same? Just with your face and figure?'

The contact is so unexpected I stand wide-eyed and frozen. A truth settles on me. That Caroline has watched bitterly as women like Harriet and me use our charms to rise faster and more surely than she. And she detests us for it.

'Let go of my arm,' I say, fighting to keep my voice calm.

Caroline looks down at her hand as though it belongs to somebody else. She drops the grip and steps back. She is smiling again now. A dangerous bitter smile.

'You have made a dangerous enemy in me,' she says. 'Do you think that your charms could hold a man such as Edward? That you would ever be accepted in London society?'

'No,' I retort, my composure returning in a flash of temper. 'Nor do I wish to be part of society which holds women like you.'

Caroline's face darkens.

'You will *never* be accepted,' she spits. 'I will make sure that every fine person knows *exactly* who you are. That you came from the streets, whoring yourself . . .'

Caroline is shouting now, her voice rising in an ugly pitch. She is so consumed with vitriol that she doesn't hear or see Edward come into the room behind her.

'Caroline.' Edward makes the word echo around the room with displeasure.

She whips around to face him.

'Edward!' Caroline's society smile manoeuvres back into place, but it is twisted and her shock is apparent. 'I was just telling Elizabeth . . .'

'That she is a whore,' finishes Edward. 'I heard you.'

He steps forward and eases the wine glass from her unresisting hand. Caroline stands rigid, her mouth hanging open. It occurs to me that she has probably never been touched so intimately by Edward before. I suddenly feel very sorry for her.

'I think you should leave,' says Edward. 'You will not be received at my house again.'

'Edward,' says Caroline, 'you cannot banish me from your society. After all my brother has done for you.'

She is outraged.

Edward makes a grim smile in reply.

'I was blind to Fitzroy for so long,' he says. 'All he ever wanted was to use my family name.' Edward shakes his head. 'He was helping himself, not me.'

He draws back a little and Caroline licks her lips, eyes darting from Edward to me.

'Already the ladies talk of her low ways . . .' begins Caroline. 'She will drag your family name into the gutter with her.'

Edward is shaking his head. His face is dark.

'Enough,' he whispers.

'Edward—' Caroline makes one last feeble appeal.

'Leave now.' Edward is too much of a gentleman to shout. But the force of his voice is enough. Caroline turns and virtually runs out of the door.

In a moment, Edward is at my side.

'Are you well?' he asks. 'Did she upset you?'

I shake my head.

'This is your second rescue of me in two days,' I say, laughing to disguise how shaken I am. 'It is a not a habit I am deliberately encouraging.'

He smiles, but I think he knows the truth.

Edward leads me to the chaise longue and we both sit for a long moment.

'I am sorry,' he says after a pause. 'For Caroline. It is not true what she said. The ladies do not talk of you badly.'

'I would not care if they did.'

We sit a little longer holding hands. Then I turn to him.

'You will not marry her?'

He smiles a little.

'No.'

I stare at his fingers taking this in. I am too cowardly to ask what I really want to know. So I ask something else.

'You changed your plans to deal in slaves?' I say, remembering Caroline's words.

Edward nods thoughtfully, his eyes glancing up at me.

I press his hand tighter.

'Your words on slavery were very moving,' he says. 'And Mr Vanderbilt is a fine man. To hear him speak of exploration is inspiring. His journeys to America sound enthralling. Perhaps I shall travel there one day, on one of his ships.'

'And take a Red Indian wife, like Mr Vanderbilt?' I tease, wondering if he has any idea of my own thoughts about travelling to America.

He glances away.

'You made a fine decision,' I say. 'Mr Vanderbilt will make you an excellent partner. You shall have joy from your business together.'

Edward smiles and then frowns.

'Elizabeth, have you thought about my offer?' he asks. 'That I will keep you in the city? In your own house.'

I look down.

'I have thought about it.'

There's a long pause and Edward's eyes dart over my face.

'But you mean to refuse? Because of Caroline?' His jaw sets angrily.

'Perhaps a little in part,' I admit. 'Certainly she will make it her business to defame me.'

Edward lifts my chin, so I am looking directly at him.

'In part?' he says. 'What is the other reason?'

I gently take his hand from my chin and enclose it in my fingers.

'Do you remember what I said that first day we met?' I say. 'That as a girl, I liked *The Faerie Queene* because I used to believe in fairy tales?'

Edward nods.

'Perhaps I still do believe in them,' I say.

'What do you mean?'

I sigh and look directly at him.

'You have done me some good,' I say. 'A lot of good. And it has ... it has changed things. I can no longer accept what once would have made me content.'

'You want more than to be my mistress,' he says, in a flat little voice.

I nod and take his face in my hands.

'I know,' I say gently, 'you cannot give it. And I do not blame you.'

Edward looks away.

'It is not just for me,' he says. 'If there were children ...'

I nod, for I am a grown-up street girl and not a child any more.

'I am not bitter,' I say. 'It is the way things are. I am truly grateful for everything you have given me.' I bite my lip. 'Your offer to keep me is more than generous. But I cannot be your mistress,' I conclude. 'Perhaps another man's. But never yours.'

Edward makes an angry kind of sigh and there is hurt in his eyes.

'Stay,' he says, suddenly fierce. 'Stay with me tonight. If not as my mistress, then stay as my lover.'

'I am sorry,' I whisper, my words coming braver than I feel. 'I cannot.'

Chapter 44

'You will not stay?'

Sophie is carefully packing my fine clothes into the trunk. I can tell she has been wanting to ask this since she started, but has only just worked up the courage.

'Oh Sophie,' I smile, 'London society is too small for a woman like me.'

Her face colours a little and she looks down. I know she is not foolish enough to truly believe I am a lady. But I think she had begun to enjoy the masquerade almost as much as I did.

Sophie frowns, as though remembering something. She fumbles in her hanging pocket.

'His lordship bid me give you this,' she says, passing me a parcel of velvet.

I take it with a question on my face and unroll the fabric.

Inside are the hair ornaments. The bird of paradise and the butterflies.

'He must have had the jeweller send them on,' I murmur, turning the dazzling bird, with its jewelled wings.

Sophie peers at the ornament in my hand.

'His lordship is perhaps not so wise,' she says, 'to let go of something so lovely.'

And then she turns quickly back to packing, as though fearing she has said too much.

I stand there, feeling idle while she works.

'Come here a moment,' I say, summoning her from the packing to where I am standing. She obligingly shuts the trunk and walks to me.

'This is for you and Mrs Tomkinson,' I say, closing the two butterfly ornaments in her hand.

Her eyes grow wide.

'You are sure?' she breathes, gazing at them.

I nod. 'I have the bird,' I say. 'That is my favourite.'

I meet Mrs Tomkinson on the stair on my way out to the carriage. She is preoccupied with directing a footman, but stops when she sees I am dressed in outdoor clothes.

'You are leaving?' she asks.

I nod.

Her face flickers through a spectrum of emotions.

'I will walk you out to the carriage,' she decides.

We step out into the sunshine, to see the carriage already awaits.

'It was a pleasure to serve you, Miss Lizzy,' she says.

Her hand reaches out and uncertainly, she pats my arm.

'I had a daughter once,' she says. 'Had she lived, I think you might have looked alike. For she had a grace to her too.'

'Thank you,' I reply.

'Here,' Mrs Tomkinson adds, moving to open the carriage door, 'allow me.'

I step up, far more easily now I have mastered my fine skirts.

Once inside the carriage the velvet walls feel suddenly stifling. I lean from the window.

'Goodbye, Bridget,' I say. 'I left a gift for you with Sophie.'

She smiles. 'Thank you, child. You were already a gift in yourself.'

Then she steps back from the carriage, collecting herself.

'You will do well,' she continues, in a slightly stiffer voice. 'And if you are ever in need, you must come to me.'

Until this point I was controlled. But my eyes fill with tears and my throat tightens.

'I am grateful to you,' I breathe, finding it hard to speak. 'For everything.'

The driver flicks his whip and the horse jolts to life.

And as the carriage rolls away from the townhouse, all I have just lost suddenly becomes apparent.

Chapter 45

*K*itty barely recognises me when I return to our old room.

As I climb the ancient staircase, the familiarity of it all is so strange. It feels like I have been away a lifetime and not a week. The smell of cheap tallow candle hangs on the air, and I realise I never noticed it before.

When I open our creaking door, Kitty's eyes grow wide as if ready to challenge me. Then her face makes a comical shuffling of expression, as she finally recognises her roommate.

'I thought a lady had got lost,' she says, standing with a wide grin. 'Look at you! There is even a little plumpness to your figure!' she adds, squeezing my arms approvingly.

I laugh, moving to hug her. 'Did you get the money I sent?' I ask.

She takes my hand and leads me to sit beside her on the bed.

'Yes. God bless you,' she says. 'For it became very close for a day or two. Creditors and all kinds of bad men came out of the woodwork.'

She presses my hand.

'But what of you?' she demands. 'I heard Harriet has been talking. You are a fine lady now.'

I smile and look down.

'Did Lord Hays fall in love with you?' she asks, searching my face. 'That is what Harriet thought.'

I shake my head.

'Harriet always did live in dreams,' I say. 'It was a business arrangement. Nothing more. But we both got what we wanted.'

'Where will you go now?' she asks.

I chew my lip.

'I had thought to set up a house in Mayfair. I have enough money to rent for a few months. And Lord Hays gave me fine clothes. I should have been able to make a try at being a courtesan.'

'But now you think different?'

I nod slowly. 'Remember Rose?' I say.

Kitty understands immediately.

'You will go away?' she asks, in distress. 'But anything might happen to you!'

I take her hand in both of mine.

'I made a friend in shipping,' I say. 'He promised me safe passage and told me about America. Women may make a fine life as rich widows. No one should know my reputation.'

Kitty shrugs.

'You never did fit in Piccadilly,' she says, her eyes skirting my face and figure admiringly. 'I always knew there would be some fine future for you.'

'For you too,' I insist.

But Kitty only smiles.

I take her hand, pressing coins into it, and at first she tries to pull away.

'Take it,' I insist. 'It is no charity I give you. I know you will use the money wisely. Buy some gloves. Find a good suitor.'

She nods, her eyes flicking backwards and forwards on mine, as if trying not to cry.

'When will you sail?' she asks after a pause.

'As soon as I can gain passage.'

Kitty's eyes widen.

'Why so quickly?'

I look away.

'Oh no,' says Kitty, shaking her head.

I bite my lip and try to stop the tears coming.

'You fell in love with your lord?' she breathes.

I nod and it feels so good to make the confession that the tears fall freely. Kitty crushes me against her and I sob on her shoulder.

'My little Lizzy bird,' she says softly. 'Your heart always was too soft for this business. You'll make a fine life in America. I am sure of it. Find yourself a husband and have that ordinary life you always sought.'

I sniff and give a little laugh.

'And you shall live the outrageous life that others dream of,' I reply.

Kitty grins. 'That is my only purpose.'

She sighs and then stands, pulling me with her.

'Come then, let us put together your things.'

Chapter 46

With my possessions all packed, I walk to the Exchange and make my arrangements. I am luckier than I dreamed. As chance would have it, a ship bound for America sails this very afternoon.

The providence of it almost gives me doubts. But I steel myself, remembering I have done far braver things. I hand over my forty guineas with my eyes closed. And receive back a bundle of papers for my passage.

Once the ticket is bought, I arrange for my trunks to be sent for, and say my final goodbyes to Kitty. Then there is nothing to do, but journey the three miles to Canary Wharf. It occurs to me that most ladies would take a sedan chair, but I do not mind the walk and should rather save my pennies.

Rather than go straight, however, I go the way of the bird market to make one last purchase.

The familiar jumble of makeshift cages and squawking occupants brings a smile of remembrance to my lips. I step slowly among the well-worn sights, wondering at how they look so different after only a week. I cannot quite say what has changed. Only the market seems smaller and duller than I remember it.

I am a little out of place now, a finely dressed lady with no man at her side. Stallholders stare openly, as I make my way through the cage walkway. A few shout hopeful pitches, but I ignore them, heading towards my usual seller.

To my relief, the birdman recognises me immediately, despite my new clothes.

'Queenie!' he grins delightedly. 'Well, now you are all fine. To match your name.'

I smile at him.

'You would like your usual bird?' he asks, uncertain now I am so well attired. I nod.

'Yes please,' I say. 'It shall be my last, for I am going away.'

The birdman seems to expect this, for he shows no surprise.

'Where do you travel to?' he asks.

'America. I start a new life.'

He digests this for a moment.

'Then I shall get you the fleetest fellow in here,' he promises, delving into the fluttering cage.

He cages the little bird expertly in a twist of paper and hands it to me. I pass him several large coins and he beams wide in gratitude.

'God speed you wherever you journey,' he says. 'May all the saints smile on you.'

The bird is light in his paper cage, as I make the walk to Canary Wharf. During the journey, I realise I am no longer the overlooked street girl I once was. My wealthy clothes attract attention. When I arrive in America, I decide, I had best travel by coach or chair.

The docks at least have an area where fine folk may gather. There is a little roped area near to the gangplank, where the handful of passengers watch burly dockmen load up endless barrels and equipment for the voyage.

My company is several young explorers, a missionary family and a brave young lord who ventures further than Europe in his Grand Tour.

They are all interested in why I am travelling alone. But as we wait to board the ship, I am become too nervous to make conversation. My eyes follow a wiry sailor, shinning up the masts to set the sails. And I find myself wondering yet again if I am making the right decision. America suddenly feels very far away.

The final arrangements are being made to the ship. The broad loading gangplank is taken in and replaced with a slimmer version, with a rope handrail, for passengers.

The bird is still safely wrapped, in my hand. And as the call comes to board, I hold him carefully. My last part of England.

Once on board, the other passengers go straight to be sure their trunks are loaded right. The passengers are the last cargo and the ship is being readied in earnest now. Any remaining barrels and goods are being secured on deck. Sailors race back and forth at breakneck speed. The last dockmen are exiting the ship.

Instead of joining the other passengers, I wander onto the deck, taking in the wide sails and the motion of the water beneath us. I know I should check on my trunks. But I am in a kind of daze, now we are so close to setting sail.

Beneath me, I see a huddle of dockmen collect to heave away the gangplank.

I breathe in the salt air. The docks of London are before us and the great wide sea ahead. It feels like freedom.

My nerves have all gone. I raise the little paper birdcage in my hand.

'I shall part from you here,' I whisper, through the paper. 'You shall be my last memory of home.'

I close my eyes, trying to drive away the memories of Edward's face and replace them with happier thoughts. America. Freedom. I resolve deep inside that this will be the last bird I set free.

Somewhere on the ship comes the cry to haul up the anchor.

Carefully, I begin to unwrap the paper. I can feel the little bird inside, jittering like a nervous heartbeat, anxious to be liberated.

There is a moment's pause and then a tiny beak peaks out the end. The bird's head pokes out after, considering me in a succession of swift movements.

Then the whole body flies free, winging out and up into the sky.

I watch him fly, trying to send my heart with it. But somehow, it seems to catch in my chest.

Instead of settling in a tree, the bird swoops downwards, back to the shore. My eyes follow him, wondering why he does not take the chance to vanish away.

'Elizabeth!' A shout comes from near where the bird has landed.

I start to hear my name. And when I see the man standing on the docks, my heart pulses in my chest.

Edward.

The sudden riot of feelings threatens to overwhelm me.

How did he find me here?

'You must hear me,' he shouts.

I stare at him dumbstruck.

'I understood what you read to me in the park,' he says. 'And I must make you an answer in person. I will come aboard.'

'It is too late,' I protest, feeling suddenly helpless. 'We are casting off.'

My eyes switch to the gangplank, which is being drawn in.

Edward glances at it too. And then, with a run and a leap, he lands on the juddering plank.

There is a cry of alarm from the dockmen, who were not

expecting a stowaway. But Edward ignores them, balancing deftly and taking cautious steps until he is level with the boat.

'Be careful!' I call, terrified for him. 'It is not secured at the top!'

Edward glances at me and then his hand catches on the prow of the boat. He heaves himself up and over, with the dockmen still shouting in his wake.

I can scarcely believe it as Edward walks across the deck to where I am standing. My only thought is that the ship must leave soon and he will be trapped aboard.

'Elizabeth,' he says, taking my hands.

He pauses, gazing into my eyes. And then he speaks again.

'"Let baser things devise, to die in dust,"' he says, '"You shall live by fame."'

He is finishing my poem.

I feel a smile creeping onto my lips.

'"I shall dedicate my life, to eternalising your rare virtues,"' Edward continues. '"And in the heavens write your glorious name."'

I am dimly aware that people on the docks are looking. There are tears in my eyes.

Edward recites on.

'"And when death shall all the world subdue,"' he finishes. '"Our love shall live, and later life renew."'

'I . . .' My throat is stopped. I hardly know what to say, only to see him is overwhelming.

He moves his hands around mine.

'How did you find me here?' I ask, blurting the first thing in my head.

Edward smiles.

'You told me, in Vauxhall,' he says, 'that you freed a bird when you were sad. I flattered myself you might be sad.'

I nod, not trusting myself to speak.

'I asked at the bird market,' he continues. 'It is not hard for a few pennies, to find out where a girl as pretty as you might have gone to.'

'So you found me out,' I say.

'Yes,' he says. 'I found you out.'

Edward hands are still clasping mine.

'You must leave the boat,' I protest weakly. 'We are setting sail. You shall be taken along to America.'

He pauses for a long moment. 'I made a mistake,' he says finally. 'I should never have let you go. And I do not want you to be my mistress.'

'You do not?' I ask, swallowing hard.

'No,' says Edward slowly, 'I want you, to be my everything.'

Now the tears come fast.

'The boat . . .' I whisper. 'It is setting sail.'

'I know.'

'So you must depart, or be swept away to America.'

Edward shakes his head.

'I have done a little thinking on this matter,' he says. 'I should like to come with you.'

'You do not know what you are saying,' I murmur, my eyes blurred with tears. 'You cannot give it up to be with me.'

'We could have a new life together,' he says. 'There would be no society to trouble us. We might start our own farm, on good land.'

'But you have no money in America. And what of your family here?'

'I have Mr Vanderbilt's trading contacts. My estate can easily spare funds, to support us in our life abroad. And my mother is well taken care of,' he adds.

'You decide too sudden,' I protest. 'You have a whole life here.'

'Yet I find it is not much of a life, without you in it,' he replies. 'I have given the matter thought enough.'

'You can't . . .'

'I can. I will,' he says, studying my face. 'But can you give up some of your freedom, to be at my side?'

'I . . .' My throat is still choked.

Slowly, I pull my hands from his grip, keeping my eyes on his. I feel into the front of my stays. My fingers close on the shape of my banknote.

I take it in my hand and pass it to Edward.

'If you take this journey, you should need a ticket,' I say, folding his fingers around my banknote. 'This will help buy your passage.'

Edward looks at the banknote in his hand and back into my eyes.

Then he takes me in his arms and kisses me. For a long moment, the world melts away and it is just the two of us.

The ship lurches beneath us, as the wind catches the sails.

I break away gently. Our faces are still nearly touching.

'America,' I say softly. 'I thought you did not take risks?'

He smiles. 'Yet I find I am greatly changed on that matter this last week.'

We cling together and the ship turns majestically, bringing the wide Channel into view.

Ahead of us is endless water, stretching out as far as the eye can see. The wind blows warm on our faces and Edward's arms are wrapped tight around me, as we gaze into the great blue expanse.

'Besides,' he whispers, as the ship carries us out and away, into our future, 'I do not take a risk. For everywhere with you is an adventure.'

Acknowledgements

Behind every published book are a thousand unsung heroes. And since it's boring to list names, let me tell you their story.

Once upon a time there was an author. Her greatest wish was to take readers on magical journeys. But the road to publication was full of trials, rejections and rewrites. Worse still, the author didn't have a marketable style. If she wanted to be published, she needed to be more like Philippa Gregory.

One day the author was sat bemoaning her lot. 'Woe is me!' she cried, 'how will readers ever discover my stories?' Fat tears rolled from her cheeks. Then to her amazement a beautiful fairy appeared.

'Stop complaining!' said Susannah Quinn (for that was the fairy's name). 'You don't need to go the publication route. You can self-publish and people will read your books that way.'

The author wiped away her tears. 'But that's vanity publishing,' she said.

'Nonsense,' said the fairy. 'It's a viable route to market,' and she waved her magic wand. In a flash a self-publishing platform appeared with worldwide distribution and one-click purchasing power.

'Goodness!' said the author, 'I can upload my books in an instant. But . . . oh dear. I don't have a book cover. Whatever shall I do?'

There was another flash and a genie appeared. He was bearded, rakishly handsome and really fond of the colour orange. 'Behold your cover!' said Simon Avery, (for that was the genie's name). 'Upload your book. I bet it will sell thousands!'

The author was nervous, but did as she was bid. And to her amazement her books did go on to sell thousands. And then thousands more. And thousands after that.

By and by the author had a thought. 'Do you know,' she said to herself, 'I do have an idea for a Philippa Gregory-style book after all.'

The words were hardly out of her mouth when there was another flash. Of course the author was rather used to flashes by now, but she blinked her eyes just the same. And what did she see, but a second genie? He was just as handsome as the first but in a different, debonair way.

'I can help you with your Philippa Gregory-style book,' said the genie. 'And other books besides.'

'Thank you, but I already have a genie,' said the author politely (because her parents Jean and Don Quinn had always taught her to be polite). 'His book covers are the best you can get.'

'You have the genie of graphic design,' said Piers Blofeld (for that was this genie's name). 'I am the agent genie, who can sell your books to big publishers and make all your dreams come true!'

'I like the sound of that,' said the author. 'How do I go about things?'

'Rub this copy of *The Other Boleyn Girl* three times,' instructed Piers, 'and we shall see what we shall see. Most likely, I shall work miracles for you.'

Well, the agent genie was as good as his word and he worked many, many miracles for the author. And for his last wonder, made her a book deal with Piatkus, the best romance publisher in existence.

There the author met fairy-queen Anna Boatman and publicity fairies Clara Diaz and Kate Doran. They performed the highest magic of all by loving the author's book and preparing it for market. Then the author wrote to Philippa Gregory who showed herself to be a really lovely woman by getting the joke.

And they all lived happily ever after.

Joanna Taylor took her inspiration for

Masquerade

from one of her favourite films.
Can you guess what it is?

Go to http://www.piatkusentice.co.uk/
masquerade-secret-scene/ to answer,
and unlock a FREE secret scene
from Lizzie's past.